Mr. R
1109 S.
Hudson, WI 54016-1409

P9-BZH-513

TRAPPED!

"What's the point of throwing us down here?" McGraw wondered aloud as Casey again crawled up on his hands and knees. "We can walk right out to the beach and back to the city." He could hear the relief in his own voice.

Casey made no comment. He was looking carefully around. Then he got to his feet and, crouching, made his way toward the opening in the rock. McGraw followed. As they neared it, McGraw's heart sank. The irregular opening was closed off with iron bars from top to bottom, spaced about six inches apart.

"Oh, no!" McGraw gripped the bars and sank to his knees on the hard sand.

"I think I know this place," Casey said thoughtfully. "When the surf is up and the tide is high, with an onshore wind, the waves surge into this cave. From up above you can see the spume spouting up through that blowhole we came down. Looks like a regular geyser."

"Damn!"

"Yeah. It's quite a sight. A few years back a couple of kids were playing in here and got caught by the high tide. Their bodies were never found."

McGraw shivered. It was immediately clear what their fate would be. He didn't trust himself to say anything. Casey was likewise silent as they stared out at the clear night through the bars of their prison.

"Is the tide going in or out?" McGraw finally asked, trying to keep his voice steady.

"It's coming in. . . ."

OTHER LEISURE BOOKS BY TIM CHAMPLIN:
THE TOMBSTONE CONSPIRACY
THE SURVIVOR
FLYING EAGLE
SWIFT THUNDER

TIM CHAMPLIN

DEADLY SEASON

LEISURE BOOKS NEW YORK CITY

For Lenny Steinauer,
in memory of all our great adventures.

A LEISURE BOOK®

January 2003

Published by special arrangement with Golden West Literary Agency.

Dorchester Publishing Co., Inc.
276 Fifth Avenue
New York, NY 10001

If you purchased this book without a cover you should be aware that this book is stolen property. It was reported as "unsold and destroyed" to the publisher and neither the author nor the publisher has received any payment for this "stripped book."

Copyright © 1997 by Tim Champlin

All rights reserved. No part of this book may be reproduced or transmitted in any form or by any electronic or mechanical means, including photocopying, recording or by any information storage and retrieval system, without the written permission of the Publisher, except where permitted by law.

ISBN: 0-8439-5131-1

The name "Leisure Books" and the stylized "L" with design are trademarks of Dorchester Publishing Co., Inc.

Printed in the United States of America.

Visit us on the web at www.dorchesterpub.com.

DEADLY SEASON

Chapter One

Jay McGraw crouched nervously in the cold, windy darkness and fervently wished he were somewhere else. Anywhere else.

The onshore wind peeled a fine layer of sand from the top of the dune in front of him and stung his face with a gritty lash. McGraw caught his breath and ducked away, sliding from a crouch to a sitting position in the soft sand on the lee side of the dune. He rubbed irritated eyes and squinted toward a figure, showing up as a dark blob against the pale sand. "Are you sure they're coming? It's got to be past two in the morning."

Detective Fred Casey nodded vigorously so he could be seen. "They'll be here. My informant hasn't been wrong yet." He had to lean forward and raise his voice to be heard, even though they were only a few feet apart.

"Yeah, but with this fog, and the way the sea's running, why would they risk it?" McGraw yelled back, his words being whisked away by the wind. The booming of the surf on the rising tide less than fifty yards away was a constant thunder that drowned the puny sound of voices.

Casey shook his head and put a hand to his ear in a gesture that he was unable to hear.

McGraw gave it up as a fit of shivering took him. He hugged the canvas jacket to his body. If it was this cold in June along the Pacific shore, what must it feel like in winter? His hand encountered the lump that was the nickel-plated .38 Colt Lightning belted under his jacket. The pearl-handled chunk of steel was a reassuring presence, since he didn't know what they might confront out there in the dark.

He glanced up and down the irregular line of low dunes that hid the figures of four more of San Francisco's undercover police squad. They were all waiting, more or less patiently, for the expected arrival of some Chinese opium smugglers. They had been waiting for at least four hours. And this whole operation was based on a tip from a Chinese informant, Ho Ming — a man who owned some of the largest brothels in Chinatown, a man who thought no more of lying under oath in court than he did of turning out one of his girls to starve on the street, if she became diseased or unproductive. McGraw's reasons for coming here, and for staying this long, were two-fold: he had promised his friend, Fred Casey, he would be sworn in as a special temporary detective to help the understaffed police squad. And, secondly, he believed that the informant, Ho Ming, was telling the truth. Ho Ming admitted that his only reason for co-operating with white authorities to slow the opium traffic was the simple fact that those who became addicted to the opium pipe spent all of their time and money in the drug dens and did not spend time and money in his houses of prostitution.

A fine, upstanding member of the community — McGraw thought — a complete opportunist, with a total lack of moral scruples of any kind. Actually Ho Ming was not really a member of the community at all — at least not the San Francisco community. Like thousands of other men, crowded into the few square blocks of the Chinatown district in 1885, he was there to accumulate enough money to return to his homeland considerably richer, by Chinese standards, than when he left. Ho Ming had no intention of becoming a citizen of the United States.

McGraw was startled from his musings as something bumped his shoulder. Fred Casey was motioning toward the beach. They crawled around the sloping end of the dune and looked seaward. McGraw could make out nothing at first, except the dull white flashes where the combers were pounding themselves to foam on the darkened strand. Then he followed Fred's pointing finger, slitting his eyes against the wind. Finally, he caught a glimpse of something — some darker blots, moving against the white of the surf. The longer he looked, the more convinced he was they were human figures, even though he guessed they had to be at least two-hundred yards away, at an angle down the beach. There was probably a boat, but, try as he might, he couldn't see one.

Casey tugged at his sleeve and started south along the beach toward the figures, crouching low as he struggled through the sand behind the ragged row of small dunes. The other men in the police squad followed them, single file. Running in the soft sand, bent in an awkward position, was real work, even for an athlete like himself, McGraw quickly discovered. He was breathing heavily before he had gone a hundred yards.

When they were nearly opposite the spot where the figures had been spotted, they all dropped down, still concealed by the low sand hills, and looked to Fred Casey who was in charge. The thunder of wind and waves continued unabated, muffling any sounds their harsh breathing and talking might make.

"There they are, Casey, just like you said," one of the men panted.

"Patience is one thing you really need in this line of work," Casey replied, drawing his revolver from under his coat.

McGraw followed Casey's example, noting that the other men already had their guns ready.

"We should be able to take them by surprise," Casey said. "Don't do any shooting unless you have to." He turned to one of his men who had wriggled to the top of the dune. "What about it, Cal?"

Cal came sliding back down to the huddled group. " 'Bout as many of them as of us, near as I can make out. That fog is blowing in thicker. Can't see what they're about."

"A nearly perfect night for smuggling," Casey observed dryly. "Except that we're here to spoil their party. Remember," he said, twisting around to include McGraw in his orders, "stay together and rush them as a group. We have no lights, so we don't want to be clubbing or shooting each other in the dark, if things get confused. Hit them together and hit them hard. It should be a total surprise. They'll scatter like quail. Don't worry if we lose one or two. What we're after here is mainly their shipment of opium. All right?"

They rumbled their assent in unison.

McGraw's heart was pounding, and his mouth was dry. He was oblivious to the cold wind. He was coiled and ready for action — the same feeling he had experienced in college just before the start of a football match.

"Let's go!" Casey called.

The lean Casey leapt through a swale in the low dunes, followed by McGraw and the four policemen. After a few sprinting steps, McGraw had to slack his pace to keep from outrunning the others. They covered the distance in less than ten seconds. McGraw could see little but heard a faint shout above the tumult of wind and water as the smugglers saw them coming, too late. Three of the smaller figures were tackled immediately and went rolling in the sand. Two of the men reached for weapons. McGraw lunged at one figure and felt a razor-sharp knife blade slit his left sleeve, and he knew he was cut. How badly, he didn't know, but the wound served to blank out his fear and fuel his anger. Before the knife-wielder could draw back, McGraw swung his gun hand and felt the pistol barrel bounce off the side of the man's head.

Two of the smugglers ran for their longboat that had washed around sideways on the beach several yards away. Casey was in hot pursuit and caught them just as the pair reached the boat and were struggling to point it back into the surging waves.

McGraw could take only a quick look before the man who had cut him bounded up from the glancing blow on the skull and came at him again, only a blurred figure in the darkness. With a lightning move the Oriental's arm swiped at his midsection. McGraw knew there was a deadly blade at the end of that arm. He pivoted neatly away, his footing solid on the hard, wet sand. But then he caught his foot and tripped on two unseen, struggling bodies. The smuggler saw his chance and lunged, arm raised to strike. This time McGraw had no choice. He fired. Yellow flame stabbed out, arresting the man in midblow. The knife arm went limp, and he staggered sideways, yelling something in Chinese.

McGraw saw his wounded opponent was out of action for the time and sprinted toward the boat to help Fred Casey. But Casey already had one of the smugglers bent over the gunwale of the boat and was handcuffing the man's hands behind his back.

"The other one took off up the beach somewhere," Casey yelled over his shoulder. "Don't worry about him. He's gone. Maybe he'll spread the word that these smugglers aren't safe anywhere," he grunted as he pulled his man erect and started him back up the beach.

The other four members of the police squad had things well in hand. To a man they were big and burly, three of them Irish and the fourth a rawboned youth of German extraction. They had four Chinese smugglers handcuffed to each other and sitting, subdued, on the sand.

"I heard a shot. Anyone hurt?" Casey demanded, pushing his prisoner down alongside the others.

"We're okay," a man named O'Toole answered.

"I had to shoot one of them," McGraw said. "I don't think

11

he's hurt too bad. Let me check him."

"The one on the end, there," O'Toole said. "You winged the little bastard. It's his outside arm or shoulder."

McGraw cautiously approached the Chinaman. "Did you make sure they're disarmed?"

"First thing we always do," O'Toole answered. "Got four knives and two pistols. But we'd better take another look when we get 'em in the light. You know how crafty these Chinamen are."

"Where you hit?" McGraw asked.

The prisoner said nothing.

"You understand English?"

No answer.

"Don't waste your time," O'Toole said.

McGraw reached for the Oriental's unshackled arm. The man jerked away and spat something rapidly at him in Chinese.

"I'm glad I couldn't understand that," McGraw said as he turned away. He could feel a wet, stinging sensation in his own left arm. He had forgotten about the knife slash that had sliced through his canvas jacket and shirt and gotten him. He could still feel the warm wetness as he flexed his arm. Instinctively he knew he wasn't badly hurt, but he would have to get a look at the wound in the light to be sure.

"Where's the opium?" Casey asked. "Brady! Kohl! Drag that boat up onto the beach and take a good look in it. McGraw, keep them covered while the rest of us spread out and look for it. Without that drug evidence, the captain is going to have my head."

"Why?"

"This will get into the papers, and he'll look like a fool for letting his men go around, beating and shooting innocent Chinamen who are out boat riding or fishing in the middle of the night," Casey replied sarcastically.

12

"Too bad there's nothing out here to make a torch of," McGraw said, drawing his Colt Lightning again and covering the prisoners.

"We're better off not showing any light," Casey said. "There could be a ship standing offshore there. They might not have just dropped that longboat and run. If their friends are still out there, I don't want to tip them off that anything's amiss."

As they talked, the men were walking in ever-widening circles in the darkness, scuffing their feet near where the struggle had taken place.

"The tide should just about be turning. Hope that stuff didn't get washed back out to sea."

They were still shuffling around in the dark with no result a few minutes later when Brady and Kohl returned.

"Found one small packet under the thwart in the boat," Kohl said, handing it to Casey. The detective hefted the small, oilskin-wrapped package that was less than half the size of a small brick. "There has to be more than this. Keep looking."

But, after about twenty minutes, they finally admitted there was nothing more to be found.

"Heathens must have heaved the stuff into the water when they saw us coming!" O'Toole spat in disgust. "I'm tired, wet, cold, and hungry, and this is all we got to show for a whole night?"

"Never you mind, O'Toole. You and Brady just pick out a nice, soft spot in the sand back of that dune and have yourselves a nap until daylight. Then give this beach a good going over," Casey directed. "Even if they threw it in the surf, there's a good chance it'll wash back up. And I want you to take turns keeping watch in case anyone shows up to pick up the stuff."

"Where're you goin', Casey?" O'Toole asked.

"We're taking these prisoners to the station house. You

might also secure that boat while you're here."

"And to think I volunteered for this assignment," O'Toole lamented. "Those little heathens didn't even put up enough of a fight to warm my blood."

Chapter Two

"Have you ever seen one of these?" Fred Casey asked, holding up a silver dollar.

"Sure. I've a couple of them in my pocket right now," Jay McGraw said, reaching across the table to take the coin. He held it up to the morning light that was filtering through a nearby window. He turned the dollar over in his hands. "Oh, it's a trade dollar," he added, noting the annotations **Trade Dollar** and **420 grains .900 fine** on the reverse, and the figure of Liberty seated, facing left, on the obverse. The date of **1877** was stamped below the figure. The trade dollar had first been authorized by the government in 1873 with a weight of four hundred and twenty grains of silver as opposed to the normal four hundred and twelve and one half grains in other silver dollars. It was designed to compete in the Orient with the silver currency of other nations. Though not as common as other cartwheels, they could still be found in circulation in the United States. Because of the value of silver bullion, the trade dollar initially bought five dollars' worth of goods in the United States. When silver bullion declined in value in 1876, Congress repealed the legal tender provision and tried to limit the minting of trade dollars for circulation only in the Orient, but they still circulated freely in the United States at face value.

"One from our own mint, too," McGraw added, noting the small S on the reverse, just below the eagle, indicating the San Francisco mint. The coin bore small scratches and about an average amount of wear for a coin that had been in circulation for most of its eight-year existence.

15

"See anything unusual about it?" Casey asked.

Kohl and Neal, the two other police squad members sitting around the table in the back of the station house, crowded around to get a closer look. They all examined it in turn for a few seconds.

"Looks like an ordinary trade dollar to me," McGraw finally said, speaking for all of them.

"Observe closely," Casey said, taking the dollar. He slipped a thumbnail along the milled edge, wiggled his thumb, and pried up slowly. The face of the coin opened on an inside hinge to reveal a hollow compartment. There was just enough of a solid rim inside the edge to give the coin weight and rigidity, but most of the metal inside had been removed, and the coin was now filled with a pale substance.

"I'll be damned!" McGraw exclaimed.

"As you can see," Casey explained, "a man can carry his own personal supply in his pocket with no one being the wiser." He pressed a thumb into the pliable opium that filled the hollow.

"How did you get on to that?" McGraw asked.

Casey winked conspiratorially. "I have my sources."

"Leave it to the Chinese. Clever little devils," Kohl said.

"That's a neat trick, but there's no way there could be enough of these little hollow trade dollars coming into the country to account for a tiny fraction of what's smoked in those opium dens in Chinatown in one day."

"Right enough," Casey agreed, becoming serious again. "If O'Toole and Brady don't show up here soon with a lot more of the stuff, then these smugglers have somehow given us the slip again."

McGraw rubbed his irritated eyes. Staying up all night on these raids was not exactly something he could get used to, even though he had gotten back with only minor injuries from this one. Dr. Donnelly, former surgeon in General Buck's cav-

16

alry and currently a contract physician for the San Francisco Police Department, had been called at 3:15 A.M., when they brought the prisoners to the jail in a barred paddy wagon. The stocky, graying doctor had looked quickly at McGraw's arm and then had gone to treat the more serious gunshot wound in the smuggler's shoulder. The bullet had gone through the smuggler cleanly just below the clavicle, doing some muscle damage but without clipping any bone or major blood vessels. After examining, disinfecting, and bandaging the wound, the physician had the man taken to the hospital.

Then he had turned his attention to McGraw. "That heavy jacket saved you," he had remarked as he had moved the coal-oil lamp nearer and had begun roughly swabbing the foot-long cut with carbolic acid. "Not bad enough to suture," he had growled, bandaging only the worst portion of the cut on McGraw's upper arm, winding the white bandage around his bicep. Dr. Donnelly had finished, closed his bag, accepted a cup of coffee, and then had departed.

McGraw flexed the arm now to see how it felt as he reached for his coffee mug on the table. He told Casey: "Even if they don't bring in any more of the stuff, you've got enough to convict them in court."

"Conviction of a few smugglers is not what we're after," Casey said, leaning back in his chair and biting at the corner of his mustache. "If we can't put a real crimp in this opium traffic, we may all be lookin' for another job."

"Casey," Jason Neal said, "you used to be on the Chinatown squad when you were in uniform. You should know these people better than anyone here."

"No Caucasian really gets to know these people," Casey replied, "even if he speaks one or more Chinese dialects. A white man is always an outsider. But I did make the contacts that are now my informants. Most of them are pretty rotten

17

characters. But you have to get used to dealing with people like that if you expect to find out anything. So far they've been pretty reliable. But Ho Ming is suspected by the Chinese underworld of being my informant. Should the tongs decide he is actually affecting the flow of opium, I wouldn't give one of these trade dollars for his chances."

The door opened, and O'Toole and Brady came in, looking played out. Their faces told the story before they opened their mouths.

"No luck, I take it?" Casey prompted.

O'Toole shook his head dolefully, while Brady tested the temperature of the coffee pot on the stove. Both of their faces looked white and pinched with cold and fatigue.

"We searched the beach up and down for at least a mile," O'Toole reported. "They didn't have time to bury it. And nobody showed up to make a pickup." He shrugged and reached for a tin cup. "At least the department is richer by one good longboat."

Casey heaved a sigh. "Maybe we can find out what ship it's from," he said wistfully. "Could be, they dropped the stuff offshore with a marker float for later pickup."

"Then why would they even come into the beach?" Brady asked. "Why would they have just that little pack with them . . . just enough to convict them?"

Casey shook his head. "I'm too tired to think just now. We're off duty. Let's all go home and get some sleep."

The men who had been seated got to their feet, stretching and yawning, and dispersed. Fred Casey and Jay McGraw walked outside together. McGraw felt the cold morning air against his bare arm through the sliced coat sleeve and shirt, both of which were crusted with dried blood. The bandage felt good and snug on his upper arm. In spite of the three cups of hot, sugared coffee, he was beginning to feel somewhat shaky by the events of the night and his loss of blood and sleep.

A cable car slowed at a corner nearby, and a short man swung down and skipped nimbly out of the way of a passing buggy.

"Oh, no!" Casey groaned softly. " 'Morning, Captain Kingsley."

The man in the dark blue suit stopped and looked up sharply. "Ah, good morning, Lieutenant Casey. You're up early. On your way to the station?"

"No, sir. Actually, we're on our way home. It's been a long night."

The older man spread his coat open and hooked his thumbs into his vest pockets. A gold watch chain spanned his slightly thickening girth. "Ah, that's right. How did the raid go last night?"

"Not bad, sir. We captured several Chinese smugglers, landing near the point."

"Any opium?"

Casey swallowed hard. "Only one small pack."

"That's all right. They know we mean business. We'll keep the pressure on. Chinatown has been nothing but wide-open vice for years. Now, thanks to that report, the department is finally going to do something about it. As William Shakespeare put it once . . . 'The law hath not been dead, though it hath slept.' Right, men? Good day." He nodded curtly and stepped around them to be on his way.

"*Whew!*" Casey blew out his breath as his superior officer walked briskly down the hill toward the California Street substation. "Thomas Kingsley! I think that man should have stayed in the theater. He seems to have a Shakespearean quote for every occasion. Likes to show off to make people think he's very literate. If he's material for a police captain, I'm a one-legged Chinaman. Damned political appointees!"

"Do you really think this surveillance and a few raids are going to slow up or stop the opium traffic?" McGraw asked, as they paused on a corner to allow a milk wagon to pass, the horse's iron-shod hoofs ringing loudly on the cobblestones in the early-morning stillness.

"Not at this pace, it won't," Casey replied, his voice dead with fatigue. He could let down in front of McGraw. The two of them had been close friends since McGraw had come to San Francisco three and a half years earlier.

McGraw asked: "Are the city fathers really serious about stopping this traffic, or is this just a lot of political smoke so everyone will think they're doing something? Seems like they'd throw most of the force into this and maybe hire extra help, like me, to seal this port tight and search every ship and every incoming passenger. I don't see any other way of doing it."

Casey shook his head. "I have to stay enthusiastic about this to set a good example for my men. But the department can't afford to commit most of the force to this effort. The money just isn't there to pay for all the extra help. We have four hundred men on the police force now. Chief Patrick Crowley has five captains under him, including Captain Kingsley. I'm one of the more junior lieutenants, and, because I've been put in charge of this special opium detail, I'm only responsible for a dozen men. The chief has been pleading for a mounted striking force, for a police wagon system, and for prohibition of those iron doors the Chinese use to fortify their gambling dens. But the board of supervisors has turned him down, flat. No money, they say. I believe they're serious about slowing down the opium, but they're not looking at the heart of the problem. The big shots want the Chinese out of the country altogether . . . a goal they'll never achieve, in my opinion. By getting rid of the *yellow horde* . . . as they're calling them . . .

the politicians believe that will take care of most of the other things . . . the filth, the barricaded gambling dens, the prostitution, *and* the opium dens."

"That would require some new national immigration laws, wouldn't it?"

"Sure would. That's why city and state officials can only try to do it piecemeal, by arresting and prosecuting individuals and small groups for violation of the cubic air ordinance, gambling law violations, opium smuggling, and all the rest of it."

A cable car slowed as the gripman released the cable, and they hopped aboard. They settled into the wicker seats, and the car rolled on down toward Market Street.

The clatter of the car made conversation difficult, so McGraw relaxed and let his mind go back over the public sensation created during the past few weeks by the publication of a report on the condition of the city's Chinatown district. The report had been prepared during late winter and early spring by a special committee of the board of supervisors. The report had just been published serially in the newspaper, and it condemned, in the harshest terms, the Chinese way of life among the citizens of California and San Francisco in particular. It was the public and political outcry, created by this report, that had prompted Fred Casey's offer to put McGraw on as a temporary special detective. In a fit of boredom McGraw had accepted the offer and requested a leave of absence from his job as a Wells Fargo express car messenger. Since he had performed heroic services for the company in the past, they had readily granted him the time off. Even though he had experienced several shooting scrapes in the past, the reaction to tonight's raid was setting in, and McGraw was feeling oddly sick and weak.

The cable car reached Market Street. McGraw said good-bye to Fred Casey and got off to walk the last two blocks to his boarding house south of the slot, as the area south of Market Street was referred to — indicating the slot in the street containing the cable that pulled the cars.

He was feeling a little feverish when he fell into his bed, exhausted. His arm was beginning to pain him slightly, and, tired as he was, he couldn't go to sleep immediately. But finally, as the sun was beginning to burn off the fog outside, he fell asleep and slept the day through.

When he awoke from his deep sleep in the early evening, he felt restored. His fever was gone, and he was hungry. The arm felt a little sore, but it had not stiffened up. He smiled to himself. He could still swing a bat. The other major reason he had asked for leave of absence from his job at Wells Fargo was to give himself a chance to test his skills as a baseball player. A team called the Stormy Petrels had been formed in San Francisco to play teams of part-time professionals from other towns. It was something he had wanted to do since he had narrowly missed being selected to play for the Cincinnati Red Stockings some six years earlier when he had lived in Iowa. An untimely injury had kept him from turning professional at that time. Now he just wanted to play for love of the game and to test his skills against others, regardless of the pay, which amounted to only a pittance. His skill as a hitter and outfielder had been immediately recognized by Tub Moran, the club manager, when he saw McGraw at the spring try-outs.

As McGraw poured some water from the pitcher into the bowl on the night stand and splashed some on his face, he was aware of the slight wound. It would not be enough to keep him out of tomorrow's game with the Seattle Woodmen, but he would be sure to keep his sleeve over the bandage in any case, so Tub Moran would have no reason to replace him with a second team player.

He wiped his face, and then poured more water into the

22

bowl to soak his bloody shirt and jacket. He was glad his landlady, an Irish widow by the name of Bridget O'Neal, had not seen him come in early this morning. He didn't feel up to any explanations. In fact, had she seen him, she might have assumed the worst, without asking any questions, and evicted him as an undesirable boarder. If he could get most of the blood out of his clothes, he'd take them to one of the Chinese laundries later in the day, and then have them sewn up.

He debated whether to take advantage of the one meal a day the widow cooked and served in the dining room. He really felt like being alone just now. But, on the other hand, the boarding house suppers were usually very tasty and plentiful. He decided to eat in the dining room.

He pulled on a clean shirt and pair of trousers and went downstairs. There were only six other boarders at the table, and, after greeting them, he said grace silently. Most of the others were more interested in their food than in conversation. The grown daughter of the widow served them, going back and forth to the adjacent kitchen. Even though McGraw was absorbed in his own thoughts, he couldn't help but notice the girl. He had been conscious of her beauty since the first day he had come to live here, several months before. She wore a white apron over a dark blue, full-length dress and had a maid's cap on the back of her head that did nothing to hide the dark, wavy hair. She had regular features, a short, straight nose, black brows and eyelashes, and blue-gray eyes. On the few occasions when he had seen her smile, it was as if the sun were bursting through a San Francisco fog. She had the type of healthy white skin that showed a blush easily. But, most of all, McGraw had been struck by her charming personality. However, lately, she had seemed withdrawn and worried, or at least preoccupied about something. Of course, he did not see her on any regular basis, since his jobs kept him coming and going at odd hours and absent from the boarding house for weeks at a time when he was working for Wells Fargo. Even so, he could only admire her from afar, since the widow was very protective and had apparently decided that her lovely daughter was to marry above her station in life, and that did not include any man who had only the means to live in this boarding house. "Catherine the Great, imprisoned in an ivory tower," the girl had once laughingly referred to herself, but, at the age of twenty she had apparently decided not to rebel against this treatment for the time.

McGraw glanced around the table. An elderly couple he had not seen before were at one end. Mr. Ivan Sarkoff, a retired bachelor of independent means who always dressed in a coat, high collar, and tie to come to dinner, was at the other end. The remaining three diners were young, men in their twenties who were laborers and had been boarding here for about six months.

"Katie, might I have a little more coffee?" McGraw asked when the girl leaned deliciously close to him to set a bowl of boiled potatoes on the table.

"Certainly."

She disappeared into the kitchen and returned with a large, blackened coffee pot, holding it with a hotpad. She filled his cup and gave him the briefest of smiles as he thanked her. Something was troubling her, but this wasn't the time or the place to ask about it. As the door to the steamy kitchen opened and closed, he could see her mother, sleeves rolled up, apron on, hair disheveled, and face reddened, doing the cooking. She looked harassed and cross. McGraw sighed as he wiped up the last of his apple pie and sipped his coffee. No wonder the widow wanted a better life for her only daughter. In any case, Katherine O'Neal was a fine-looking lass and brightened his day, whenever she was around.

He finished his meal and went back to his room. Casey had told him there was no need for him to come in tonight due to his injury. Casey had planned a clandestine trip to some of the opium dens in Chinatown to see if any of the efforts at stemming the flow of opium could be detected. He was not optimistic. They had managed to intercept only a few small shipments of the drug in the past few weeks. Now that the smugglers knew the pressure was on, they were not as blatant as before. They planned to go, posing as tourists, since travelers and visitors to San Francisco were allowed into the opium dens, the brothels, but not usually into the gambling dens which were normally barricaded against police raids. Even if they weren't closed to outsiders, ignorance of the Chinese tongue and Chinese games of chance would effectively prevent any gambling. The Chinese reserved this particular vice to themselves.

McGraw lighted the lamp on the bedside table, turned up the wick, and sat down on the bed with a contented sigh. He was pleasantly stuffed from the evening meal and, having slept most of the day, wasn't tired. The arm wasn't even paining him. If he kept it clean, the cut should have no problem healing. He would read for a while and then take a walk.

He reached for a thick pamphlet on the night stand. It was called REPORT OF THE SPECIAL COMMITTEE. Normally something with a title like that was a guaranteed sleep-producer, but this was different. It was the report that had stunned the city and created so much turmoil among its politicians. It had just finished running in the *Chronicle*. When the printers of this government document had seen what a sensation it caused, they had rushed out another press run and begun selling it at the newsstands and bookstores. McGraw had obtained a copy through the police department. In fact, all the men on the Chinatown squad as well as the men who were attempting to stop the smuggling were required to read it.

McGraw had perused it rather hurriedly, but then had gone back and re-read various portions of it carefully. The author had pulled no punches. On the basis of his committee's findings, and on the personal testimony of policemen and missionaries, he had blasted the Chinese race in general and the thirty thousand Chinese in particular who were packed into the several square blocks of San Francisco's Chinatown district.

He flipped open the report and scanned down one of the first pages.

All great cities have their slums and localities where filth, disease, crime, and misery abound, but in the very best aspect which Chinatown can be made to present it must stand apart, conspicuous and beyond them all in the extreme degree of all these horrible attributes, the rankest outgrowth of human degradation that can be found upon this continent. Here it may truly be said that human beings exist under conditions (as regards their mode of life and the air they breathe) scarcely one degree above those under which the rats of our waterfront and other vermin live, breathe, and have their being. And this order of things seems inseparable from the very nature of the race. . . .

He turned the page and let his eyes drop down the print, picking another paragraph.

Your committee have found, both from their own individual observations and from the reports of their surveyors, that it is almost the universal custom among the Chinese to herd together as compactly as possible, both as regards living rooms and sleeping accommodations. It is almost an invariable rule that every bunk in China-

town (beds being almost unknown in that locality) is occupied by two persons. Not only is this true, but in very many instances these bunks are occupied again by 'relays' in the daytime, so that there is no hour, night or day, when there are not thousands of Chinamen sleeping under the effects of opium, or otherwise, in the bunks which we have found there. . . .

Leafing over a page or two, the section on prostitution caught his eye.

The most revolting feature of all, however, is found in the fact that there are so large a number of children growing up as the associates and perhaps the protégés of the professional prostitutes. In one house alone, on Sullivan's Alley, your Committee found the inmates to be nineteen prostitutes and sixteen children. In the localities inhabited largely by prostitutes, women and children who apparently occupy this intermediate family relationship already alluded to, live in adjoining apartments and intermingle freely, leading to the conclusion that prostitution is a recognized and not immoral calling with the race. . . .

He skipped over a couple of pages and read part of an interview with a Dr. Toland, a practicing physician and a member of the Board of Health. He was quoted as stating he had treated many boys as young as eight to twelve years old who had contracted syphilis from visiting Chinese houses of prostitution which welcomed anyone for a very cheap price. He and another doctor testified that the number of diseased youngsters in San Francisco was growing alarmingly high.

The report continued on in other areas where the residents

of Chinatown were flouting the civil laws concerning unsafe cooking and heating fires and deplored the fact that about one-seventh of the population of the city was pretty much doing as it damned well pleased, and nothing was really being done to enforce the law.

In a sanitary point of view Chinatown presents a singular anomaly. With the habits, manners, customs, and whole economy of life violating every accepted rule of hygiene; with open cesspools, exhalations from water closets, sinks, urinals, and sewers tainting the atmosphere with noxious vapors and stifling odors, with people herded and packed in damp cellars, living literally the life of vermin, badly fed and clothed, addicted to the daily use of opium to the extent that many hours of each day or night are passed in the delirious stupefaction of its influence, it is not to be denied that, as a whole, the general health of this locality compares more than favorably with other sections of the city which are surrounded by far more favorable conditions.

The committee could not account for the fact that no serious plagues or contagions were sweeping Chinatown, except for the fact that the twelve-square-block area was constantly being fumigated by wood smoke, coal smoke, cigar smoke, opium smoke, and incense. Under the heading — *Opium Resorts in Chinatown* — McGraw read:

The following table shows the number and location of the public Opium Resorts. The 'opium layout' is found in nearly every sleeping room in Chinatown and is nearly as common as the tobacco pipe; but these dens are for the general accommodation of those who have no sleeping

28

bunks and conveniences for opium-smoking of their own, and who therefore frequent these resorts to indulge in the habit.

The bunks are occupied night and day, and the spectacle of pallid men in a condition of death-stupor, wrapped in the dirty rags which constitute their bedding, may be witnessed in these dens. . . .

A list followed of the addresses, floor levels, numbers of bunks, and general condition (ranging from filthy to very filthy) of twenty-six different locations, containing three hundred and nine bunks. Then the following:

The use of opium is so general among the Chinese that no visitor to Chinatown, night or day, can enter many sleeping rooms without finding men indulging in the habit. Nor will the explorer travel far without finding them under every stage of its influence down to the dead stupor such as would seem to furnish fit subjects for the coroner and the morgue, rather than as beings to whom life is ever to return again.

McGraw continued flipping through the report, pausing every page or two to read a couple of paragraphs. A section dealt with murders that went virtually unpunished because the crimes were committed against fellow Chinese, and, if any witnesses could be found and the murderer arrested (unlikely), more witnesses would come forth at the trial to swear that the accused was nowhere near the scene of the crime. The tongs took care of avenging their own, without the interference of the meddlesome white men who were attempting to enforce the laws of the city and state. The report went on to quote various policemen to the effect that the Chinese habitually used the law

29

to their own advantage, such as when they wanted a runaway slave girl returned.

The report devoted several pages to the complaint that the Chinese were undercutting the native work force by taking labor jobs at very low pay. It also took issue with the fact that the district was filled with illegal gambling dens. The committee professed to be appalled at the audacity with which these places flouted the law. But the author concluded that the number of police on the force was inadequate to patrol Chinatown and raid these gambling dens, and the property owners were unwilling to put a stop to it. The report called for:

. . . Nothing less than a police force large enough to constitute a constant army of occupation that must be kept in Chinatown, with battering rams and dynamite, if necessary, to enable them to open and raid these dens of vice.

A list of one hundred and fifty gambling dens was attached as an appendix. Under a heading — *The Heathen Chinee* — the report took issue with the joss houses and the idolatrous temples, mentioning that more than one altar had even been erected to the Goddess of Prostitution. The report quoted several missionaries who confirmed the abject failure of their efforts to convert the Chinese to Christianity.

The Chinese brought here with them and have successfully maintained and perpetuated the grossest habits of bestiality practiced by the human race. The twin vices of gambling, in its most defiant form, and the opium habit they have not only firmly planted here for their own delectation and the gratification of the grosser passions,

30

but they have succeeded in so spreading these vitiating evils as to have. . . .

He slapped the report shut, yawning, and stood up, wondering idly how many members of that committee had sampled the vices that they condemned so eloquently. *Enough of that.* It was very clear that the report, authored by Willard B. Farwell and signed by committee members, John E. Kinkler and Mr. Pond, was in favor of vigorous enforcement of existing laws and the passage of new ones that would restrict immigration and eventually rid California of the Orientals altogether. The opium problem seemed to be only one of several reasons that made the Chinese unwelcome residents in the midst of the city.

McGraw wondered what had prompted the formation of this committee, back in February. Obviously the situation had been the same or worse for years. Maybe some political big-wig was trying to lay a foundation for reëlection, intending to campaign on a law-and-order platform. Pure altruism hardly seemed a likely reason for wanting to clean up Chinatown. He wondered if the mayor's term would be up soon.

He rose and slipped on a light coat, still absently pondering the situation. He usually paid little attention to politics, local or national, but now he was curious. He hated to be risking his life for the career of some corrupt politicians. Fred Casey had assured him that corrupt office-holders had been the order of the day as long as Casey had been in the Bay city, but, after all, McGraw had volunteered to do this more for the excitement and adventure than for any other reason. It certainly wasn't for the low pay. Yet, if he could indirectly save even one person from the enslaving addiction to opium, then his time and effort would be well spent.

Thus feeling justified to himself, McGraw extinguished the

bedside lamp and went out, locking his door. Time for a long walk in the chilly night air, maybe a stop for a light, frothy steam beer at Boyle's Saloon, and then back home to bed.

Chapter Three

Jay McGraw reported to the baseball field at Twenty-Fifth and Folsom in the Mission District just before eleven o'clock the next morning. He was early. Only the club manager, Tub Moran, was already there, raking the dirt of the infield and preparing to mark the baselines.

McGraw waved at him and went under the wooden stands to a small, stuffy room that served as a dressing area for the home team. The Stormy Petrels were a source of civic pride to the citizens of San Francisco, but the team was constantly in need of funds to continue operating. Tickets were priced low in order to continue drawing the hundreds of working men who crowded the stands at every home game. There was talk of improving the field, building better dressing rooms and dugouts, but wrangling over spending public money was always a wearisome process.

The baseball diamond had been located at this site since 1868, but the Petrels had only existed for about ten years as a semi-professional team. The team had been modeled after earlier teams in Boston, New York, Cincinnati, and other Eastern cities by being initially organized as a social club whose activities included many other pastimes besides baseball, such as cricket and Rugby. But like the older clubs it had quickly evolved into an American baseball team to the exclusion of most other sports or forms of entertainment. Besides baseball, one of the few remaining activities was an annual picnic for the team members, the wives and girl friends and other guests. He had invited Katherine O'Neal to this year's picnic that was scheduled for late September. Much to his surprise and delight she had accepted.

He sat down on the unpainted wooden bench and untied his shoes. Even with the door standing open, the room smelled of liniment and old sweat. He never lingered but was always glad to get outside into the cool, fresh air to begin warming up. Even though he had taken part in many athletic contests from his schoolboy and college days, he never failed to be nervous to the point of nausea before each race, wrestling match, football, or baseball game. Fear of playing badly was not the cause of the nerves. In fact, once play began, the nervousness vanished, to be replaced by total concentration on the job at hand. Former coaches had always told him pre-game nerves were a good sign that he was taking the contest seriously and would play or run better because of the pent-up energy. He doubted this theory. Nevertheless, he privately believed that his innate athletic ability was enough to overcome what he considered a draining nervous experience. In any event, he could never face food within six hours of a game and always arrived early so he could avoid his teammates as they dressed, since he knew his state of mind made him poor company. Today was no exception.

He pulled a long undershirt down over his bandaged arm and then put on his uniform shirt with the seabird logo stitched onto the back of it. No one would be the wiser as long as the injury didn't affect his play. He picked up his glove and ran out onto the field, his stomach churning, as usual. He was irritated with himself. Why should he be nervous? He was the best outfielder on the Pacific coast, and he knew it. He was also one of the best batsmen.

The top of the seventh inning saw the Stormy Petrels clinging to a six to five lead over the Seattle Woodmen. Two men were out. Runners were at second and third. From his position in left field McGraw did not recognize the batter but could see he was a big man. Tub Moran was frantically waving for McGraw to play deeper. Just as he started to back up, the batter swung. McGraw got a late start on the ball as it was driven hard toward the left field corner. His metal cleats tore the turf as he accelerated to his full stride toward the foul line. Even with his fluid speed he wasn't sure he could reach the ball. If he pulled up and played the bounce, two runs would score. If he went for the catch and missed, two runs would score.

At the last instant he lunged for the ball. It struck his glove and ricocheted upward. McGraw twisted in the air and grabbed the deflected ball just as he hit the ground on his side. The jarring impact drove the air from his lungs, and everything spun in his sight, but he instinctively gripped the ball as he skidded to a stop. He lay there a few seconds until things came back into focus. Then he rolled over and flipped the ball to the center fielder who had run over to back up the play.

"Good catch, McGraw," Jim Bellson said with a straight face, "but did you really have to make it that spectacular?"

"Moran thought he would hit it deeper," McGraw gasped, shaking the sand out of his pants and retrieving his cap. He tossed his glove at Bellson who dodged and let it fall near the foul line as they trotted toward the bench.

"Helluva stab out there," Kevin O'Toole grunted as he slumped down on the bench beside McGraw. A layer of dust coated the catcher's damp forearms as O'Toole mopped his broad face with a towel. "Nothing's gotten past you today," he added.

"And you stopped everything behind the plate, too," McGraw said.

They grinned at each other.

"Snuffy's got his good stuff out there," O'Toole said. "He's got 'em swingin' at his high, hard ones. Like chasin' smoke."

He looked down, and his grin faded. "Lord, man, what'd ye do to your arm?"

McGraw looked at his left arm. Blood had soaked through the sleeve in several spots. He was aware of a slight stinging sensation. He glanced around quickly to see if any of his teammates had heard. *"Shhh,"* he motioned for O'Toole to be quiet, "that's where that smuggler knifed me the other night. Must've pulled it open when I hit the ground. It's not that bad, but, if Tub sees it, he'll pull me."

"Damned Chinee. You should've plugged him for good. That's the only way. Either shoot 'em or run 'em outta the country, I say. This tryin' to stop the opium is no way to handle the problem." He picked up a towel and wiped his arms, and McGraw noted the broken nails and the meaty, callused fingers. The hands were beet-red from the pounding of the ball.

"You may need to try stuffing a little more padding into that mitt," McGraw remarked, gesturing at the catcher's hands.

"Yeah, they *are* a sight, aren't they, now!" The nail of his right forefinger was split to the quick. O'Toole held it up. "And to think the catcher used to stand back several feet behind the plate and catch the ball on the bounce."

"Yeah, and it used to be a fielder only had to catch the ball on the bounce in the outfield to put the batter out. The rules makers thought that made it too easy . . . too much of a boy's game."

"Baseball has really changed in the last twenty or thirty years. Do you really believe we're being paid enough to play this game?"

"Probably not, but it sure is fun. Where else are you gonna find a crowd to cheer at the sight of your ugly mug when we take the field?"

"At least my mug won't be gettin' any uglier, since it's behind a mask." He held up the face gear. "I'm glad somebody

. . . probably a catcher . . . had the good sense to invent this thing about ten years ago."

The sun was bright, but the usual chilly afternoon breeze was gusting in off the Pacific. McGraw squinted at the field through the blowing dust as the Woodmen's pitcher completed his warm-up throws, and the batter stepped up to the plate to begin the eighth inning.

The Petrels managed to hold onto their one-run lead and won the game. McGraw had another time at bat but grounded out to the second baseman. As he trotted back to the bench, Tub Moran noticed the blood on his sleeve and demanded an explanation.

"Hurt it when I hit the ground out there a couple innings ago," McGraw said, brushing past the coach.

"You must've hit a rock or something sharp. If we go into extra innings, you sit down and Finney will go to left."

McGraw nodded. He was through for the day, but the game ended with the third out in the top of the ninth.

The blood had coagulated, and McGraw left the bandage in place when he changed into his street clothes under the stands, following their win. He would clean it up when he got to his boarding house. He wondered if he should show his injury to Katherine O'Neal but put the thought swiftly out of his mind, since he knew his real motive would be to solicit sympathy. She had promised to come and watch a game soon but apparently had not been in the stands today, or she would have somehow gotten his attention.

When he came out, carrying a small satchel containing his uniform, glove, and shoes, most of the crowd was gone. As he started for the street to catch the cable car, he noticed O'Toole, still in uniform, talking to two men on the sidewalk on the far side of the stands. *Maybe signing autographs,* McGraw thought. The big, bluff Irish catcher was a hometown favorite and the only policeman who was a member of the team.

One of the men was carrying a white cane and wearing dark glasses. However, from this distance McGraw could not tell if he was actually blind, since he seemed to move with some assurance and turned to face his companion and O'Toole as the conversation went back and forth. There was something that struck a familiar chord in the back of McGraw's memory about the man with the cane as he turned away and swung aboard the cable car that had approached the corner. He had seen the man somewhere before, and it seemed odd that a blind man would be attending a baseball game. Maybe he had partial sight.

He was too tired and hungry to think any more about it as he dropped into his seat. His arm was aching and feeling a little stiff, but he had the satisfaction of knowing he had played a good game. In addition to his diving catch he had played errorless ball, and his three-for-four at bat had helped the Petrels to another win.

Chapter Four

"I'd like you to take a little jaunt with me to Chinatown this afternoon," Fred Casey said, stepping inside McGraw's room late the next morning.

"Fine. What's up?" McGraw asked, motioning his friend to a chair as he lounged back on the unmade bed. He was bathed, shaved, had gotten a good night's sleep, and was feeling fit again.

"Your arm all right?" Casey asked, indicating the fresh white cotton bandage that swathed the left arm from mid-forearm to above the elbow.

"Never felt better. In a day or two I'll take this wrap off and let my sleeve keep the dirt out of it while the air finishes healing it up."

Casey nodded and looked away absently as he chewed on one corner of his mustache.

"What's wrong? You look pretty dragged out. Been taking your work home with you again?" McGraw asked. "When you were in uniform on the Chinatown squad, you didn't let things bother you. How long since you took some time off, or went to the theater, or had a date? I can't even get you to sit still long enough to have a beer at Boyle's with me. You're always in a hurry, or you're on duty, or something."

Casey looked at him. There were dark circles under his eyes. The face was still handsome, but the usual ruddy color was gone from his cheeks. "Life was a lot more fun, then," he replied somberly. "Maybe because it was all new and different. Now. . . ." He paused. "Now things are just . . . more frustrating, I guess. I have more responsibility as a detective, and, if I can't produce results and solve the puzzles, then I don't feel I'm earning my money."

"So you're working yourself day and night to figure out how this opium traffic is getting in so you can stop it," McGraw finished. "If you keep up this pace, you're going to be out sick, and then who's going to do the work?" He shook his head. "Hell, you're not the whole police department. You can't do it all yourself. Ease up. There are a lot of people in on this with you."

"I know you're right, but it's just hard to let go, when you've been given a job to do and it feels as if you're failing."

Casey would never have shown this more human side of his nature to anyone other than McGraw, his most trusted confidant.

"What do you want to do in Chinatown today?" McGraw asked, to lead his friend away from his self-castigation.

"I'm not sure. Just groping again. I haven't been there lately. When I was on uniformed patrol there, I used to be able to get a feel for what was going on sometimes, even though I couldn't speak the language. I could pick up on little things . . . the way merchants were acting with customers, how many people were on the streets, the bulletins that were posted on certain buildings about tong activities, and how excited the men reading them got, the number of patrons in the opium dens. That sort of thing. I could usually tell if something big was up, especially in regard to the tong underworld activities."

"I read that report commissioned by the board of supervisors," McGraw said. "That committee certainly got a feel for Chinatown when they surveyed it," he said dryly.

"Yeah," Casey grinned, "they sure did." It was good to see his friend hadn't lost his sense of humor. "Actually Ho Ming was due to contact me again, but I haven't heard from him.

40

Because of fear of retaliation he can't be seen with me or near the station house."

"How does he do it?"

"Writes a message in English and gives it to a Chinese street vendor he knows who can't read or write English. The street vendor has a certain route he travels, selling fresh vegetables and fish on Friday afternoons. I always contact this vendor one block from the ferry building on Market Street. The last two times I've met him, he's had nothing for me. The last message I got from Ho Ming was two weeks ago, and that was to tell me about the smugglers we caught the other night. Nothing since."

"Maybe he just hasn't had any more to tell you."

Casey shook his head. "We arranged to communicate at least once a week, regardless. I'm afraid something has happened to him. Ho Ming is a police informant . . . a low-down character, but I believe he's a man of his word. As a dealer in slave girls and an owner of the largest brothels in Chinatown he has a vested business interest in helping the white authorities slow this opium traffic. I actually believe he's opposed to the use of the drug on principle. It's debilitating and killing his people. And he impresses me as a man who has a lot of pride in his race."

McGraw had his doubts about any motives not prompted by greed, from what he had heard of this man, Ho Ming, but he kept silent. After all, Fred Casey had dealt with the man face to face on a few occasions and knew him better. Casey had told him Ho Ming could speak passable English.

"So you think someone in the opium traffic might've had him killed if they discovered he was an informant?"

"Exactly."

"How would we ever know?"

"That's why I want to go to Chinatown. By just walking

41

around and asking a few innocent questions among the merchants, I might be able to pick up some clues as to whether he's still alive. After all, he's a man of great influence, albeit bad, in the Chinese community. If I go down there in my official capacity, demanding answers, I'll never find out anything. I did manage to make friends among some of the honest Chinese merchants and workers when I walked a beat there. Most of them who deal with the public have learned to speak English."

"Let's go, then."

"Relax, there's no hurry. We'll go about three o'clock, and we may stay until well after dark when the gambling, opium dens, and whorehouses get going full blast. I'm scheduled to be off tonight, but my squad is patrolling the Bay in boats. All indications are it'll be a clear, moonlit night."

McGraw gave him a pained look. "Working on your night off again?"

Casey shrugged and admitted: "When your job's your whole life, what else is there to do?"

"You used to be interested in other things, too," McGraw remarked softly, getting up and pacing to the window. There was silence between them for a few seconds. "Let me ask you something," McGraw said then. "Is there anything to these rumors I've been hearing about some kind of ghost ship that's been seen slipping into the Bay with no markings, no name, and no lights? I've heard it may be dropping the bulk of the opium that's coming in here."

"Who told you that?" Casey asked sharply.

McGraw was somewhat startled by his reaction. "Well, I don't really remember. I think a young man who lives in this boarding house and works at a shoe factory told me he and a friend were out fishing one night and got sucked out by the current. He told me he saw this ship . . . he described it as a small schooner . . . discharging something over the side into

42

small boats. Since they were lost in the fog, they yelled for assistance when this schooner loomed up out of nowhere with no lights showing. Someone on deck pulled a pistol and took a couple of shots at them. He said he jumped on the oars and pulled away as fast as he could. They finally found their way ashore after the fog lifted the next morning."

"What made him think they were opium smugglers?"

"He just assumed they were up to something by the way they acted. When he yelled for help, he heard someone say something in Chinese, and the men stopped loading suddenly like they had been startled."

"The imagination of a couple of guys lost and scared," Casey replied.

"Why would anyone shoot at them if there was nothing illegal going on?"

"Don't know, but that's no proof of anything. Maybe they were over somebody's private oyster beds. There are some tough characters around this seaport when it comes to defending against oyster pirates."

"I've heard similar stories discussed by two fishermen near the ferry building a couple of weeks ago. They had gone out before dawn and had come up on what might have been this same schooner, heading for the open sea through the Golden Gate. There was a light breeze blowing seaward, and they crossed the stern of this ship in their lugger almost before they saw it. They heard a man's voice very clearly, coming from somewhere near the wheel, speaking with a pronounced British accent. He was giving commands to the helmsman. The fishermen were showing a lantern in their rigging and were seen just as they went by. They said the Britisher, or Australian, cursed them as if they had been the ones who nearly caused the collision. The fishermen looked in vain for some name or port of call on the stern of the craft but saw none, and the lightless ship was swallowed up in the darkness a few seconds later. The men I overheard telling this to a friend weren't calling it a smuggler, but they were damned mad about the danger the vessel presented to other craft on the Bay."

"Sounds like a problem for the Port Authority, not for us," Fred Casey replied. "But, just in case, I'll have my men keep an eye open for it."

"Well, rumor or not, it might be worth checking out," McGraw said. "Let's go get a bite of lunch. I'd bet you haven't had anything to eat since yesterday."

"Just some black coffee at the station house this morning."

While they consumed ham and cheese sandwiches, washed down with beer at Boyle's Saloon, McGraw voiced his concern about the politics behind the committee report.

"Of course, it's political. It's all political," Casey said impatiently around a mouthful of food.

"I guess I'm naïve when it comes to that sort of thing," McGraw said. "I take things too much at face value."

"While you're working for the city, you'll have to start reading the papers and paying attention to what's happening around you."

"I've never been interested in all the shenanigans of politicians."

"Have you ever heard of Blind Boss Buckley?"

"The name sounds familiar."

"It should. He's the biggest political boss this city has seen in its history. I'm ashamed to say he's an Irishman from the old country. He learned his politics at Tammany Hall in New York before heading out here to the Coast. He and a partner named Fallon set up a saloon down on Bush Street in the 'Seventies. They cater to office holders and seekers and hangers-on. Buckley wheels and deals, puts a little bribe here, a little

44

pressure there. He's gradually gained a following and wields a lot of votes. It's gotten to the point where anyone seeking a building contract with the city has to deal with him rather than directly with city officials to go through the bidding process. In fact, he's backing a whole slate of candidates for city offices who are running in the fall elections. Odds are that most or all of them will be elected."

McGraw nodded. "So you think he had a lot to do with this investigative report on Chinatown?"

"That seems to be the common belief. His tactics have always been to stir up the voters by creating some big issue a few months before an election. Next time it will probably be taxes or some other issue. He's a master at simplifying complex problems, making popular slogans out of them, and then hand-picking candidates who support his views. He's got enough influence now that office holders come to see him, instead of the other way around."

"Why do they call him Blind Boss?"

"His eyes are so bad he can't see to write his name. But that doesn't seem to slow him down any."

"Does he wear dark glasses outdoors and carry a white cane?"

"Yes. And he invariably wears a brown suit. Don't think I've ever seen him in anything else. Very unimposing-looking little man. Why? Have you seen him?"

"I think so. At the ball game yesterday."

"The ball game?" Casey paused in his chewing.

"Yeah. He was talking to O'Toole on the street just after the game. There was another man with him."

"What were they talking about?"

McGraw shook his head. "Don't know. I paid no attention. They were a good way off, and I was headed home. I thought O'Toole was signing autographs at first."

"Odd." Casey resumed eating.

"Why?"

Casey shook his head as if brushing off a bothersome fly. "Nothing. Just that I can't imagine what Buckley, who can hardly see at all, would be doing at a ball game or why he and O'Toole would have anything to talk about."

"Maybe O'Toole has political aspirations. After all," McGraw smiled, "he's Irish. And don't most Irish gravitate to politics, saloon-keeping, or police work?"

"Think I'll ask him first chance I get." Casey didn't smile. "Let's walk. I want to show you something on the way."

Five blocks away from Boyle's, on a street south of Market, Casey led the way through the front door of a two-story brick building. A big man with one cauliflowered ear sat just inside the door, reading a newspaper.

"Yeah?"

"We want to take a look inside."

"Why?" The tone was belligerent as the barrel-chested guard stood up.

Casey flashed his silver badge. "Official police business."

The guard deflated like a gas balloon with a large hole in it. He followed curiously as Casey and McGraw brushed past him down a short, dark hallway and opened another door. McGraw stopped in surprise at what he saw. A large room was filled with row after row of Chinese men, hunched over sewing machines. The whole room was whirring and chattering, the overhead drive belts being powered by an unseen steam engine. McGraw could feel the wooden floor vibrating as he watched the nimble fingers of the workmen, guiding the cloth under the flashing needles. The room lacked ventilation, and a strong odor of dye permeated the place. At the far end of the room McGraw saw long cutting tables stacked with bolts of cloth. Near the row of windows on one side, where the light was better, men were doing some kind of hand stitching.

The noise was so overwhelming McGraw could not hear Casey when he turned to say something. No one looked up or acknowledged their presence, even though a white supervisor was walking among the workers.

The guard still stood at their backs, glowering.

Casey motioned McGraw back outside. "You noticed this sweatshop was filled with Chinese," he said when they were again on the sidewalk. "No telling how many hours a week they work in there."

McGraw nodded.

"They'll work for much less than any white worker, so the factory owners gobble them up. The Chinese are good with their hands which makes them very adept at this type of work. Cigar-making is another industry that is dominated by Chinese workers, for the same reason. It means big profits for the employers. But that's one of the major reasons for the riots and the beatings some of the Irish gangs have given the Chinese workers. They're undercutting American workers and taking thousands of jobs . . . one of the main reasons the city fathers want to get rid of them."

"How can they afford to work so much cheaper?"

"Their lifestyle. They can live on what would starve a cockroach. Probably learned to do it in their poverty-stricken homeland. You've been in Chinatown and you've read the report. They crowd together, share bunks, eat meals in common. Almost no expenses. One of those Chinese workmen back there earns fifty-five cents for each dozen pairs of overalls and does well on it, by his standards. The average white worker would need a minimum of five times that much, just to get by."

"So this opium business is just a smoke screen the politicians are using to try to get rid of the Chinese."

"Not really. The opium traffic is a legitimate concern.

Opium is just an easier issue to focus on. After all, there's no law against working for a pittance. There *are* laws against opium smuggling, gambling, and prostitution, and the lesser violations of sanitary laws, fire codes, cubic air ordinances, and the like."

McGraw nodded.

"These workers you just saw were making work clothes. This factory supplies most of the work clothes for the whole West Coast. There's a big shoe factory here in the city that turns out thousands of pairs each month . . . mostly done by cheap Chinese labor. The owners are getting fat and rich on the backs of this cheap labor. They don't want to see the Chinese out. The biggest influx of Chinese labor came here to build the Central Pacific Railroad in the Eighteen Sixties, just after the war. And many others have come since to make their *fortune* and then go home."

They had reached the corner of Clay and DuPont Streets and started up the hill into Chinatown. The view changed immediately. All the signs were in Chinese. The pedestrians were nearly all Oriental, most wearing the pajama-type clothing, round caps or dark felt hats. A few wore combinations of Oriental and European-style clothing.

Even with a cool breeze fanning their faces, McGraw's nose was assaulted with a mixture of smells — sweet spices and unidentifiable cooking odors. Now and then, as they passed an alleyway, he got a whiff of rotting vegetables and clogged drains. He felt very conspicuous as a Caucasian, but they occasioned only one or two stoic glances.

Fred Casey stepped into a shop that dealt in scented candles and various types of ambrosia as well as brass incense burners and ornaments. He picked up and examined a figurine, admired an ornate jade goddess, sniffed a pinch of incense.

The proprietor of the tiny shop appeared in a yellow and

green embroidered silk outfit. "May I be of service?" he inquired in soft, docile tones, bowing slightly. He was tall for an Oriental and thin, with concave cheeks, eyes so slanted and slitted they almost appeared to be shut.

"The wares of your shop are a delight to my nose and eyes," Casey responded.

The proprietor inclined his head in acknowledgment of this standard compliment, a thin smile affixed to his face.

"It would please me to spend more time enjoying all this," Casey continued, "but I am on official business today. I am wondering if you might have seen or heard of Ho Ming in the past two weeks?"

The smile vanished from the shopkeeper's face, and he cast his slanted eyes quickly about to see if anyone was within earshot. "Ho Ming is not a man I wish to see or have any dealings with."

"I know what he is and that honest men such as you do not associate with men like Ho Ming. I thought perhaps, since you see many people, you might have heard someone mention him, or you yourself may have seen him on the street or in your shop."

"No, no." He shook his head. "No see Ho Ming. Do not wish to see Ho Ming."

"You have not heard anyone mention his name?" Casey persisted.

"His name has not soiled my ears," the Oriental replied.

"Thank you, my friend. I wish all people in Chinatown were like you," Casey added in a softer tone as he guided McGraw out into the street once more.

Their next stop was at Li Po Tai's Chinese Tea Herb Sanitarium on Washington Street at Brennan Place. The two clerks here were young men Casey did not know. He showed his badge and made polite inquiries. But they, too, disavowed any knowl-

49

edge of Ho Ming or his whereabouts.

The result was the same at two more legitimate businesses they visited. Although the men who ran these small stores knew Casey from his days as a patrolman on the Chinatown squad, most did not address him by name. McGraw assumed it was because they did not want to be seen by their fellow Chinese as being too friendly with white authority. If any of them had seen or heard anything about Ho Ming, they were not admitting to it.

Casey was plainly worried. "I don't like the sound of it," he said as they paused on a corner after almost an hour of casually probing for information. "I would think that if these men had heard anything of Ho Ming, they would have told me. It could be he has been lying low. But I think he would have contacted me as we agreed. The man may be scum, but I think he's as good as his word. I would go straight to one of his whorehouses and inquire, but no one there would tell a white detective anything. And none of the girls or anyone else there would probably know anything about the comings and goings of the owner."

"You think he's dead?"

Casey didn't reply for a few seconds. "I don't know," he said slowly. "I have a hunch he's not. The world wouldn't be any worse off without him, but he's been a very co-operative informant for the police."

"What now?" McGraw asked.

Before Casey could answer, a blue-uniformed policeman approached them from around the corner.

"Ah, there you are, Lieutenant Casey. I was told you were in the area."

"Yes, Sergeant Davis?"

"Sir, we've found a dead body in an alley about a block from here. I think you should come and take a look."

"Ho Ming?" McGraw asked, arching his brows at Casey.

The patrolman shook his head. "I don't know who this Ho Ming is, but this body is white."

Chapter Five

"The wagon has been sent for, but I thought you should have a look before anything is moved," Sergeant Davis said as the three strode quickly toward the alley.

"Any identification on the body?" Casey asked.

"No, sir. His pockets were empty. And. . . ."

"Yes?"

"Something else was very odd about this killing."

"What's that?"

"The way he was murdered. Apparently an axe was used."

"The signature of the *boo how doy,* the hatchet men of the Chinese tongs," Casey stated. "You should know there's nothing unusual about that, Sergeant."

"Right, sir. But this body has been mutilated. The head is missing."

Casey stopped in his tracks and stared at the uniformed policeman for a few long seconds. Then he motioned for the sergeant to lead on.

In the middle of the block they turned into a narrow alleyway. Nothing else seemed amiss. The alley was thick with Chinese pedestrians, going and coming on their various errands. The alley was overhung with protruding second-story balconies. About a hundred feet from the street McGraw spotted a uniformed patrolman, standing guard over a pile of rags. As they approached, the patrolman reached down behind a row of garbage cans and pulled the rags away to reveal the body. Even though McGraw had been prepared for it, the sight of a headless corpse sent chills up his spine. The body was lying on its back, dressed in a plain pair of beltless cotton pants and a blue cotton work shirt that was soaked with dried blood on its upper half. McGraw averted his eyes from the ragged stump that protruded from the neck of the shirt. Flies that had been buzzing around the rotting garbage quickly settled on the mass of dried blood as the body was uncovered.

"Who found him?" Casey asked as he knelt on one knee to take a closer look.

"I did, sir. Patrolman Todd. Actually, it was the cook from one of these eating places who came out here to pitch some slops into the alley and tripped over him. I was makin' my rounds, and he sent someone to fetch me."

"Where's this cook now?" Casey asked.

"Gone. Before I could hold him for questioning, he slipped away. You know how some of these people are . . . don't want to be mixed up in anything that smacks of the law."

"No matter. Probably couldn't tell us anything, anyway. If he had been mixed up in it himself, he wouldn't have sent for you."

Beside the body was a bloodied axe that McGraw took to be the murder weapon. It was of an unusual shape and design.

"Nothing's been moved?" asked Casey over his shoulder as he looked around.

"Not by us, sir. Everything's just as we first saw it."

Casey took a notebook and pencil from his shirt pocket and began jotting something in it.

McGraw could see that the murder victim had been a big man — probably taller than six feet, with a stout build to match. What he could see of the skin on the arm, where the shirt had been torn, was pale and freckled with reddish-brown hair. The hands were big and callused. Obviously a working man who had been used to hard labor. McGraw tried to concentrate on the details of what was before him to keep the nausea from overwhelming him. He moved a few steps away from the garbage to get a breath of fresh air and to see the body from a different angle. Another chill went up his sweaty back, and he knelt quickly beside the body and picked up the right hand. The natural paleness of the skin in life had been made almost a fish-belly white by death and the massive loss of blood. But it wasn't the color he was looking at; it was the fingers. The nail of the forefinger was split to the quick.

"I know who this man is," he said in a choked voice.

"Who?"

"Kevin O'Toole."

"What? How can you tell?"

McGraw felt tears blurring his eyes and had to swallow a time or two before he could answer. "We were joking about how beat-up his hands were yesterday at the game. That right forefinger had the nail split exactly like this. And look at his coloring and size."

McGraw stood up with a sigh and looked at Casey. The latter's face had gone slightly pale, and his mouth beneath the black mustache was drawn into a grim, compressed line.

With a sudden clatter of hoofs on cobblestones, the black police wagon turned into the alleyway, scattering several passers-by. The team and wagon came to a stop in the narrow passageway. While the driver held the horses, the attendant and the patrolman lifted the body onto a stretcher, covered it with a strip of canvas, and slid it into the back of the makeshift hearse.

McGraw leaned against the nearby brick wall. In spite of the cool air sweat was bursting from every pore, and he was wet all over. Fred Casey had walked over to have a few words with the attendant as the latter closed the back doors of the black wagon. Then the attendant heaved himself back up to

54

the high seat, the driver snapped the lines over the team, and they moved off.

Through a haze McGraw was aware that Casey was taking another close look around in the area where the body had been found. Then he spoke briefly with Sergeant Davis who had retrieved the bloody axe. Wrapping it carefully in one of the dirty rags that had been used to cover the body, Davis handed it to Casey.

"Let's go," Casey suggested to McGraw. "I want to take this back to the station house and look it over." When McGraw didn't reply, Casey looked at him sharply. "You all right? You don't look well."

McGraw swallowed and ran a sleeve across his sweaty forehead. "Yeah, I'm okay. It's just . . . well, finding O'Toole like this and all. . . ."

"I know. He was a friend of mine, too." Casey led the way down the crowded alleyway, through the curious onlookers toward the street. "We'll forget about locating Ho Ming for now. I want to examine this weapon. You look like you could use a good cup of coffee. You want to sit down for a minute?"

McGraw could feel the blood draining from his face, and his knees were weak. But he saw the oily water, the dirt and soggy newspapers in the gutters, and resisted the impulse to sit down on the curbing. A Chinese vendor was hunkered down, tending a curbside brazier, cooking and selling some concoction whose foul smell made McGraw feel even sicker.

"This is ridiculous," McGraw gritted through clenched teeth. "I'm supposed to be a temporary city detective. I've seen violent death before."

"But not the beheading of a teammate and co-worker," Casey reminded him. "Nothing to be embarrassed about. You'd be something less than human if you didn't react to a sight like that, even if it wasn't somebody you knew."

55

"I'll be all right. Just a little shaky. Give me a few minutes. Let's walk."

Casey took his arm as they made their way downhill, away from Dunscombe Alley. But the horrible sight would linger in Jay McGraw's mind long after the alley was left behind.

The ocean breeze was kicking up and swirling dirt and trash out of the streets. By the time they reached the station house a few blocks away, the later afternoon shadows were stretching long, and McGraw felt he had himself under control again. The violent reaction had passed, his knees were stronger, and he was rapidly returning to normal.

Casey went first past the desk sergeant, down a hallway, and into a back room where he shut the door behind them. It was the same room where they had gathered following the clash with the smugglers two nights before.

Casey put the axe on the heavy oak table and carefully unwrapped it. He studied it for a few moments and then asked: "Do you see anything unusual about this weapon?"

"Turkish, maybe?" McGraw replied, noting the curved edge. "Looks like pictures I've seen of a headsman's axe, only it's smaller."

Casey nodded. "Could be. Or possibly Oriental, although I've never seen anything quite like it in Chinatown. If there was ever any kind of engraving on the blade, it seems to have eroded away. Notice how old and rusted and pitted the iron is. But somebody has sharpened it with a grindstone or a file." He ran his thumb gingerly along the gleaming edge. A few strands of hair were stuck to the dried blood that covered about a third of the axe head. An ash handle, about three-and-a-half feet long, protruded from the head of the axe. Casey picked up the weapon carefully, with the rag around the handle, and gave it a couple of tentative swings. "Feel this. Grip it where my hand is. Don't want to mess up any latent fingerprints."

Casey handed the weapon to McGraw who whipped it around. It was much lighter than he had expected, as well as being well-balanced. "Amazing! Look how thin the blade is. Probably doesn't weigh over two pounds. This thing was made for battle. I almost feel like I need to be wearing a helmet and armor to be wielding it."

"Some of the Chinese hatchet men actually do wear armor, you know. A chain mail vest made in China costs two hundred and forty dollars . . . a very small price when you're talking about preventing a fatal wound. And most of the other *boo how doy* wear bullet-proof, heavy quilted coats . . . much thicker and denser than the usual quilting of Chinese clothing."

"Do you think this axe might have come from China?"

"I don't know. But it looks like an antique of some kind. Probably stolen."

"Wonder why it was left with the body? Maybe the killer was interrupted, had to get away in a hurry, and couldn't be seen running away with the murder weapon in his hand," McGraw said.

"No. Dropping the weapon by the body is a hatchet-man custom. Whether it be a gun or a blade, leaving the weapon is what you might call their trademark. That murder was committed somewhere else, and the body dumped in that alley. Did you notice there was hardly any blood on the ground? A decapitation would cause massive amounts of blood. And the head itself is missing. Sergeant Davis said they made a thorough search of all the garbage cans and trash heaps in the alley and found nothing."

"Why would the murderer take the head?"

"I wish I knew. Until now the criminal element in Chinatown has been very careful about confining its murders to others of its own race, to avoid confrontations with white man's law. And even though beheading is a common form of execution in China, the hatchet men in the tongs usually just split a victim's skull and let it go at that. Now some of these highbinders have even taken to using Colts."

"Are you saying this wasn't the work of a Chinese high-binder?"

"I'm almost sure it wasn't. My theory is poor O'Toole was beheaded somewhere else, probably with this ancient war axe, and then hauled to Chinatown some time last night and dumped in Dunscombe Alley to make it look like the work of the Chinese *boo how doy* hatchet men. The axe was left in case we didn't get the hint. The pockets were emptied, and the head disposed of to disguise the victim's identity . . . at least for a time. By the way, had you ever seen O'Toole wearing the clothes that were on the body?"

McGraw thought for a moment. Plain canvas work pants and a pale blue shirt. "Not that I recall. But he could have owned those clothes. I just don't remember."

They fell silent for a few moments.

"I can't believe O'Toole is gone," McGraw then mused, half to himself. He felt an emptiness in the pit of his stomach when he pictured the big, brash Irishman, subduing and handcuffing a smuggler, or swinging for the fence as the hard-hitting catcher of the Stormy Petrels. They hadn't been close friends, but he would certainly miss the rough-hewn Irishman. "If it wasn't the work of highbinders, then who? And why?"

"That's what we'll have to find out, somehow. I didn't know that much about O'Toole, other than he was a good, depend-able policeman. He was a single man. What he did on his own time was strictly his own business."

"Maybe it was simply a robbery and murder. O'Toole was a big talker. With a few drinks in him, he may have bragged about having a lot of cash."

"Possibly, but I doubt it. If someone wanted to rob him, and then kill him to keep from being recognized later, why go to the trouble of cutting off his head? There are murders in this town every day, but most of them are simply shootings, stabbings, or clubbings. Why would a robber want to call attention to his crime of murder by making it so horrible that it would stand out and get more publicity? He wouldn't."

"O'Toole had an eye for the ladies. In spite of the fact that he had little use for the Chinese in general, I've heard him mention visiting a Chinese brothel a time or two. He might have taken a fancy to one of those doll-like sing-song girls and got crossways with a male Oriental over her. You know how rough he talked. He was not a diplomat. He had no trouble making enemies."

"Possible," Casey said dubiously. "But I think there's more to this than just that. Did O'Toole have any family or close friends . . . possibly a regular girl friend? His employment file probably has something. I'm sure they'll routinely check all that out."

"I've heard him mention his mother, but she lives in Philadelphia, I think. He also has a brother and a sister back East some place."

"What about friends here?"

"Hmmm . . . don't really know. I never saw much of him except on duty or on the baseball field. I'll ask some of the other guys on the ball team."

"Did he ever mention any particular girls?"

"I remember him dating someone named Susie, but he never mentioned her last name. I heard him talk about a blonde named Trixie, or Tessie, or something like that." He shook his head. "Sorry. Much as I liked O'Toole, I didn't know much about his private life."

"No matter. I'll ask some of the other men. Maybe we can get some leads on what he did on his time off. Surely we'll find some clue as to what led to this. I don't think it was just happenstance. Too grisly. I'll put one of the other men on tracking down any leads we can find. We'll start by going through the stuff at his rooming house."

"I'd hate to be the one who has to tell his mother," McGraw said. "Especially the gruesome circumstances and the fact that we don't know who did it, or why."

"*If* we can find her," Casey said. "Whether his death has anything to do with our push on this opium smuggling, I don't know. But tough as it may be, we've got to put his murder behind us and let someone else in the police department work on it. You and I and the special squad can't be diverted from our main job."

"Unless we find out there's a connection," McGraw finished.

"Unless we find out there's a connection," Casey agreed.

The body was positively identified by matching the corpse's fingerprints to those in O'Toole's personnel file at the police department. Doctor D. L. Dorr, the coroner, performed an autopsy and ruled the body free of poisons or other injuries or defects that might have contributed to death. His official ruling was that Kevin O'Toole had met his death as a homicide at the hands of parties unknown.

At first the newspapers carried only sketchy items of an unidentified body found in Chinatown. But two days later, almost before the coroner had finished his job, newsboys on the streets were hawking copies of the *Chronicle* emblazoned with the banner head:

POLICEMAN MURDERED IN CHINATOWN
Kevin O'Toole,
Popular Catcher for the
Stormy Petrels,
Beheaded by Hatchet Men

The article went on to describe what little more the reporters had been able to find out and padded with information about O'Toole's work on the opium squad and his record as a baseball player.

As a result of this splash of publicity, the funeral next day was thronged with friends, acquaintances, and the morbidly curious. The entire Stormy Petrel baseball club was in attendance, along with many of the team's followers. In addition, many of O'Toole's fellow policemen, including the Chinatown squad and the opium squad, showed up, resplendent in their dark blue uniforms and brass buttons. They looked on, silent and grim, as the big Irishman's casket was lowered into the earth, following a moving eulogy by a young priest from the San Francisco Mission.

The leaden sky was leaking a light, steady rain, and the smell of damp wool was prevalent as McGraw's eyes scanned the crowd. There were several unattended young women present, and, before the service was over, McGraw quietly pointed them out to Casey who signaled his men to maneuver themselves to head the women off before they could leave. Gleaning any information they might have about O'Toole's private life was imperative, and this was easier than trying to find them later for questioning.

The final prayer was intoned, and damp clods of dirt were thudding onto the lid of the coffin as the crowd began to disperse.

"Casey!"

Casey looked up sharply at the sound of his name.

"Yes, Captain?"

"I don't think this is an appropriate time for your men to be socializing with those young ladies."

"They're not socializing, sir. I've given orders that these women be questioned as quickly and thoroughly as possible about their knowledge of O'Toole and his movements the last few days of his life."

"That should be done at the station house . . . not here. His last rites should not be profaned. As the bard wrote . . . 'So may he rest; his faults lie gently on him.'" The short, slightly balding Captain Kingsley frowned as he replaced his uniform hat. "How do you know these women even knew him?"

"Nothing like a funeral to bring out old girl friends and acquaintances, Captain," Casey replied. "If they were interested enough to dress up and come out here to stand in this rain, they *knew* him."

"Your men have plenty to keep them busy on their special assignment. Leave the homicide investigation to the ones who've been assigned to it. 'Truth will come to light; murder cannot be hid long.' Shakespeare."

Casey nodded glumly.

McGraw looked across a stunted forest of headstones and saw a woman, edging away from Jason Neal, obviously annoyed and making an impatient gesture as she climbed into a closed carriage.

"I don't want any complaints from the public about being harassed by your men, Casey. Call them off." Captain Thomas Kingsley turned up his raincoat collar and walked away without another word.

Casey muttered something under his breath, his face as dark as the weather.

"What'd you say?" McGraw asked.

"As long as he's quoting Shakespeare, I've got one of my own . . . 'I dote on his very absence.' "

McGraw covered a sudden snort of laughter with a quick cough.

Chapter Six

"Here he comes."

Casey straightened up and tapped the dottle out of his stubby pipe against the brick wall where he had been leaning. It was the following Friday, and he and McGraw were near the lower end of Market Street.

A slim figure was meandering toward them up the street. He was an Oriental, dressed in a conical straw hat and the dark blue pajama-type clothing so familiar in Chinatown. Across his shoulders, side to side, he balanced a long pole with a basket suspended from each end, loaded with freshly caught fish from the Filbert Street wharf.

Casey and McGraw approached the peddler, but a woman shopper reached him first to look over his selection. She picked out a fish with some deliberation, and the vendor put down his pole and wrapped her purchase in a piece of brown paper torn from a roll he pulled from somewhere under his loose-fitting jumper. She stashed the fish in her cloth shopping bag and walked away. As the vendor was raising the pole to his shoulders, Casey came up and casually palmed his badge so only the Chinaman could see it. The Oriental's dark eyes betrayed no sign of recognition or surprise. He simply reached into one of the baskets, shoving the slippery, shiny bodies aside, and finally selected one he had apparently marked, and brought it out. Casey passed him a silver dollar and took the fish in a fold of brown paper.

Without a word having passed between them, the exchange was accomplished and Casey and McGraw retreated up the street. When they were a half block away, Casey stopped and glanced casually around before stepping into an alleyway. He probed inside the gaping mouth of the fish. Muttering something under his breath, he wiped his hand on his pants and then dug out a clasp knife and handed the fish to McGraw while he opened the knife. Then he slashed open the fish's belly, raking out the viscera with his fingers. A tight wad of soaked paper fell out. McGraw threw the fish into a nearby trash barrel as Casey was wiping his hands and carefully unfolding the paper.

He scanned the figures on the small paper square. McGraw saw his brow crease as he held the stained message to the light.

"Well?"

"It's from Ho Ming, all right, so I guess he's still around and unharmed."

"What's he say?" McGraw asked after a few seconds when Casey paused with a thoughtful look on his face.

"He wants to meet with me."

"Why? I thought this whole elaborate message system was to prevent you having to be seen with him."

"It was. That's what puzzles me."

"He doesn't say why?"

"There's not much you can put on a scrap of paper this size, even writing in code."

"Are you going?"

"I'll have to. He's my only real contact. And we've about run out of leads. The night patrols on the Bay have been coming back empty-handed. Truth is, I need this man."

McGraw smiled. "So why are you trying to convince me?"

Casey chewed at the corner of his mustache. He looked uneasily at the note again. "This is not like Ho Ming. He was the one who was most insistent that we not see each other."

"Maybe he changed his mind. Maybe something urgent

came up that he can't convey in a note." McGraw shrugged. "Maybe it's not as dangerous as he first thought."

"There's no sense of urgency in this note."

"Orientals are good at not showing their emotions, especially to Caucasians."

"Something's wrong," Casey stated, unconvinced.

"Well, you know him better than I do. You think the note's a forgery?"

Casey shook his head slowly. "No. It appears to be his handwriting. I'll compare it to the others I have, but I feel sure it was written by him."

"Where do we meet him, then?"

"*We?*"

"You want to go alone?"

Casey thought a moment. "Well, if Ho Ming wants to break the rules of this game and have a face-to-face meeting, I guess it won't hurt for me to bring another person."

"Besides having another gun to watch your back. Think we should take one or two more of the boys on the squad, just in case?"

"No. I'll tell Brady I'm going, and that I'm taking you. He won't care, since you're just temporary, anyway. Besides, I don't think any of the others are that crazy about going into China-town at night."

"We meet him somewhere in Chinatown, then?"

Casey nodded. "In one of his whorehouses at ten tomorrow night."

The next day, Saturday, McGraw's team had a ball game with the Central Pacific Stars, a team from the Bay area made up entirely of railroad workers. The Stormy Petrels won handily, eleven to four, but McGraw struck out twice and misjudged a fly ball in left field, allowing two runs to score. Although he felt fine physically, his mind was not on the game. Finally Tub Moran benched him.

"Guess I'm just upset about O'Toole," he told Moran as the manager called him back for a pinch hitter in the bottom of the fifth.

"We all miss him, son, but we can't let that interfere with our play. Your mind's not here today. You should have pounded that pitcher."

McGraw nodded and sat back down on the bench. The second team catcher, P. J. Vanderpool, a young, rawboned, six-footer, was now doing full-time duty behind the plate. The youngster had good skills and quick hands, but he was somewhat awed by his responsibilities and was much quieter than the flamboyant O'Toole. The gaps were filled, and the game went on. *No one is indispensable,* McGraw reflected.

The game ended, and McGraw got back to his boarding house just in time to clean up, change clothes, and get to supper in the dining room. He had brought his appetite. The smell of fresh-baked bread filled the room, complimented by the delicious aroma of Irish stew.

"Ah, your mother outdid herself tonight," McGraw remarked to Katherine O'Neal as she set a butter dish on the table.

She straightened up and put her hands on her hips. "I'll have you know, Mister McGraw, that I made that stew myself while my mother was busy with other things. You must think I can do nothing a-tall," she finished, but only half seriously.

McGraw flushed as the other diners looked up. "Sorry, Katie," he mumbled.

As she hustled off to the kitchen, McGraw couldn't decide whether or not she was really irritated, or was just joking with him and enjoyed seeing him squirm. Women, he thought, were completely incomprehensible. He put her out of his mind and concentrated on doing justice to the meal. He had a feeling he was going to need the strength this food provided.

McGraw stretched out on his bed and closed his eyes for a few minutes of rest after supper. When his eyes flew open, someone was pounding on his door, and the room was dark. Instantly awake and alert, he sprang to the door and opened it.

"I fell asleep," he said, admitting Casey. "Sorry."

"Never mind. Let's get going. It's half past nine."

McGraw fumbled for some wooden matches on the bedside table and lighted the lamp. He took his gun belt from the bedpost and slipped it over his head, so the holster hung beneath his left arm. He checked the action and the load of his pearl-handled, nickel-plated Colt Lightning. It was working smoothly. He eased the hammer down on an empty chamber and checked the cartridge loops to be sure they were full. Satisfied, he reached for his wool jacket to cover the whole arrangement. He took one last look around, blew out the lamp, and went out.

They walked to Market Street, caught a cable car, and rode it a few blocks before dropping off and walking on toward Chinatown. Both men were wearing hats, but it was a clear night, and there was no mistaking them for Orientals. At least with their faces concealed in shadow, no one would recognize or know they were policemen. McGraw hoped that anyone who saw them would assume they were only a couple of Caucasian tourists who had come to Chinatown to sample the delights of the sing-song girls.

Casey led the way directly to a brick structure on DuPont Street. He stopped before an unmarked wooden door. A small gas light hissed quietly in a wrought iron sconce above the door. Underneath the pale light the shadows were even blacker as Casey pulled a short chain that hung from one side of the doorway. A chime sounded faintly from somewhere inside.

Almost immediately the door swung inward, and one of the biggest Chinese men McGraw had ever seen stepped aside to admit them. The man had a completely bald, bullet-shaped head. He wore a pair of western pants and a loose-sleeved, belted jacket made of some type of dark velvet.

They passed through a small anteroom that was nearly dark. Casey brushed aside a hanging bamboo curtain, and they entered a larger room. McGraw was immediately struck by a cloying, sweet odor of heavy incense. Candles, flickering through red glass hoods, illuminated the ornate Oriental rug and the pale couches around the room. Decorating these couches were six doll-like Oriental figures in various reclining poses. They were fully dressed and heavily made-up with black hair swept back and eyebrows penciled in arches over black, slanted eyes that showed no sign of warmth as they were turned toward these newcomers. The heavy, brocaded silk *cheongsums* they wore were slit to the upper thigh on both sides to reveal small, but shapely, legs.

A woman of indeterminate age, dressed the same, but obviously older, rose to greet them. "Gentlemen, welcome to our house of celestial delights." She bowed slightly from the waist, never changing expression. "Our girls are here to serve you. If you have any. . . ."

"We're here to see the owner, Ho Ming," Casey interrupted her.

She looked at him, and then at McGraw, squinting slightly to see their faces beneath the hats which they had not removed.

"Don't worry. He's expecting us," Casey said.

She bowed slightly again. "This way."

She led them through another hanging bamboo curtain that closed off the far side of the room. At the end of a short, gaslit hallway she stopped at the foot of a stairway that led up sharply to the left. She pointed upward. "It is the door at the end of the hall." Presently she was gone, the pale silk stretched across her bowed back, shining in the gas light as she shuffled back to her parlor.

Casey took a deep breath and started up the dark staircase as McGraw slid a hand inside his coat to be sure the Colt Lightning was still in place. He had a prickly feeling up his back. Why hadn't their informant contacted them in some place other than his own whorehouse? Some place safer for Ho Ming? It didn't make sense. But, then, there was no accounting for the Oriental mind. If they were seen coming here by Ho Ming's enemies, of whom there were apparently many, any of the criminal tongs who controlled the flow of opium into Chinatown could have Ho Ming's name on a street corner poster in a matter of hours for all to see that he was slated for elimination by the dreaded *boo how doy*.

The stairs in the old building creaked and groaned under their weight. When they reached the second floor, they came out into a dimly lit hallway with a strip of thin carpeting down the middle and three rooms on each side. The door of the first room on the left opened, and a small Chinese man emerged, his jacket over one arm. He gave them a quick glance and then ducked his head and hurriedly started down the steps.

They proceeded to the closed door at the end of the short hallway, as McGraw began to have a claustrophobic feeling. There were no windows and apparently no back stairs. He felt as if he were going headfirst into a badger's den.

Casey rapped softly on the door. There was a pause, then the door opened. "Come in. You are just on time."

The man who spoke was of medium height, obviously Oriental with black hair slicked straight back from his face and lying close to his head. As he turned to close the door behind them, McGraw noted that he wore a short queue, in the style of many older, traditional Chinese. In contrast, he wore western-style clothing — a black business suit with a soft white shirt and no tie.

The room was a small office with a desk and was lighted by an overhead oil lamp. McGraw noted almost unconsciously that the desk top was clean, and the walls were devoid of any type of decoration. It was almost as if the man conducted no business here, or had just moved out.

"What is it that you wished to see me about?" Casey asked abruptly. "It's not good for us to be seen together."

McGraw had never before laid eyes on Ho Ming, but the man was obviously nervous. His pale forehead glistened with perspiration in the light of the lamp. Though not above average height he was large-boned for an Oriental, with flat planes to his face. The hooded eyes were slightly more oval and were topped by heavy brows.

"It was imperative that I see you in person," Ho Ming began. "This information could not be trusted to some fish-mongering courier . . . even one who does not read English."

"What is it?"

The door burst open, and three Chinese men with guns entered, fanning out along the wall as the last one slammed the door behind them. McGraw's hand was halfway to the holster, hanging under his coat, when the loud clicking of the three .45s being cocked stopped him. A cold feeling of dread settled in him.

"What is this" Casey asked, his tone deadly even.

"What are you doing?" Ho Ming cried, his voice rising. "Get out of my office!"

Whether the three intruders did not speak English, or just were not inclined to talk, McGraw didn't know. But one thing was obvious. These three were members of the murderous Chinese *boo how doy*. All three wore round black hats with short brims, western-type trousers, and the heavy, quilted jumper-style tops. But, more importantly, they had the upper hand at the moment. *Cold, professional assassins,* McGraw thought as he braced himself for the slugs he expected to tear into him at any moment.

On some unseen signal one of the intruders circled behind them and quickly felt them up and down for weapons. McGraw felt his Colt being deftly removed from its holster. A small revolver was also taken from Ho Ming's coat pocket, and Casey's service revolver likewise was lifted. The hatchet man didn't seem concerned that McGraw kept his full cartridge belt.

There was no talking. There was really nothing to say. The next move was up to the three hatchet men. McGraw thought their time was up, but his anger was almost as strong as his fear — anger that he would not go down fighting. He had been surprised and disarmed.

"You will come with us," one of the hatchet men said in halting English, motioning with his gun toward a door that McGraw had not noticed before on the far side of the office. They had no choice but to obey. Refuse, and they would be shot on the spot, McGraw was sure. But, if they could stall these triggermen, there might be a chance of escape. He had no idea where they were being taken, but the three of them were herded through the door and down a steep, dark stairway. At the bottom McGraw, who was in the lead, encountered a heavy, iron-backed door that was both barred and locked.

One of their captors said something in Chinese, and another one of them pushed to the front and lifted the bar and stood it aside. McGraw could hear locks grating, and the door suddenly swung outward. McGraw was pushed outside into the dim light of an alleyway. Each of the hatchet men took one of them by an arm, a gun muzzle in their ribs as they were walked down the alley.

McGraw was alert to everything — the irregular row of two-

and three-story brick buildings, pressing close on either side, the strip of starlit sky dimly seen overhead between them. Except for the light on the streets at either end of the block, the alley was dark, yet there seemed to be an unusual brightness. Then he twisted his head to one side and noticed an almost full moon, rising over his shoulder and beginning to cast a cold, dimly white light on boxes and barrels and trash heaps and overhanging balconies in the narrow passageway. There was no sign of human life. In McGraw's experience the Chinese quarter usually was swarming with activity, day or night. It seemed unusually dark and still. Maybe the night-prowling Chinese had somehow gotten the word that the *boo how doy* would be on a mission tonight and decided to stay clear, like a school of fish avoiding sharks.

Then McGraw's eyes caught a slight movement, and he heard a clicking and shuffling noise. It was a horse — a horse hitched to a dark, closed carriage with no sidelights, about thirty yards away. All his senses jumped to the alert. Maybe there was a chance to jerk away and run into the darkness before they reached this coach or whatever was waiting for them. But his captor had a grip on his arm just above the elbow like the talons of an eagle, and the gun was still pressed firmly into his back. Even as quick as he was, McGraw knew he couldn't outrun or dodge a bullet. This thought was hardly gone from his mind before they were at the carriage, the door was opened, and they were quickly pushed up and inside. The door slammed, and McGraw was thrown back into the forward-facing seat as the coach lurched into motion.

McGraw realized he was as tense as a coiled spring and tried to concentrate on relaxing. He might later need this energy he was using up. As the coach rocked along, he decided to watch the slits of light sliding past the curtained windows.

Wherever they were being taken, it had to be a long way

from Chinatown, McGraw reasoned, as they kept going for what seemed like nearly an hour. Either that, or they were just being driven around in circles to confuse them. Not a word was spoken by anyone as the iron rims of the carriage wheels ground along on the cobblestones and the clopping of the horse's hoofs came faintly to them through the closed coach. Once McGraw reached for the window curtain and started to pull it aside, but one of the Chinamen gave an exclamation and cracked McGraw's wrist sharply with the barrel of his Colt. McGraw dropped his hand as pain shot up his arm. He had to bite his lip to keep from lunging at the man.

Eventually the outside lights ceased, and they rode for a long time in total darkness over what sounded like a dirt road. Finally the coach halted, and the *boo how doy* jumped out, pulling a man with each of them. To McGraw's amazement they were somewhere on the coast. The cold, onshore wind bit at them, and the fully risen moon made the long Pacific rollers look like liquid silver. The coach had stopped on a sand rise where clumps of seagrass had taken root. Then the sandy soil ended, and the rocks began — big rocks that bastioned the shoreline against erosion and took the force of the heavy rollers, shattering them into white spray.

The shoreline was deserted. They were apparently quite a distance from the city, on the outer ocean shore and nowhere on the Bay itself. McGraw did not recognize this section of the coastline as the hatchet men marched them away from the coach toward the huge rock formations that overlooked the beach. *Was there a boat waiting for them?* McGraw's mind was reeling, and he looked over at Casey as they were hurried along.

"You have any idea where we're going?"

"No talk!" The command was punctuated with the sharp jab of a gun barrel.

Casey shook his head in reply.

They were led out onto a shelf of solid rock and then down into a cleft about three feet deep. From there the solid rock layer was broken into a fantastic labyrinth of shapes and fissures where centuries of pounding waves had eroded and shaped the formation.

Their captors seemed to know where they were going, since they never hesitated. If they were headed for the narrow, sandy beach below the rocks, there were certainly easier ways of getting there. They had almost reached the edge of the rock formations, and it appeared they would have to jump or climb down about twenty feet to reach the beach, when they halted.

"Here!" one of the captors said, jerking Casey to a stop. A cold shiver swept over McGraw that had little to do with the night wind. This, then, was where they were to be shot and their bodies thrown into the ocean for the tide to carry out. Unless their decomposed remains washed up somewhere, no one would ever know what had happened to them. As prevalent as sharks were along this coast, it was unlikely that even their remains would wash ashore.

Now would be the time to make a break for it, if they were ever going to. McGraw tried to get Casey's attention, but Casey's captor was shoving him down into the rock, or rather a hole in the rock that McGraw had not seen until now. It wasn't the normal fissure they had been climbing in and out of for the past few minutes. This was an irregular, round hole about four feet across that went straight down into the surface of the rock table. As Casey disappeared into this hole, his personal captor did not follow.

Next it was McGraw's turn. *Was this hole filled with water? Were they to be drowned?* McGraw cringed at sliding down into the blackness where he had no idea what awaited him. But the muzzle of the .45 persuaded him, and he sat down, lowering his legs into the hole. When he hesitated, his captor put a foot on his back and gave a quick shove. He plunged into the blackness, feet first, his arms flailing as he went. He banged off the walls of the narrow hole, sliding and scraping his hands as he instinctively tried to protect his face and head. The sides of the hole had been worn relatively smooth by water action, and fortunately there were no sharp outcroppings. Then he was falling free for a second before his feet struck sand and jarred him clear to his head. McGraw crumpled to one side and gasped for breath, his insides feeling as if they had been crimped when he had jackknifed on landing.

He rolled over on his back and slowly straightened his legs, hoping he had no internal injuries. After a few seconds he was fairly sure no bones were broken. Except for some scrapes and bruises he seemed to be intact. He lay still a few more seconds, recovering, and wondering what had become of Casey. He finally rolled up to his hands and knees with a groan and looked around. Dim light was coming from somewhere, casting just enough illumination to see a lump a few feet away. It began to move and gave a low grunt. McGraw crawled to his friend.

"Fred! You all right?"

Casey coughed and then drew a shuddering breath.

"Say something! Can you hear me?"

"Yeah," came the weak reply. "Quit hollerin' in my ear." Casey sat up, brushing sand from his face. "Must've blacked out when I hit. Knocked the breath out of me." He started to rise, but gasped, and sat back down.

"What's wrong?"

"Just turned my ankle a little. It's O.K."

"Where are we?" McGraw asked. "On the beach?"

Casey turned his head. "No. We're in some kind of opening under the rocks."

McGraw's eyes were adjusting to the dimness, and he could now make out where the faint light was coming from. It was an opening in the rocks that looked out onto a glittering, moon-lit patch of Pacific.

Casey spat sand out of his mouth and pushed gingerly to his feet, wincing as he bumped his head. He sank back down, rubbing the sharp pain in his scalp. The rocky roof of the cave was no more than five feet high.

"What's the point of throwing us down here?" McGraw wondered aloud as Casey again crawled up on his hands and knees. "We can walk right out to the beach and back to the city." He could hear the relief in his own voice. "Maybe they were just trying to scare us . . . let us know the *boo how doy* can kill us any time they want."

Casey made no comment. He was looking carefully around. Then he got to his feet and, crouching, made his way toward the opening in the rock. McGraw followed. As they neared it, McGraw's heart sank. The irregular opening was closed off with vertical iron bars from top to bottom, spaced about six inches apart.

"Oh, no!" McGraw gripped the bars and sank to his knees on the hard sand.

"I think I know this place," Casey said thoughtfully. "When the surf is up and the tide is high, with an onshore wind, the waves surge into this cave. From up above you can see the spume spouting up through that blowhole we came down. Looks like a regular geyser."

"Damn!"

"Yeah. It's quite a sight. A few years back a couple of kids were playing in here and got caught by the high tide. Their bodies were never found. Even though the city fathers weren't responsible, there was a lot of pressure put on to do something since the beaches close to the city are popular places for outings. Our old friend, Blind Boss Buckley, got into the discussion, and it wasn't long before the city had workmen out here and

77

cemented these bars in here to keep kids from playing in this cave."

McGraw shivered. It was immediately clear what their fate would be. He didn't trust himself to say anything. Casey was likewise silent as they stared out at the clear night through the bars of their prison.

"Is the tide going in or out?" McGraw finally asked, trying to keep his voice steady.

"It's coming in. Hear the thunder of those waves? Take a look at the surf line."

McGraw studied the breakers, hitting the beach several rods away. Using a snag of driftwood as a reference, he noted how high each succeeding wave washed, before it receded. It soon became obvious that the tide was definitely surging, aided by a stiff onshore wind. Ironically the one thing that was creating a beautiful night outside — the full moon overhead — was helping create a deadly situation for the two of them, by pulling the tide even higher. Yet, this method of execution was not like the *boo how doy*. They usually just used a knife, hatchet, or gun.

"Probably because we're white," Casey replied when McGraw voiced his question. "They probably took Ho Ming somewhere back to Chinatown and executed him, tong-style, as a lesson to any other Chinese who might be tempted to work with the white authorities."

"How long do you think we have?" McGraw asked, changing the subject to what was uppermost in his mind.

"I'd guess maybe two hours before we're knee-deep in here. Less than three before this cave is full."

McGraw gripped the bars and stared in fascination at the marching succession of waves that were gradually pulsing higher and higher on the sloping strand, like some hungry monster, crawling back to its cave to devour two unwelcome intruders.

Chapter Seven

"We have to figure a way out of here . . . *McGraw!*"

McGraw tore his gaze away, jolted out of his hypnotic depression by the harsh yell.

"We've got time," Casey continued tersely. "Let's make good use of it."

McGraw forced his mind to focus on the problem, to break the paralysis of fear that had momentarily gripped him. "Is there any other opening into or out of this cave?" he asked.

"I doubt it, but let's take a quick look to be sure. Might as well eliminate the obvious first."

"Start on that side, and I'll start here, and we'll work our way around the walls in opposite directions. Give a holler if you find anything."

"Wish I had a light," McGraw said.

"I wish we were out of here, as long as we're wishing," Casey answered, moving away.

McGraw began feeling his way along the wall. The rock was fairly smooth under his fingers, worn by many years of pounding, surging water. But the wall itself was irregular, bending in and out. As it went back under the cliff, the sand floor sloped gradually upward until McGraw was forced to his hands and knees. As he crawled toward the back of the cave, the thunder of the surf receded slightly, giving the illusion that he could somehow get into the farthest reaches of the cave and escape the rising water. But the wet sand that was soaking the knees of his pants told him otherwise. This cave had been drowned during the last high tide, only a few hours earlier.

Irregular as the walls of the cave were, there was not a crevice or an opening large enough to allow a rat to escape. After running his hands over the rough rock McGraw, with a growing sense of panic, heard Casey, scuffling along near the rear of the cave.

"Find anything?"

"Nothing. But I didn't think there would be an opening."

"What about the way we came in?" McGraw asked, thinking of the next most obvious possibility — the rock chimney.

Casey scooted over to get himself under the blowhole. McGraw could look up and locate the opening by the faintly lighter circle and a few winking stars in the night sky.

"How high, do you reckon?"

"About twenty feet, I'd guess," Casey replied.

McGraw stood up and put his arms over his head. At this spot the ceiling was about six feet high, or higher. In addition, the opening that sloped up into the base of the narrow chimney was wide and roughly cone-shaped. The chimney was narrow enough that one could possibly wedge himself into it and walk his way up, feet braced on one side and back on the other. It would be difficult and exhausting. One release of pressure, one slip of the foot, and the climber would be right back at the bottom. But before McGraw could worry about falling, there was one major hurdle that had to be overcome.

"Think we can get up there?" he asked.

"We have no choice. We've got to try. But you're the athlete. Maybe if you stand on my shoulders, you can reach it."

McGraw brushed the sand off his hands and hunched his shoulders inside his jacket. Casey knelt on one knee, and McGraw stepped up onto his bent knee, gripped both of Casey's hands in his to keep his balance, and then carefully put one foot on Casey's shoulder and thrust himself upward. Casey wavered, McGraw got overbalanced, let go, and dropped lightly to the sand.

"Again," he said.

They repeated the maneuver, with the same result. The third time McGraw was able to stand upright, his shoes rocking on Casey's shoulders as he held his balance. He finally steadied himself, let go of one of Casey's hands, and reached upward. Cold air was rushing upward past him. He could easily touch the inside of the cone-shaped rock. Then he let go with the other hand and quickly stretched upward to place both hands against the rock to steady himself. He swung one hand out and around in the darkness to feel for the other side of the chimney. Nothing. He was not yet high enough. A wave of despair washed over him. Even if he could contact both sides of the chimney, he would not be able to swing himself up into the chimney if he could find no handhold to grip. He crouched and jumped down.

"Not high enough," he grunted. "Think we have time to scrape a pile of sand here to build up this spot?"

"Yeah."

"That rock's worn too smooth. No handholds. I've got to get high enough so I can get at least waist-deep into the narrow part of that hole. Otherwise, I won't be able to wedge my feet and back up in there to try to start the climb."

Conscious of the increasing noise of the pounding surf outside, they began to dig frantically with their hands, scraping the damp sand up into a mound. Precious minutes dragged by as they worked, panting and not talking, keenly aware of the rising tide. Finally they paused and leveled off the top of the little sand hill. It was only about two feet high.

"It's not high enough. Has to be at least four or five feet," McGraw said. "Of all places for this ceiling to be so high!"

They renewed their efforts, scooping the sand with cupped hands. The mound grew slowly higher and higher as they dug out a trench around the base. Precious time ticked away as they worked.

At last McGraw called a halt and leveled off the top, packing the sides of the slope. "Let's try it."

Casey crawled up the mound, followed by McGraw. They positioned themselves, and Casey nodded. "Now."

McGraw stepped nimbly up, gripping his friend's hands. When he had gained his balance, he slowly straightened up. His head and shoulders were up inside the narrower part of the hole. He felt with his hands until he could visualize the contours of the rock. He took a deep breath. "Okay, when you feel my weight go off your shoulders, get out of the way in case I slip."

"Right."

McGraw pressed his back against the smooth rock and put both hands out to the sides, trying in vain to get some sort of purchase against any little rough spot.

"Brace yourself. I'm going to push off."

"Go ahead," came the muffled reply from below.

McGraw shoved hard, kicking his right leg up. He slammed his shoe sole hard against the opposite wall, wedging himself into the narrow chimney. Holding his breath with the strain, he swung his left leg up so he had both feet braced, with his back pressed against the opposite side. The hole was almost too wide at this point to get enough leverage to squirm and walk his way upward. His legs were nearly straight out. Chill air was rushing upward past him, but he could feel himself perspiring. He could also feel the cartridge belt diagonally across his back which he had forgotten to remove from under his coat.

With his elbows and shoulders he began to wriggle his body

upward. He gained a few inches, and stopped a moment to rest. Then, pressing his feet against the opposite side, he took a deep breath, hunched his shoulders, and tried to scoot his back a little higher. Again he gained a few inches. He felt encouraged. Maybe he could do it. When his upper body was higher than his feet, he moved one foot up, pressed it in place, and followed with the other. He repeated the process, trying to guess how many feet he had to go. Even as he struggled upward, a disturbing thought crossed his mind. If he were able to reach the top, he still had to find a rope or a long pole or log to use as a ladder to rescue Casey . . . and he would have to do it quickly.

The hole was still too wide for him to be able to use his hands effectively. He was only able to use his elbows and the backs of his upper arms to squirm upward. He continued to slide and walk his way, an agonizing few inches at a time. Progress was very slow, and he would have to go faster or his legs would never stand the strain long enough to reach the top. His legs were already beginning to quiver from bracing his back across the opening. He was panting, and sweat was beginning to trickle down his face. He couldn't look up or down. He could only exist with the darkness, and the hard rock against his back and under his shoe soles.

After a few seconds of rest to gather himself he pushed upward once more — and suddenly stopped, snagged by the cartridge belt under his jacket, catching on a crack or some kind of rough outcropping. He gasped and struggled to free himself, but he couldn't move. He had reached the point where he could no longer slide upward without somehow getting past this snag. To do it, he would have to rock his back and shoulders outward, away from the wall. When he couldn't immediately push himself past it, he paused a moment to consider. If he could press his hands against the sides for a few seconds, he could take the pressure off his back enough to slide past the obstruction, whatever it was. The problem was, he couldn't reach out far enough on either side to press his hands against anything solid. He would have to use his elbows. He pressed his elbows back and thrust his shoulders forward and upward. The cartridge belt was still caught on something. He pressed more of his weight against his elbows and wiggled his shoulders.

In a flash the slick leather soles of his shoes slipped off the rock face, and he shot downward, feet first. He hit the pile of sand and rolled off, coming to rest in the trench they had scooped out to build the mound.

"You all right?" Casey asked.

McGraw could hardly trust himself to speak. "Yeah," he finally muttered. "Yeah, I'm okay." He was close to despair. He would have to start all over again. And, from the way his legs and back felt, he wasn't sure he was up to it.

"Want to give it another shot?" Casey asked.

"Let's go."

They repeated the maneuver, but this time McGraw shrugged out of his jacket and took off the offending cartridge belt that had been looped across his chest and back like a bandoleer. Before he climbed to Casey's shoulders, he had the detective face a different direction. Trying to ignore the thundering of the surf that was pounding closer and closer outside, McGraw hopped up nimbly, and then pressed himself up into the chimney once again. This time he managed to squirm and walk his way up a good six feet. But then the chimney grew so wide he could only brace himself across the opening by pressing only his shoulders against the rock and straightening his legs out. He placed his hands back over his shoulders to press against the smooth rock and aid in his pushing. Unless the chimney narrowed above, it was hopeless.

After catching his breath, he tried again. But just as he started to move, his shoulders lost pressure against the rock, and he plunged down, head first, throwing out his arms to break his fall. He hit and rolled, spraying sand into his mouth and eyes.

"You hurt?"

"No." McGraw stood up and looked toward the cave entrance. "How much time do we have?"

"Not sure. Maybe an hour or so."

McGraw was brutally plain. "I can't get up there. Even if I could, I don't know where I'd find something like a rope to get you up before this cave fills with water."

"Worry about that when you get out." Casey paused. "Even if you made it alone, you could tell what happened."

"Forget that. We either both make it, or we don't." He thought for a few moments. "Is there any possibility that we could ride up with the water and swim to the top of this chimney? Maybe pop us out the top like corks from a bottle?"

Casey was not encouraging. "The surf slams into this cave with unbelievable force. We couldn't hold ourselves in position under this hole until the waves got high enough. It would first wash out all this sand we've piled up. And that hole's only wide enough for one at a time. We'd be battered to a pulp before we could ever get up there. Not a chance."

"What about those bars?"

"What about them?"

"How are they fastened? Were holes drilled in the rock, were they set in cement, or what?"

"I don't really know."

"Let's check." McGraw scrambled toward the mouth of the cave. He was shocked to see how high the water had already risen while they had been trying to climb the chimney. The

85

water was swishing in and out past the bars with each wave. As he went to his knees and grasped the bars, he gasped at the shock of the cold water. How could water be so cold and not turn to ice? — probably the salt and the constant motion of it. He steeled himself and gritted his teeth to ignore the pain. He had more important things on his mind.

"Help me see if any of these bars might be loose," he yelled at Casey as a wave broke, and its creamy lip curled in around the bars, wetting their legs. "If these things have been here for several years, the salt and exposure must have rusted them some." He jerked and tugged one bar at a time. "Maybe the wave action has loosened some of the underpinning."

Casey threw his weight against the bars, but nothing gave. "Feels really solid," he muttered, tugging with both hands at one of the middle bars.

McGraw had quit pushing and pulling and was digging with both hands in the sand at the base of the bars.

"What are you doing?"

"Trying . . . to . . . see . . . if I can . . . reach the base to see how these things are fastened," he panted. He paused as a wave burst just outside and water surged over his arms. "If they're set in rock, with holes individually drilled, or they're several feet down, we're out of luck. But if they're just set in cement and covered with a foot or two of sand, we may have a chance."

"A chance for what?"

"Cement crumbles with age and water and pressure. Maybe we can break one or two of these loose. C'mon, help!"

They both dug into the wet sand like badgers, digging a burrow. But it was almost too late. The water was already surging into the cave with each wave, collapsing and sliding the sand back into the holes as fast as they were scooped out. When McGraw got his hands down a foot before the next wave came, he held them in the hole as the water broke and washed around his shoulders. The water receded. He was shaking now from the chill and the desperation, but he kept digging frantically before the next onslaught of water.

"Hey! Look what I found!" Casey yelled. "As that wave washed out, it sucked back a piece of driftwood. A board. Looks like a piece of packing crate." He began to dig with it.

"Ah, here it is," McGraw said. "I feel the cement base. And it feels rough and cracked. Help me over here. Let's both work on this one bar. I thought I felt it give a little."

Casey moved to McGraw's side and used the narrow board to help dig. Another wave burst just outside, and they had to grab the bars to keep from being swept back from the entrance as the creaming water surged in.

"Quick! Use that board for leverage!" McGraw yelled, coughing out brine as the wave ebbed, leaving water several inches deep on the floor around them. "Stick it between this bar and the next one and see if you can force it out at the bottom!"

They worked feverishly together, their arms submerged up to the shoulders as they knelt and groped under the sand and water. "Careful we don't break the board. Just work it back and forth near the bottom." McGraw pushed and pulled on the base of the rusted bar.

Casey used one end of the board to punch and chip at the crumbling cement he could not see. "Hang on! Here comes another one!"

A wave burst with a thunderous roar a few feet away, and the ice-cold flood completely engulfed them. McGraw's head went under, and there was a sudden silence except for the muted gurgling and swishing sound. Then the wave receded with nearly as much force, and they were thrown against the bars.

"Quick! Dig!" McGraw gritted. "We don't have much time."

They struggled to push and pull the rusty bar loose from its moorings.

"Look out!" yelled Casey.

They grabbed the bars and rode out another bursting wave. The tide was almost at flood stage, and each breaker now nearly filled the cave entrance to the top. The wave surged back violently, tons of cold water sucking out through the bars. McGraw thrust his leg down at the base of the bar and kicked hard — once, twice. He gripped the bars on either side and kicked with both heels simultaneously, while Casey was using the board as a lever. The bottom of the bar came loose suddenly, just as another breaker burst through the opening. Caught off guard, they were swept and rolled backward several yards. When the wave surged back, they both popped to the surface, sputtering. There was barely headroom between the water and the low cave roof.

"The bar is loose," McGraw gasped. "I'll dive and force it the rest of the way out. Stay here and hold on."

McGraw struggled back to the entrance, took a deep breath, and disappeared. He felt for the bar in the icy blackness and silence. He pushed forward and back. Then one more hard shove forward, and the bar came out. He felt another wave pulling at him and forced himself to wait several seconds for it to recede before popping to the surface, gasping. There was hardly room to breathe, and he swallowed some water. He coughed and choked and finally cleared his throat. "Now! Now! It's open. Go down and squeeze through!"

Casey sucked in a deep breath and ducked under. McGraw braced himself against the low ceiling as the surge of water pulled at him. He waited until he could no longer touch Casey's legs with his foot. Then, just as another breaker pounded in, filling the cave to the top, he dove and worked his way to the opening, twisted his body sideways and, with the ebb surge wiggled his way through the small opening and stroked hard two or three times to get away from any rock overhang before he shot to the top.

"Casey!"

"Over here."

"Quick! Swim out. Dive under."

They both dove, and McGraw swam like he had never swum before as he felt the swell lift and carry him backward toward the deadly rocks. He was helpless in the grip of the relentless ocean, but then the surge slowed and stopped before he hit the rocks. His desperate stroking had carried him just beyond the surf line. He thrust himself upward, his lungs burning, and popped out to his armpits, blowing, sucking in the life-giving air.

"McGraw!"

The voice came from his left in the darkness. Casey's head appeared, bobbing on a swell in the bright moonlight. "Swim this way. The surf's hitting the coast at an angle. Let the current carry you down. About a hundred yards farther there's a break in the rocks. See it?"

McGraw kicked around, treading water, and saw the white smother of foam, beating itself against the steeply sloping sand beach, pale in the moonlight. "Let's go."

McGraw's teeth were chattering, but he no longer felt the freezing water as he pushed off in a long, gliding sidestroke. They were going to make it.

Chapter Eight

"I still can't believe your mother let you come with me."

Katie O'Neal dismounted and smoothed her divided riding skirt with one hand before replying.

"Jay, my mother doesn't dislike you," she said, glancing mischievously at him out of the corner of her eyes as the two of them stood, side by side, holding their horses.

"But to go riding on a picnic, into the Oakland hills, unchaperoned? That doesn't sound like her."

"I believe she's thinking you're some kind of hero after that episode the other night." Katie smiled.

"I wasn't able to sleep well after that," McGraw said, grimacing. "Every time I started to doze off, I'd feel like I was smothering, and I'd jump and wake myself up."

She glanced sideways at him as they walked their horses along the crest of a grassy hill in the bright sunshine. Off to their left was a stunning view of the Bay and San Francisco in the distance, but McGraw hardly noticed. Even with this lovely creature walking beside him, he was preoccupied with recurring memories of that black cave under the rocks and the trapped feeling as the icy water rolled in on them. Fred Casey's reaction to the ordeal had been more physical — he had contracted a bad cold with fever and head congestion and had taken to his bed for a couple of days. McGraw would have almost welcomed a physical sickness, instead of the black fear that lurked in the recesses of his mind and only crept out when he relaxed for sleep at night. This outing with the lovely Katie was partially an attempt to provide himself an antidote for the memory and to bring some sunshine back into his life. Then, too, he had been interested in her for some months, and this just seemed like the right time to ask her out. To his surprise and delight she had accepted. And her mother, Bridget O'Neal, had even told them to "have a lovely time."

"Oh, that looks like a good spot," Katie said, breaking into his reverie. She pointed toward a level, grassy area, partially shaded by trees.

McGraw nodded, and they led their horses into the shade and tied them. While he loosened the cinches, Katie dug into the saddlebags for the food they had packed. McGraw had originally planned to rent a buggy for this outing, but she had insisted that he rent two saddle horses. "It'll be a lot more fun," she had said. "We can go anywhere we want. I'm a good rider. And don't you dare get me a sidesaddle," she had warned him as they stepped off the ferry on the Oakland side, early that morning. The fog had lifted about ten o'clock, and the warm summer sunshine bathed the Bay area. The entire setting was balm for McGraw's physical and mental condition. He was bruised and scraped in more places than he could count, in addition to the lingering fear that had been implanted in his mind by the ruthless *boo how doy*.

"Katie, my compliments to your mother. This fried chicken is delicious."

"Jay, that's one thing I like about you. You always know the right thing to say to make a girl feel good. I fried that chicken myself last night."

McGraw grinned. "Well, I did it again. Sorry."

"That's O K," she said, taking a roll from the small basket. "You know I was only trying to get you flustered." She hesitated. "You seem pretty nervous. Are you sure you're all right?"

McGraw forced himself to smile. "I'm fine. Just a little tired.

91

Haven't slept too well the past couple of nights."

"I can understand why. Have you been back to work?"

"Yes, but it was the day shift. Just doing some routine reports in the office. Also did some follow-up with the men in the lab to see if anything was found on O'Toole's body or on that axe that would give a clue as to who killed him."

"Did they find anything?"

McGraw shook his head and poured some wine into a tin cup. "Not really. They did confirm the body was O'Toole's. But there was nothing on the body . . . you know, under the fingernails, and such as that. There was one fingerprint on the axe, but there's no way of knowing whose it is. The axe is definitely not Chinese, but the lab men aren't real sure just what it is. It appears to be very old, or at least of some very old design. But you don't want to hear about all this gruesome stuff, especially while we're eating."

"No, no. I think it's very interesting. It's sure a lot more exciting than the life I lead . . . cooking and serving and washing clothes and cleaning house and changing bed sheets. Helping mother run that boarding house is a lot of work, but there is no way she could do it alone. And she can only afford a little part-time help . . . like some school boys coming to help shovel coal in the winter and chop wood for the stove . . . you know, the heavier work."

McGraw felt a wave of shame for thinking of himself and his own problems when this girl went about the daily drudgery of her life without complaint or rebellion, out of filial love, or some sense of obligation. "Well, I tell you, I'll be glad to get back to my regular job as a Wells Fargo messenger. This police work is too dangerous for me." He grimaced. Then he smiled at her. "I'd rather just enjoy the day, the fresh air, and the sunshine, and the food . . . and you. Let's not spoil all this by talking about work. We both get enough of that every day.

Maybe I can tell you about it later. Pass me one of those pickled eggs."

It was mid-afternoon before the couple finished their wine, packed away the remnants of the food, rolled up the blanket, stowed everything in the saddlebags, and set off for Oakland. McGraw was more relaxed than he had been since the hatchet men had tried to kill him.

"I want you to get that serious look off your face," she told him as they rode side by side down the trail. "We've had a good time today, and you just put that awful business out of your mind, you hear me? You are a better man than those Chinese criminals. I know you'll be more careful next time. They caught you once, but they were just lucky. It wasn't your fault, anyway. Detective Casey is much more experienced at police work, and he had been dealing with this Ho Ming, and *he* was taken in by that phony message."

"You're right. I'll have to put it behind me. From now on, I think we should be the aggressors. We'll take the initiative, and I'll make sure Casey has some of the others on the Chinatown squad backing us up."

"There's only one thing I ask," she said seriously, squinting at him in the light of the westering sun.

"What's that?"

"If you ever again go into a Chinese house of prostitution, I want you to close your eyes and ears until you're safely outside again."

Her silvery laughter washed over him as she spurred her horse to a gallop down the slope toward the valley below.

"Any word from Ho Ming?" McGraw asked as he sat in the station house the next morning with Casey.

"No. The men on the Chinatown squad have been routinely

inquiring about him, but nobody admits to having seen him since that night he was grabbed with us."

"Even the girls at his houses of joy?"

Casey nodded. "We took two of the madams into custody for questioning. Brought them here to the station, away from their familiar surroundings, to impress them with the force and authority of white man's law. Scared the hell out of both of them, but they still denied having seen or heard from their boss. The captain believes they were telling the truth. It doesn't really matter, in any event. Ho Ming has lost whatever value he had to us as an informer, whether he's dead or alive. If the tong's enforcers didn't kill him, he's probably in hiding or running for his life."

"Well, all I can say is you and I had better watch our step. We can't count on being so lucky next time."

"If it's any consolation, that was completely my fault. And the chief let me know about it, too. I was a fool to fall right into that trap. Maybe I've been at this kind of work too long. Careless or reckless, I don't know which. When I got that note from Ho Ming by way of the fish peddler, asking me to come and meet with him, it rang an alarm bell in my head, but for once I ignored the warning. Ho Ming was so afraid of dealing directly with me that he was the one who set up that elaborate way of communicating."

"If the note was out of character, it must have meant he had something urgent he couldn't tell you in writing, even in a coded note," McGraw suggested.

"I don't think he had anything to tell me at all. I think he was forced to write that note to lure me into a trap. It was no forgery because it was in his handwriting, and he was expecting us when we got there."

"Then why didn't he try to warn us?"

They looked at each other.

"Maybe he didn't have a chance," Casey said slowly.

"We had a minute or so before the hatchet men came to the door," McGraw persisted. "We could have all made a run for it out the back door."

"I don't think so. Remember, when we got to the bottom of those stairs, the door was both barred and locked. And one of those hatchet men had a key to unlock it."

"That's right. The whole thing had to be planned, if he had a key . . . unless it was a common type lock that can be opened with a skeleton key. If Ho Ming knew they were coming, or were close by, he could have made some move to save us, and himself. We were armed. We could have fought them. Or . . . it was an intentional trap set with Ho Ming's help."

"But why? The *boo how doy* took him, too."

"A cover. So we wouldn't suspect him."

"It wouldn't matter if we suspected him or not, we were about to be very dead."

"You're right. It makes no sense. Ho Ming wasn't thrown into the cave with us. And he's dropped out of sight now that the whole world knows we escaped. So, he was either part of the plot and is in hiding, or he was an innocent victim, like we were, and has been executed, tong-style."

"Could be they meant for us to escape that cave."

"Huh! I don't remember seeing any obvious escape routes," McGraw said dryly.

"Why would he betray us to the tong's hatchet men after being our informant for several weeks?" Casey wondered aloud. "After all, it was in his best interests to stem this flow of opium."

McGraw shrugged. "Maybe he had a change of heart. Could be the tongs who control these opium dens found out what he was up to and threatened him with death if he didn't lure us into a trap. After all, a couple of dead or missing detectives would put a damper on this crackdown on smuggling."

"Or, he could have been feeding us false information all along," Casey said thoughtfully. "Several of the tips he gave me turned out to be of little value. You remember that tiny bit of opium we got on the last raid you were on? Ho Ming was probably feeding us little token amounts of the stuff to make us think we were really accomplishing something. Damn!" Casey banged his fist on the table and got up to pace in frustration. "Whether or not Ho Ming was in on the trap we walked into, I think he suckered us, intentionally or unintentionally, if *his* informants were giving him bum steers. I feel like a fool. We've wasted a lot of time, chasing false leads while the bulk of the opium continues to flow in with no interruption."

"Don't let it get you down. Look at the positive side. You and I are still alive. And the department does have a few smugglers in custody to wring some information out of before they go to trial."

"Those prisoners have been grilled. And they either don't know anything, or we can't threaten them with any punishment bad enough to make them tell us how the drug is getting into the city in spite of our best efforts. I suspect they just don't know anything. They were probably set up to be caught."

"So, where does that leave us? Do we try to follow up on O'Toole's murder to see if there's a possible connection? If so, we might find a crack in this wall of silence."

"Yes, we'll try that, if I can do it through the homicide people without Captain Kingsley being aware. And we'll also continue our nightly routine boat patrols on the Bay. Maybe we'll get lucky."

"All ships entering port are being searched, aren't they?"

"Only ships from the Orient. We don't have enough men to search them all. Big steamers like the *City of Peking* take a lot of time to search. And we've found nothing. The opium's either being very cleverly concealed in those ships, or it's being dumped somewhere before they enter port."

"What about the passengers?"

"All passengers, crew, and baggage debarking are searched. But, as I say, it's a laborious, time-consuming process, considering the number of ships constantly arriving and departing. And it's possible the stuff may be coming off one of the ships from another country right under our noses. We make random spot checks of some of the other ships, but it's strictly hit or miss. So far, no luck. Meanwhile, Chief Crowley is coming under more heat from the mayor and the board of supervisors and the public, with Blind Boss Buckley helping keep things stirred up, of course."

"Has anybody really investigated Buckley to see if he may be connected with this opium smuggling? He seems to turn up everywhere. Remember, I saw him talking to O'Toole outside the ball park after a game. Then O'Toole turns up dead a day later. And you told me Buckley was behind the big push to get the bars installed at the mouth of that cave . . . the cave we just happened to be dumped in to die."

"Supposedly some of the big wheels in the department have checked him out, and he's not involved. Of course, that's just hearsay. Personally I believe that Buckley's so intertwined in the political fabric of this city that I can't imagine him not being involved in this opium business, even if it's only indirectly."

"This whole thing smells more and more like a dung heap," McGraw snorted.

"This is my job, and I do what I'm told to do. I try not to think about the political corruption that may be involved. You're always going to have that."

"How are you to ignore it?" McGraw demanded. "Unless you're satisfied to just go through the motions of an investigation, making a token arrest now and then, risking your own life and the lives of your men."

Casey looked at him sharply and then averted his eyes, leaning on the back of a chair and looking out a window. "You don't make it easy."

"Hell, Casey, you and I almost died together a few nights ago. I'm calling this thing as I see it, whether it lines up with what you think it ought to be or not." When Casey did not respond, McGraw continued in a softer tone. "You and I have been friends for several years, ever since I first came to this city. We've been *good* friends. We've confided in each other, and we've told the cold, hard truth to each other, even when nobody else would face that truth . . . when it was hard to face it ourselves. Isn't that one of the things friends are supposed to do?"

Casey heaved a sigh. "All right. It's something I've been struggling with . . . trying to reconcile the two halves of my mind. And I guess there's no way I can have it both ways. You're right. I'll either have to give it my best effort, go wherever the leads take me, and report everything honestly with my eyes open, or . . . or quit and get into some other line of work. Maybe it took somebody like you, from the outside, to make me face it." He turned and grimaced. "I almost wish I were back in uniform on the Chinatown squad, just walking my beat on the night shift, now and then helping chop down the door of a gambling den. Life was a lot simpler then."

"Responsibility and supervision make life a lot tougher and a lot more complicated," McGraw agreed. "You're the detective," he continued briskly. "Where do we start?"

"We've already started. It's just a matter of focus and tireless pursuit. I'm afraid some of it is going to be boring, compared to what we've already been through."

"I could use a little boredom at this point."

"Okay, here's what we'll do. The investigation will take two directions. First, I'll put one of my men on checking O'Toole's background, starting with his application for a job here two years ago, talking with any friends and people at any saloons he frequented, his landlady, and all of that. Some of that has already started. It may give us a clue as to what type of man he really was. Did we know the real O'Toole? Or was he leading some kind of double life? We'll also try to trace his path from the time you saw him after the ball game, talking to Buckley, until his body was found in Chinatown. I'll have another man take that axe to a professor of medieval history I know. Maybe he can give us a clue as to the origin of that weapon. There's something incongruous there."

"Were the lab men able to get any more fingerprints from the axe?"

"No, just that one clear print in blood on the handle. Of the right index finger. Problem is, there's no telling if or when we'll be able to match it up to anyone's hand. This new science of fingerprinting is a great thing, but it's got a long way to go. I understand Sir Francis Galton in England has established a bureau for the registration of civilians by means of fingerprints and measurements for the purpose of identification. A large file of prints must be established, at least of all the known criminals, before we can ever hope to find a match. Of course, if you have a suspect, that's a different matter." He shrugged. "Meantime, we've got a good, clear print, and no way of finding its owner."

"And what will you and I be doing while this is going on?"

"You and I will go have a talk with Blind Boss Buckley. But I wouldn't get my hopes up, if I were you. This man has more twists and turns and blind alleys than a maze. He's one of the shrewdest political bosses you'll ever meet. As one native-born Irishman to another, I may be able to see through some of the smoke he's bound to throw up when we start probing. He may have bad eyesight, but his instincts for personal survival are razor-sharp. In any case, it won't do any harm to go down to his saloon and see what we can find out."

"How come this wasn't done when this investigation first started?" McGraw inquired. "Buckley should have come to mind right off."

"As I said, supposedly he was checked out by some of the higher officials of the department. In fact, my captain . . . Kingsley . . . gave me specific orders to leave Buckley alone for fear of embroiling the department in a lot of political controversy."

"That by itself would have fired my curiosity."

"It fired mine, but I couldn't very well disobey a direct order."

"You plan to start now?"

Casey nodded. "I told you I was going to follow up on any leads, no matter what. I know some of the men on the Chinatown squad were on the take when I was a member of the squad, although we couldn't prove it. That's why, when I became a detective and was assigned to this opium-smuggling business, I insisted I be allowed to select my own, hand-picked squad of men to help, because I knew the honest ones." He frowned and bit the corner of his mustache. "I may have made a mistake where O'Toole was concerned. But, as I started to say, if low-paid uniformed Chinatown squad members were taking bribes to keep their mouths shut about things happening on their beats, you can imagine how many payoffs are taking place in the world Buckley moves in."

Opening time at Buckley's Star of the West saloon was noon. McGraw and Casey arrived a few minutes after twelve and strolled into the dim, cool interior. A burly man in a white shirt, galluses, and with sleeves rolled up to reveal massive, hairy forearms was removing inverted chairs from table tops and setting clean cuspidors at strategic locations.

"Combination swamper and bouncer," Casey said under his breath as he and McGraw turned toward the long bar.

"What'll it be, gents?" the lanky barman asked.

"Two steam beers."

As the bartender set two pint glasses under a keg on the back bar, Casey asked: "Is Mister Buckley in?"

"Too early. He never comes in before three or four o'clock," the barkeep replied over his shoulder. "Who wants to know?"

"Fred Casey."

The bartender shook his head.

"When he comes in, give him the word that Detective Fred Casey of the San Francisco Police Department would like to have a word with him."

The bartender turned and set the two foaming glasses in front of them. Casey was cupping his badge in the palm of his hand for the bartender to see. The lean barman glanced up quickly at Casey's steady blue eyes. He picked up a towel to wipe his hands. "I'll see if he might have come in early by the back door. Roscoe!" he said sharply as he moved away.

The swamper looked up, and the barman jerked his head at a ragged figure, shuffling into the saloon. The burly swamper in one jump was on the tramp like a cat, grabbed him by the scruff of the neck, and pitched him back outside into the sunshine. He returned to his work without a word.

McGraw looked at his partner. "Regular customer?"

"Apparently."

They burst into laughter and turned their attention to their drinks. But they had time for only a swallow or two before the bartender emerged from the back room.

"The boss will see you," he said. "Right through that door."

"Oh, arrived a little early, did he?" Casey remarked.

The bartender ignored the sarcasm as they headed toward the rear office.

"Gentlemen, gentlemen, come in. What may I do for you this fine morning?" The voice was deep and carried traces of its owner's Celtic origins, but the figure behind the desk was less than imposing. Blind Boss Buckley wore a pair of gold-rimmed spectacles with lenses so thick they made his eyes appear to be peering out of twin tunnels. He was a small man with thinning, reddish hair. The face was clean shaven, and he wore a starched white shirt with a new celluloid collar. A diamond stickpin affixed the knot of his yellow tie that was tucked into a brown vest. His white cane hung on the back of his chair.

"I'm Casey of the city police department, and this is my associate, Mister McGraw," Casey began.

"It's an honor to finally meet the both of you." Buckley bowed cordially, leaning forward in his chair, weak eyes straining to see them more clearly. "I'm very familiar with the heroic exploits of the both of you over the past few years. What brings you to my establishment? I assume this is not a social call."

McGraw glanced pointedly at the only other person in the room, apparently a personal servant or bodyguard who sat reading a newspaper near the room's only window. "Who's that?" he asked Buckley.

"Who? Oh, Harvey. Don't mind him. He's been with me for years. Anything you have to say to me, you can say in front of Harvey Bascomb."

"I just have a few questions, Mister Buckley," Casey resumed. "Won't take up much of your time. We're trying to trace the movements of one of my policemen shortly before he died."

"And who might this policeman be?"

"Kevin O'Toole."

"O'Toole?"

"Yes. A big, rawboned lad. He was found beheaded in

Chinatown. We understand he frequented your place. Maybe you knew him."

"I heard about that grisly murder. Terrible thing. A big lad, you say? Was he blond, by chance? Yes? Rather loud and boisterous, especially after a few drinks?"

"That was O'Toole," Casey agreed.

"It's possible he's been here. Hmmm . . . hard to say. As you probably know, hundreds of people are in and out of my saloon every day. I'm pretty good at names, but . . . with my eyesight, you know . . . it's more difficult to identify faces. I believe I do remember him being here. He was an athlete of some kind, was he not? That's it. A baseball player. He played for the Stormy Petrels. Am I right?" He smiled at his memory.

"Yes, that's the man," Casey said. "When did you last see him?"

"Now, that's a more difficult question. As I said, there are hundreds of people in and out of here every day. I'm sure I haven't seen him for at least a week or two."

"Is it possible you could have seen him somewhere other than this saloon?" Casey pursued.

"No. Not unless I ran into him on the street somewhere. And I always wear dark glasses when I'm outside. I'm nearly blind in the sunlight. I would not have recognized him on the street. Anything else I can help you with while you're here?"

McGraw thought the words came out like the lines from a well-rehearsed play.

"During your political dealings, have you ever known or met a man named Ho Ming?" Casey asked.

"I take it from the name that he is Chinese. No, the name does not ring any bells."

"Chinese," Casey prompted. "A larger than average Oriental, wears a queue, but dresses well in western style. Runs two of the largest brothels in Chinatown. He's a well-known man in the Chinese community."

Buckley shook his head. "Can't say as I've ever heard of him."

"Did you put political pressure on some members of the board of supervisors to get an investigation going into conditions in Chinatown?" Casey asked.

"Are you asking if I was responsible for the report that's got the gentle folk of San Francisco in an uproar?" He chuckled softly. "You give a poor, blind saloonkeeper too much credit. I did mention it to a few men I know. And some of the candidates for public office who come in here for drinks have discussed it. But, no, I didn't put any political pressure, as you call it, on anyone. I have no means or inclination to do that. My only concern is that of a involved citizen who has the interests of my adopted city at heart."

"I think I may throw up," McGraw muttered under his breath.

"What's that?" Buckley asked, swinging his impaired gaze toward him.

"Nothing," Casey interrupted. "Do you know the men who actually authored the report?"

"Not personally. I've seen them at public gatherings. But why all these unrelated questions? Am I under investigation or suspicion for something?"

"No. We're just trying to get a few leads on some things we're working on."

"Fine. Then, if there's nothing else, I have several business matters of my own to attend to." He stood up and put out his hand to Casey who was still standing. "Good day to you, gentlemen. It was a pleasure meeting both of you."

Casey took the proffered hand. "Likewise."

They went out and closed the door. As they passed out through the saloon, McGraw noted that a half dozen men had come in and were lined along the bar, nursing drinks and helping themselves to the generous free lunch Buckley always provided for one and all. But the place wouldn't really begin humming until after dark.

"I told you he was a slick one," Casey said as they emerged onto the sidewalk.

"I got the distinct feeling he was lying about everything he told us. And I know for a fact he was lying about never having met O'Toole outside this saloon, since I saw them with my own eyes. And that Harvey Bascomb in there was the man I saw with them."

"Buckley's a political boss. He knows we're investigating a murder. Even if he's in no way involved, he's not going to allow any suspicion to come his way by admitting to having known or met O'Toole outside his saloon."

"He's the kind of oily character I'd like to grab by the Adam's apple and shake till his gold teeth rattle."

Casey was chewing at one corner of his mustache and frowning as they threaded their way through the busy lunch-time pedestrian traffic of businessmen, well-dressed young women, laborers, and a few factory workers.

"I'm sure our little session with Buckley will get back to Captain Kingsley, and I'll be called in to explain what I was doing," Casey grumbled. "I only wish something productive had come of it."

"Where do we go from here?" McGraw asked, hurrying to keep up with the long-striding Casey.

"I wish I knew. Let's get some lunch and talk it over."

Chapter Nine

At five-thirty the next morning McGraw and his teammates boarded the passenger cars for a run down to Salinas
for a game against the Pumas. The game started at three
o'clock, the hottest hour of a hot, windless day. At first, the
heat was a blessing for McGraw who had not played or practiced for two weeks. It took him less than a quarter hour to
work up a sweat and get his muscles supple. Then his natural
ability took over, and he played with his usual timing and
co-ordination. He batted three for five and played his position in left field flawlessly, throwing out a runner at third base
in the fourth inning. The Stormy Petrels won the contest four
to one.

After the game McGraw shared a hack with four of his
teammates when they returned to the depot. The stationmaster
peered at them through his barred window. "Train's delayed
south of here," he told them. "Not expected in until nine-fif-
teen."

There was a collective groan.

"Sorry. I'll chalk it on the board if there's any change."

The station clock pointed at six thirty-five.

"Boys, I'm tired," McGraw said. "I think I'll get a room
and stay the night. See you Saturday at practice." He picked
up his small grip and walked across the dusty street to a two-
story wooden hotel.

"Is there a bathhouse close by?" McGraw asked as he signed
the register.

The desk clerk wrinkled his nose at the sweaty, grass-stained uniform McGraw still wore. "Two doors down." He jerked a thumb over his shoulder.

McGraw went straight to the bathhouse, carrying the small bag with his clean street clothes. Ten minutes later he was soaking away his fatigue in a steaming tubful of water. The female Chinese attendant poured the last bucketful of hot water and withdrew.

He lay his head back on the wooden rim of the tub, closed his eyes and drowsed. The slightly pulled thigh muscle, the raw spot on his left knee from the slide into second base, the bruises on his arms from the fall down the blowhole in the rocks, the barely healed cut on his left forearm inflicted by the smuggler, the tightness in his back muscles from the unaccustomed exercise — all faded from consciousness in the steamy balm of the hot water.

He was nearly asleep when he became aware of someone stirring next to the tub. He roused himself enough to crack his eyelids and see a bare-armed Chinese girl in yellow silk.

"No more water. It's hot enough," he mumbled, and closed his eyes again.

"You maybe need something else?" a silvery voice asked.

McGraw opened his eyes again. The girl was young and attractive, although rather heavily made up. She was wearing a *cheongsam,* slit up both sides nearly to the hips, exposing shapely thighs as she sat on the edge of the tub. McGraw sat up and glanced around quickly. Low partitions separated his tub from the others in the room, but the place seemed to be empty at the supper hour.

"Need what?" he asked, looking at her again, trying to focus his relaxed mind. "No, no. Nothing. I've got all I want . . . soap, towel. I'll call if I need anything."

"I am here to serve you when your bath is done. If you wish, I am just outside." She trailed her fingers up his bare arm and

107

across his shoulder. McGraw shivered and felt his face flushing as her meaning at last came clear. He had not expected to find Chinese sing-song girls operating in Salinas, much less openly soliciting. But then he remembered that Chinese prostitutes were in demand not only in San Francisco's Chinatown district but also throughout the state, by Orientals and Caucasians alike.

He had to remind himself that this girl had no attraction or affection for him. She was merely doing a job for some master or overlord she was bound to serve. Slave girls were routinely bought in China for about three hundred dollars and sold in San Francisco for about seven hundred dollars, and someone like Ho Ming could afford to buy these girls several at a time. This volume buying and selling could bring the price down to as low as three hundred dollars a head. He found himself wondering, as he stared at her, how much she had cost. *Amazing how humans could demean one another,* he thought. Legal slavery in his own country had been abolished only two decades earlier. But, since McGraw had been merely a child during the Civil War, the end of slavery seemed like ancient history to him.

He was suddenly aware that the girl was staring at his naked body through the dirty water. Instinctively he leaned forward onto his drawn-up knees.

"You are sure you want nothing?" the soft, accented voice asked again. "I am here to serve you."

"Can't say I'm not tempted," McGraw groaned, mostly to himself. "But what I really need you can't give me . . . like information about how opium is being smuggled into China-town."

She looked at him with a curious blankness.

He shook his head. "Never mind. Just thinking out loud. I don't want anything else."

"How much will you pay?"

"I told you I didn't want your services," McGraw repeated

with some irritation. He wanted this girl to leave so he could relax a few more minutes before the water cooled off.

"How much will you pay if I tell you about opium?"

"What?" McGraw was so startled he forgot about his modesty.

"You pay much money, I find out about opium."

"How?"

"I find out. How much you pay?"

McGraw was suddenly on the spot. "I don't know. I was just talking."

The girl got up quickly to leave.

"Wait."

She paused and looked down at him with cold disinterest.

"How can you find out about the opium shipments?"

"I know a man. He come to me from San Francisco."

"Is his name Ho Ming?"

Her expression was inscrutable. "I get information. You pay."

This slave girl reduces things to their simplest terms, McGraw thought. He made a quick decision. "You find out for me, and I'll pay."

"How much?" Her tone and manner were no longer seductive.

"Whatever it's worth," McGraw countered, his voice also hard and business-like. "I'll have to verify the information is correct first. If it is correct, I'll be sure you are well paid." He had no idea how he would keep this promise, or what amount he was talking about, but it was best not to shut out any possible lead. He was equally dubious about any information this girl might relay to him.

She simply nodded. "I will meet you here one week from tonight."

"Do you want to know my name?"

She shook her head. "You want information. You meet me here. Bring money."

Then she was gone, silently and quickly.

The water had grown tepid, and McGraw was no longer drowsy. He climbed out, shivering, and reached for the rough towel on the low stool. By the time he had dried off and pulled on his clean clothes, the girl's visit seemed like some unreal apparition.

When he got outside, the girl, as he expected, was nowhere to be seen. The old Chinaman who ran the bathhouse was chatting with his neighbor next door at the laundry. No one else was in sight.

McGraw shook his head in wonder and started back to his hotel. *Where had the girl come from? Was she on the street, or did she have a crib in some local red-light district?* He suddenly realized he hadn't asked her name, and he wasn't sure he would even recognize her, if he saw her again. The glossy black hair, pulled back in a chignon — a knot at the back of the head, the painted black brows, the rice-powdered face, the slit-skirted *cheongsam* — were features that many Oriental prostitutes shared. *She had promised to find him a week from tonight. She had said to bring money. How much? Should he just ignore this as some attempt to pry money out of a gullible white man, or did she really have some well-connected underworld contact from San Francisco? He'd let Casey decide,* he thought wearily as he climbed the stairs to his room. McGraw felt he did not have the instincts of an experienced detective.

McGraw rode the steam cars back to San Francisco the next morning. He arrived at the depot late in the morning, caught a cable car to within a few blocks of his boarding house where he dropped off to leave his dirty uniform at a Chinese laundry. It was such a beautiful, sunny day, and he felt so well rested, he elected to walk the rest of the way home.

As he reached his boarding house and was climbing the steps from the street, thinking of seeing Katie, he met Fred Casey coming out the door.

"There you are. Thought you'd be in last night."

"Too tired, so I got a room and spent the night. But I think I might have stumbled across a lead."

Casey looked blank. "A lead for what?"

"Haven't you been getting enough sleep again? What do you think we've been working on for the past several weeks? The opium smuggling, of course."

"In Salinas?"

"Yeah."

As Casey led the way back down to the sidewalk, McGraw began filling him in on his encounter with the Chinese prostitute. When he had finished, Casey frowned and chewed at the corner of his mustache. "She didn't tell you who this man was?"

"No. I guess she thought it would ruin her bargaining position if I could find him first and force the information out of him."

Casey shook his head. "Forget it."

"What do you mean, forget it?"

"Just what I said. Forget it. She'll take whatever money you give her, and you'll never see her again."

"I wasn't planning on giving her anything up front."

"Do you know how many so-called informants we've had since this investigation began? At least three dozen people, from factory workers to housewives, have come forward to offer tips about this opium smuggling. About half of them have offered information for money. I've had my men check out most of these tips, and they've all led to nothing. Just people wanting to sound important by repeating rumors or some chance remark they heard, or tell of some suspicious-looking co-worker or servant. You name it. All it has done was waste a lot of police time and energy. So don't get excited about anything this whore may want to sell you besides herself."

McGraw felt chastised and foolish, and said nothing.

Casey took a deep breath and squinted around at the quiet street in the morning sunshine. Then he looked back at McGraw. "Sorry. Didn't mean to sound so harsh. It's just that I've been so damn' frustrated by this whole business, I'm really getting irritable. Tell you what, I'll see if I can pry a hundred dollars from the department for you to use. Go ahead and check her story. Just don't spend any more than you have to."

"I won't take more than seventy-five dollars with me, just in case it's a trap to rob me. And I'll go armed . . . wish I hadn't lost my Colt Lightning when the *boo how doy* captured us. That was a handy little Thirty-Eight. In any case, I'll work the best deal I can. I'll just have to take a chance on losing that much until I can check out any information she gives me."

"If you think she's sincere, take her with you, just in case."

"She'll have to go willingly, or it's kidnapping. I can't arrest her without a charge."

"Charge her with prostitution, if nothing else. It's technically illegal. If you give her any money and then let her out of your sight, she and the money are gone."

"Don't all of these slave girls have to turn over whatever they earn to their masters?"

"From customers, yes. But these men know about how much a girl can earn. She probably just saw a chance to do a little business on the side . . . in peril of her life, I might add. These sing-song girls are susceptible to threats, like everyone else. Use your badge on her. She'll never know you're only a temporary on the force."

McGraw grimaced. "Why does this kind of work make me feel dirty?"

"He who lies down with dogs, gets up with fleas. I think that's a quote from Benjamin Franklin, but I'm not sure."

McGraw laughed. "When this is over, I'll need a tub of flea dip."

"Usually detective work requires dealing with some pretty low characters. It works like a vaccine . . . you have to take a little of the disease to become immune from catching the disease yourself."

"I'll keep that in mind."

"Now, *I've* got something that might be a lead in the murder of O'Toole."

"What's that?"

"That professor friend of mine, Doctor Andrew Bennett, wasn't able to identify the axe, but a visiting professor from England at the university told him there was a man vacationing in San Francisco from London who might be able to identify it. I've found out where he's staying, and I'm going to take the axe to him tonight. I want you to come with me."

"See you tonight, then."

It was eight o'clock that evening when Casey stopped at the boarding house with an object about three feet long, wrapped in a cloth sack.

"Did you clean it up?" McGraw asked as he shrugged into his light wool coat.

"No. I think the boys in the laboratory have finished with it, but I don't want to be accused of destroying any evidence."

"Where are we going?"

"The Palace Hotel."

McGraw paused in folding down his collar and arched his brows in surprise. "The Palace? Is this English visitor royalty? That's an expensive place."

"For you and me, maybe," Casey laughed. "And any other

113

working man. But there *are* people in this world who have money to spend."

"I'm ready. Let's go."

They walked to Market Street and caught a passing cable car. The huge bulk of the Palace Hotel, a San Francisco landmark, loomed up in the distance, looking gigantic from more than two blocks away.

"What's this visitor's name?" McGraw asked above the clatter of the car.

"John H. Watson."

"Thought it might be Sir somebody or other. He's probably at least the head of some archaeological department or college at Oxford."

Casey shook his head silently, unwilling to speculate.

They dropped off the moving car at the corner by the hotel and entered the huge lobby. The desk clerk gave them the room number of **318** and directed them to the lift. On the third floor their footfalls were noiseless on the soft-carpeted corridor until they came to a door with the brass numerals **318** attached to the dark wood.

Casey rapped sharply. There was a pause, and the door was opened by a man of medium height with graying, sandy hair. He sported a thick mustache and was dressed in a smoking jacket.

"John H. Watson?"

"Yes. I'm Doctor Watson."

"I'm Detective Fred Casey of the San Francisco police, and this is my partner, Mister Jay McGraw. Professor Bennett referred us to you."

For a second there was no hint of understanding in the blue eyes that regarded them, then the face lit up in a smile. "Ah, yes, Professor Bennett . . . Colin Wilson's friend at the university here. Come in, gentlemen, come in. Colin told me you might be stopping by . . . something about an antique weapon you wish examined."

He held the door open, and they stepped into the room.

"I hope we're not interrupting your dinner or anything," Casey apologized as he noticed the remnants of food on the dishes of a room-service tea cart.

"Not at all. Would you care for something to eat?"

"No, thanks."

"Some tea, perhaps?"

"That would be nice," McGraw answered for both of them.

"Allow me to introduce my friend and associate," Dr. Watson said, turning to another man in the room who was standing quietly, leaning on the mantle of the fireplace. "Mister Casey, Mister McGraw, I would like you to meet Mister Sherlock Holmes."

They each stepped forward and shook hands with the tall, lean man with the slightly beaked nose and dark hair. The name meant nothing to McGraw, but he noticed a glimmer of recognition on Casey's face.

"Sherlock Holmes . . . that name is familiar to me," Casey said, stepping back and appraising the tall man. "By chance would you be the Scotland Yard detective?"

"I am a consulting detective," Holmes corrected him pointedly, with no trace of a smile. "And I have assisted Inspector Lestrade in the solving of several puzzling cases."

"Mister Holmes is too modest," Dr. Watson said proudly. "His exploits in deductive reasoning are becoming the talk of London. I've had the privilege of being the chronicler of several of his cases."

"And they've been outrageously dramatized," Holmes added in his rich dialect as he came forward from the fireplace to accept a cup of tea from Dr. Watson.

Watson smiled as he poured the still-steaming brew from a

gilt-trimmed porcelain pot on the cart. "Actually, my prose is understated. Holmes made the inspector appear a proper fool in at least three instances."

Over the lip of his cup McGraw noted Casey, eyeing the tall detective with something between keen interest and awe.

"That's where it was," Casey blurted suddenly. "That's where I first heard of Sherlock Holmes. A friend passed me a copy of a British magazine . . . *The Strand*, I believe it was . . . that contained a story about one of your cases. A marvel of observation and deduction. And the *Police Gazette* even picked up a news item about you earlier this year."

"Some of those who fancy themselves inspectors and constables should learn to be more observant, that is all," Holmes commented in an off-hand manner. He set his cup down abruptly. "I understand you have brought a murder weapon to be examined," he continued, changing the subject.

"How did you know it's a murder weapon?" Casey asked as he picked up the cloth bag he had placed on a chair.

"No mystery about it," Holmes replied. "Professor Colin Wilson told Watson, here, that you wanted to bring a murder weapon . . . an axe, I believe, that was used to behead a victim?"

He took the proffered sack.

"Careful, it's still covered with dried blood," Casey said.

Holmes pulled out the crescent-bladed weapon by its three-foot handle. He carried it to a marble-top table. Turning up the wick on the Rochester lamp, he examined the axe carefully.

"Hmmm. . . ." After several long seconds he glanced up sharply, his eyes looking like black opals in the light shining up the chimney of the lamp. "Did the victim have a beard?"

"No. He was clean shaven," Casey replied.

There were a few more seconds of silence as Holmes concluded his examination before sliding the axe back into the sack. "This weapon has been handled and scuffed about so much, it's nearly impossible to draw much information from it," he said. "All I can tell is that it was wielded by a right-handed man of below-average strength who is unused to such a weapon. It was used to strike a rather hairy blond man."

"How in the world can you tell all that from just looking at that axe?" McGraw asked in amazement and some private disbelief.

"The single fingerprint I can see in the dried blood was made by the right index finger, as you can tell by its shape and its position on the handle. The murderer was not of great strength because he obviously had to use more than one blow, even though the edge is very keen. I can tell this since the blood had run down the handle before he gripped it to strike again, leaving his fingerprint in the blood. The victim was a hairy blond man as can be seen by the coarse blond upper chest, or lower neck, hairs still stuck to the blade. Since he was clean shaven, these are not beard hairs. And the killer was obviously unfamiliar with this weapon because he held it so high on the handle. Had he gripped it farther down, he could have swung it with much greater ease and force, since the weapon is superbly balanced. The head was not severed with one blow, was it?"

"No. The trunk indicated it was rather crudely hacked off," Casey replied. "The head was never found."

"Just as I thought. Even though it's rather light, that axe has the capability of severing a head cleanly in one blow, if handled properly. And, unless I'm rather far off the mark, that is not the first death that axe has caused."

"What do you mean, Holmes?" Watson asked.

"This is a Danish war axe, dating from approximately the Tenth Century. This may be the very axe that was found in the Thames eighty years ago. The ash handle was replaced, and it had been on display in the British Museum until it was stolen last year."

Casey and McGraw looked at each other with the same question in their eyes.

"Did you say a Tenth-Century Danish war axe?" Casey finally repeated incredulously.

"Does that surprise you?" Holmes inquired.

"Frankly, yes. I was fairly sure the axe was an antique, but I suspected it probably originated somewhere in the Far East."

"Why?" Holmes snapped.

"I don't know. I guess because the body was found in Chinatown, and the way it was done is similar to the killing method of the tong hatchet men." Casey shook his head as if to clear his mind of a mistaken notion. "That's what I get for making assumptions before I have all the facts," he muttered.

"Precisely." Holmes said. "The conclusions must follow the facts, however improbable or bizarre the facts may be."

"No conclusions can be drawn from this," Casey reasoned. "It just confounds the puzzle even more. Of course, if that axe is actually an ancient Danish war axe, as you say, it could have been used by anyone, Chinese included, to commit the murder. I just can't imagine how that weapon could have made its way to San Francisco."

"The curator of the British Museum would have to make a positive identification," Holmes said, "but I feel certain this is the same axe. I have seen it in the Museum myself, more than once. As to how it came to be here, I cannot say." His mood seemed to change abruptly, and he pulled his watch from a vest pocket and consulted it. "In any case, I wish you gentlemen a swift and sure conclusion to your investigation."

"Thank you, Mister Holmes, and you, Doctor," Casey said as he took the axe and replaced it in the sack.

"It was a great pleasure meeting both of you," McGraw added as they moved toward the door.

"Holmes, I'm going to see these gentlemen outside," Dr.

Watson said. "I'll return directly."

Sherlock Holmes did not reply. He already had his back turned when Watson opened the door for the visitors, and the three of them left.

McGraw felt something was amiss. They had found their own way here. Why did Watson feel it necessary to see them out? Maybe it was some nicety of English manners with which he wasn't familiar. He followed wordlessly as the doctor eschewed the lift and, in spite of a slight limp, led them nimbly down the carpeted staircase.

When they reached the lobby, the doctor strode across the tiles to the center of the large room before he halted and turned to face them. "Gentlemen, I had to use this ruse to get you aside for a few words in private." He hesitated, as if unsure how to proceed.

McGraw and Casey regarded him curiously.

"We have only just met, but I feel compelled to take you into my confidence. I fancy myself a fair judge of men, and I feel you can be trusted. In addition, you are policemen, and have much in common with my friend and associate. But, I will be brief, and I trust our conversation will remain in confidence."

McGraw and Casey nodded in unison.

"I wish to request a great favor. I would like one, or both, of you to accompany Mister Holmes and me on a foray into one of the opium dens in Chinatown. To act as guides and protectors."

"Why? Is Holmes here on a case?"

"No. We are here on holiday. To be blunt about it, Holmes is addicted to drugs . . . cocaine, in particular. He takes it in a solution with sterile water. Before you say anything, let me assure you that I, as his physician as well as his friend, most heartily disapprove of this activity of his. But you must realize that he is the possessor of an extraordinary brain . . . just how

119

extraordinary the world will soon become aware as his reputation grows. However, it is precisely his brilliant mind that is the problem. When he has some puzzling mystery to work on, he is at his best and happiest. He is like a hound on the scent. But when he is between cases and is at loose ends, so to speak, his mind cannot stand boredom. He plays the violin, conducts chemical experiments, takes pistol practice in our rooms in Baker Street, writes arcane monographs on such subjects as the identification of various types of tobacco ash. But his intellect must have more than this to occupy it. To relieve his *ennui*, he turns to artificial stimulants. Dangerous drugs can be purchased legally at any apothecary in England, as you know, so he has no difficulty in obtaining the drug with which he injects himself, in spite of my dire predictions as to the eventual consequences. In an effort to get his mind occupied with something else, I proposed this trip, hoping to take him outside himself until he has another case to focus his powers upon. However, he knows about the notorious reputation of your city's Chinatown district. And he is bent on experiencing the hallucinatory effects of the opium pipe."

McGraw and Casey exchanged a quick glance.

Dr. Watson looked hopefully from one to the other.

"Doctor, this is rather awkward," Casey responded. "You know, of course, that these opium dens, as well as the gambling dens in Chinatown, are technically illegal."

"So I have been told."

Another pause.

"The only reason they are still going full blast is because of the lack of enforcement of the laws," Casey continued. "And this lack of enforcement is due to individual police corruption, lack of manpower, and, until recently, a lack of interest on the part of the general public to clean it up. I hardly need tell you that any man, especially any white man, who appears to have

120

a little cash in his pocket is in real danger of being robbed or killed there, and his body disposed of. We constantly get reports of whites disappearing in Chinatown. If that doesn't happen, there is always the chance that the place will be raided, and Holmes and all of us arrested. In the latter instance, his reputation as a brilliant detective will be badly damaged, not to mention the trouble we'll be in as law officers."

"I realize that also," Watson, said, nodding, with a pained expression on his face. "That is why I am seeking your help to guide us to the safest place and to protect us from harm, both going and coming. You know the district, and I'm sure some of the Chinese there know you. They certainly wouldn't harm any members of the police force."

McGraw thought ruefully of their capture by the *boo how doy* in the brothel and their near death in the cave.

"Okay, we'll do it," Casey decided firmly. He thrust out his hand, and the doctor gripped it briefly. "If you can be ready in thirty minutes, we'll have a hack waiting near the front door of this hotel for you."

"Agreed. And, thank you. We'll reimburse you for your trouble." Dr. Watson turned and limped toward the stairway.

"No need for any payment," Casey called after him.

"Why in the world did you agree to that?" McGraw asked as they made their way among the potted plants and easy chairs toward the front entrance.

"Mostly impulse. But Holmes did do us a favor by giving us that information on the axe. Also it might give us a chance to do a little looking around. We'll just blend in with these two British tourists. Besides, it's been a custom for several years for tourists to go to city hall and hire an off-duty policeman for about two and a half dollars to protect them on forays into Chinatown. So this is really not all that unusual."

"Going to affect some kind of disguise, since a lot of the Chinese know your face?"

Casey shook his head. "Maybe change my appearance just slightly and keep my mouth shut. Shouldn't be a problem."

As they stepped outside and walked a few steps around the corner onto Market Street, a derelict lurched toward them and stopped, looking them up and down.

"Could you fine gennemen spare a little change for a hungry man?" he slurred, trying to keep his balance.

McGraw started to walk past him, but Casey stopped.

"I tell you what. I'll do better than that. You can have my coat. It's good and warm."

The bum looked startled but eagerly reached for Casey's wool jacket as he peeled it off.

"Only one thing I want for it," Casey said, and the bum hesitated.

"Whassat?"

"I want *your* jacket."

"Sure." As he tried to take it off, he lost his balance and would have fallen had not McGraw caught him by an arm. A strong odor of cheap wine assaulted his nose.

The exchange was made, and the bum went off happily while Casey shrugged into the ragged tweed jacket that was too short in the sleeves. Casey crumpled his hat out of shape and slapped it back on his head, then stooped to the gutter and rubbed his hands along the grimy cobblestones, and transferred some of the dirt to his face and neck.

"How's that?"

"If I didn't look at you close in a good light, I'd never know it was you," McGraw nodded approvingly. "Are you armed?" he asked as an afterthought.

"Yes. I got the department to issue me another gun to replace the revolver that I lost when we were captured. It's a Thirty-Two

Smith & Wesson. Hasn't got great power, but it's accurate and easy to carry." Casey patted his side pocket. "Have you got a gun?"

"No. My Colt Lightning was taken by the hatchet men. But I don't think I'll need one tonight."

"You're probably right," Casey agreed.

Chapter Ten

Watson was as punctual as his word. At ten minutes past nine he came out the front door of the Palace lobby, dressed in tweeds and a beige cape. Holmes was muffled in a black cloak and dark hat against the chill fog that was forming thick swirls in the streets. Except that it lacked the yellow pollution of sulphur coal this present fog promised to rival a pea-souper in London. As they climbed into the waiting hack, McGraw thought the two visitors might feel right at home.

Casey was the last one in and said something to the driver as he slammed the door and dropped into a seat next to McGraw. The coach lurched away.

"It's only a few blocks from here, but I thought it best to get a hack," Casey said to the two visitors, sitting across from him in the dark. The clopping of the horses' hoofs could be heard on the cobblestones, and the fog-dimmed gas lights slipped past the windows. No one spoke for the quarter hour it took them to reach their destination.

When the coach stopped, Casey opened the door and led the way out. If anything, the fog was thicker than before, and visibility was restricted to only a few feet.

"Where are we?" McGraw asked as Casey handed a few coins to the driver.

"California Street. We'll walk from here. Wouldn't do to pull up to the front door in a hack. A little too conspicuous."

The hack pulled away, vanishing in the mist almost immediately. McGraw was disoriented, but Casey apparently knew exactly where they were and led off, the three trailing him. The widely spaced gas lights did little to illuminate the street but at least showed a few feet of the sidewalk. Casey walked slowly, so as not to appear to be in any hurry. They turned into what McGraw recognized as Cooper's Alley, know locally as Rag-picker's Alley. A few lights shone from small windows in the brick buildings on either side of them. Had it not been for this illumination, they would have been groping blindly in the trash-strewn passageway where no street lights shone. When the alley reached the next street, Casey made a left turn, went another short block, and turned left again. McGraw was thoroughly confused now. He noticed Dr. Watson's limping was heavier, and he was slowing down as the street led uphill.

"Hold up, Casey," McGraw called softly. They stopped and Dr. Watson leaned against a nearby brick wall.

"Sorry, gentlemen."

"What's wrong?" McGraw asked.

"My leg bothers me when I walk up steep hills or do much running, but especially in cold, damp weather. I thought perhaps this trip would get me away from that sort of thing in London, but we came here, where it's even colder in the summer."

"What's wrong with your leg?"

"Took a ball in it during the Afghan War. Invalided me out of the service. Doesn't keep me from conducting a small medical practice, however." He took a few tentative steps. "I'm fine now. I can go on."

They walked at a slower pace for two more blocks, now and then passing an Oriental figure, drifting noiselessly past them in the fog. Holmes and Casey walked ahead, with McGraw and Watson following. No one spoke further. McGraw wondered why Dr. Watson did not continue in his attempt to talk the detective out of this foolish venture but supposed Watson had already done all he could to dissuade him. McGraw had been in Chinatown many times before, had seen the insides of gambling dens, opium layouts, and joss houses, but for some reason this was different. As he glanced at the tall, caped figure striding ahead of him beside Casey, he wondered if it was the responsibility of protecting these two foreigners that was causing his sudden uneasiness.

"Are you armed, Doctor?"

"Why, yes, it so happens, I am." Watson threw back his cape and tweed coat to reveal a flapped holster, strapped high on his left hip, butt forward. "My old Adams service revolver. I never go into any strange or dangerous situation without it."

"Good. Hope you don't need it."

"Are you also carrying a weapon?"

McGraw shook his head. "I'm afraid not." He didn't go into any explanations. "Fred has a revolver."

Casey stopped, and they gathered around him. "There it is." He pointed at a plank door several yards farther on. The door, recessed into the brick wall, was faintly illuminated in the fog by a gas light, softly hissing in an overhead iron bracket. As they looked, the door swung outward, and a man came out. He was a thin Oriental, dressed in pajama-type clothing. McGraw thought the man looked to be at least ninety years old as his bent figure shuffled past them without looking up.

"I'll hang back in case someone there might recognize me as a policeman and suspect a raid. We need to do this as quietly and unobtrusively as possible. Jay, you've been inside these places before. They're all filthy, but I don't think this one is as bad as most. I'll stay out here, and you stay inside with Mister Holmes for as long as it takes, even if we're here most of the night. Doctor, you can suit yourself after you've seen the inside of the place. There's no sign out front here, but this establishment goes by the name of the House of Celestial Delights." Casey's teeth flashed faintly white in a quick grin. "There's a back door to the place that leads out into an alley." He turned to McGraw. "Just keep your wits about you, and everything should be all right."

McGraw nodded and led the way to the door. There was no latch or knob on the outside of the solid planks — a precaution against sudden raids. He rapped softly. There was a click, and the door swung open slightly. McGraw pushed past the Oriental face, and the two Englishmen followed him inside. The nauseating stench of burning opium struck them as McGraw glanced about the room at the narrow board bunks along the walls. About half of them were occupied.

"Welcome to the House of Celestial Delights, honorable gentlemen," a thin Chinaman intoned in a heavy dialect.

"How much money?" Holmes demanded with no preliminary.

The Chinaman glanced up at the tall white man in the black cape. "For you, honorable sir, only twelve dollar."

"What?" McGraw's head snapped around. "Don't give him a penny over five, and that's still more than twice the going rate."

Holmes pulled a small purse from somewhere under his cloak and extracted a five and two ones and handed them over with no comment. Then he gave Watson the purse, slipping a gold chain out of a buttonhole and handing over his watch as well. Watson hastily put them out of sight, but McGraw ground his teeth at this public display of wealth. He glanced around to see if anyone had seen the gold watch and the purse change hands. Except for the thin Chinaman they were dealing with, the other men in the room all seemed oblivious to anything going on around them. They were in various stages of stupor. Only one other man, who seemed to be a muscular bouncer, lounged near the rear door to the alley. He was the only other person in the room who did not seem to be purposely inhaling the burning drug. McGraw wondered how anyone could breathe the air in here for very long and not come under the influence of the opium. McGraw tried to breathe shallowly against the foul air that was thick with the smoke of several tiny lamps and candles mixed with the fumes of the burning opium, not to mention the odor of unwashed bodies.

The proprietor was handing Holmes a long-stemmed pipe and a marble-size ball of the pliable white drug. His hands looked like yellow talons in the light of the smoky lamp on the table. He also gave the Englishman a tiny coal oil lamp, already burning with a low flame, for his use in lighting the pipe, and motioned toward several empty bunks along the back wall of the room. Holmes strode purposefully to the lowest bunk, unhooked his cape, and spread it on the filthy straw mattress. He slid awkwardly into the bunk sideways, tucking his long legs up. Then, as McGraw and Dr. Watson watched from a few feet away, he took the ball of opium, rolling it in his long fingers, and pressed it into the bowl of the pipe. Then, holding the long pipe sideways, over the tiny flame, he turned it around until the opium began to grow dark, melt, and smolder. Then he took a few tentative puffs, glancing at the other smokers to be sure he was proceeding correctly.

McGraw and the doctor looked at each other, and McGraw read disgust and aversion on the face of the physician. They watched Holmes take a few more puffs, then close his eyes and rest his head on his arm as the drug began to take effect.

In a few seconds he opened his eyes again. "No need for you to stay, Watson. I'll see you back at the hotel."

Holmes closed his eyes again, and McGraw motioned with his head. "Let's step out back and get some air," he muttered quietly. "He should be all right in here for now." He glanced at the cadaverous-looking bodies, lying in rags, some with eyes closed, some with glassy-eyed stares as they sucked at the pipes, the burning drug sizzling and gurgling horribly. McGraw's stomach almost revolted. "Let's go." He took the doctor by the elbow and guided him toward the rear door, past the burly bouncer.

A few seconds later the door swung shut behind them, and McGraw was gulping in huge lungsful of the cool, damp air. The fog trapped odors of sewage, rotting garbage, and stopped-up drains, but the air was sweet and fresh by comparison to the stifling atmosphere they had just left.

"Whew!" Dr. Watson removed his bowler and wiped his brow with a handkerchief. "I am ashamed for you to see Sherlock Holmes in such a state, embracing the deadly tentacles of this drug world. I know it is hard for you to believe, but this man is undoubtedly the finest human being I've ever known. When he is himself, he is a most generous, brilliant, steadfast companion. But I suppose every man has at least one weakness, and this is his. As I said earlier, it may be the result of his brilliance. His mind cannot be content with mundane affairs like other men's. It is a pity." He replaced his hat and wrapped his cape closer about himself. "If I can see him through this night of experimenting with the opium pipe, perhaps I can steer his mind to other things during the remainder of our holiday." He looked at McGraw. "How long does a smoker usually stay in one of these places?"

McGraw shrugged. "I believe it can be from an hour or two up to several hours. Some of these poor wretches who are so hooked on the stuff act like alcoholic derelicts. They live only from one state of delirium to the next. And they can usually only beg or steal a few cents at a time, so they buy only enough to last a very short while. They forget all about food. The drug is all they crave. It's food and drink to them. It's their escape to a dream world. It's their temporary heaven. Well, you saw some of those wasted men in there. And you're a doctor. I don't need to tell you what a devastating effect that habit can have on the human system. But, with the amount Holmes bought, he could be in there most of the night."

Dr. Watson took a deep breath. "Ah, well, watching out for him is the least I can do. I've seen several drug fiends in my practice, usually dragged to my consulting rooms by a desperate parent, wife, or friend. Unfortunately, there was little I could do by the time the habit got to that stage." He shook his head and leaned against the brick wall. "Would you care for a smoke? I'm afraid all I have is pipe tobacco."

McGraw shook his head. "No, thanks."

Dr. Watson reached for his pipe and tobacco pouch in an inside coat pocket and began to pack a smoke.

McGraw turned up his coat collar and thrust his hands into his pockets as the chilly fog blew more thickly around them, making the night even darker. Somewhere down the alley he heard a door slam and a few seconds later a mumble of voices. He paid little attention. The voices moved closer, and he found himself listening. They were speaking English.

Dr. Watson suddenly paused, pipe in hand, to listen as well, since the voice that now came clearly to them was speaking with a British accent.

"I tell you I cannot deliver just when you want it. There is too much pressure being put on."

"That is not my problem," a voice replied with a pronounced Chinese accent. "We must have it in one week."

"Impossible. Can't you get that through your thick Chinee head?" the British voice grated brutally.

"Keep your voice down," the Oriental cautioned, quieter.

The unseen speakers had apparently stopped only a few yards away. Dr. Watson turned to say something, but McGraw quickly motioned him to silence.

"Why can you not deliver as agreed?"

"I've been trying to tell you that my ship cannot risk the run into the Bay. There are police boats out every night. We aren't even safe in the fog any more. The last two times we were in, we nearly rammed small boats. One of them was a police gig. Had to put the wheel hard up at the last second. It was a very near thing. As it was, they may have gotten a look at us before we slipped past."

"My people on the docks say the fishermen who see your ship without lights think she is a ghost ship. We are helping to spread that story. As long as people believe that, you need not fear."

"I'm not afraid. I'm prudent. That is why I have never been apprehended these many years."

There was silence for a few seconds as McGraw hardly dared breathe for fear of being heard. It was eerie, hearing voices so close, yet seeing nothing.

When the Oriental voice resumed, the tone was sarcastic. "Maybe famous Captain Moreland should go ashore, get wife, safe job. We will get someone else to bring us opium."

Dr. Watson leaned over quickly, putting his mouth to McGraw's ear. "I thought that voice sounded familiar," he whispered. "That has to be John Moreland. He was a British blockade runner for the Confederate States during your Civil War. Bad reputation. Like a modern Henry Morgan."

McGraw nodded, then put a finger to his lips for silence as he strained to hear the voices that had suddenly become muffled. Either the speakers were moving away from them, or the shifting fog was playing tricks with the sound.

"You know bloody well I have a schooner full of the stuff, standing off the coast right now. What I'm telling you is either you wait until I feel it's safe to bring it in, or you and your slant-eyed blighters can damn' well send out some boats to offload it and haul it in here yourselves. I'm not taking the chance of getting my neck stretched or a long prison term just for the likes of you."

"You forget, Captain," the Oriental continued in a quiet, deadly tone, "that you have already been paid one-third of your fee in advance. You will deliver when we say deliver."

"The devil I will! You blinking rotters think I'll be stuck with this stuff, that I'll have to bring it in or dump it over the side and take my losses. Not bloody likely! I can always sail up to Victoria and unload it with ease. I'm a British subject and always welcome there. They never question me."

McGraw's heart was racing. After all these weeks of frustration he had struck gold! He had somehow to alert Fred Casey. But suddenly the voices grew louder again. This time it wasn't the fog. He was certain they were moving closer as they talked. If he and Watson crouched down, maybe the pair would pass them in the darkness and never know anyone was there. They were standing near the middle of the alley. They had at least to get farther back against the wall. He tugged at Watson's coat sleeve. There was a black slot behind them. As he put out his other hand, he realized it was a gap about three feet wide between the walls of two buildings. If they could just slide in there, they would never be seen or heard.

As he guided Watson toward the gap, he heard the scuffing of feet against some newspapers only a few feet from them. His heart jumped into his throat as the voices sounded nearly at his elbow.

". . . need to be dealing with your boss, not with you. Where is he tonight? I must see him, and then be off."

McGraw was near panic. The British voice was nearly in his face. He jerked Dr. Watson into the gap to hide. Just as he took another step into the blackness, McGraw's foot collided with a pile of empty tin cans that had been dumped there. The metallic clanging and clattering sounded like a bomb burst in his ears.

"Hullo! What the hell is that?"

McGraw stumbled out of the trash pile and nearly bumped into Ho Ming.

"What're you two doing? Lurking about in the dark and eavesdropping, are you?" Moreland snarled.

"Nothing of the sort," Dr. Watson blustered, pushing his way forward. But Moreland put out a hand and shoved him back against the wall.

"I say, sir, take your hands off me. This is outrageous! I was merely walking down this lane and. . . ."

"By heaven! Another Englishman! Strike a light and let's get a look at these two," Moreland said. "We'll find out if they were just passing by."

McGraw could vaguely see Ho Ming fumbling in his pocket for a match. McGraw knew the Chinaman would instantly recognize him, and then it would be all over. But there was no way he could communicate this to Watson. He reached across to grab Watson's gun from under his coat. But he missed as the doctor turned just at that moment.

A match flared in Ho Ming's hand, and McGraw made a quick decision. "Run, doctor!" McGraw yelled, shoving him. "Get Fred!"

There was a grunt as Watson collided with someone, and then the cape whipped across McGraw's face and was gone, and he heard the uneven footsteps going at a limping run.

"Stop where you are!"

McGraw ignored the double click of a revolver hammer being drawn to full cock and threw himself onto the wet paving stones, rolling hard into the man's legs.

"Damn . . . !"

The roar of a gun going off nearly deafened him, but McGraw rolled away from the staggering form and scrambled to his feet. He had to get away. He was unarmed. But the man

133

did not follow up with his weapon. McGraw saw the dim figure plunge away and then heard the pounding of shoes on the pavement. The sound was quickly receding. His fear of being shot vanished. He had to stop this man, Moreland. He was the key to the smuggling operation.

"Fred! Fred! Here! He's getting away!" he shouted at the top of his voice. The fog seemed to swallow his yell like baffles of spun cotton.

He turned and made one step in pursuit of the fleeing footsteps, and something struck him squarely across the forehead. He dropped to his knees, stunned, and felt himself rolling helplessly onto his side and back, unable to move his arms or legs. He felt as if he were falling into a hole as consciousness spun away from him. He was dimly aware of a light flaring in his eyes, the sound of a voice, and then . . . darkness.

Chapter Eleven

McGraw's unconsciousness must have been only partial, or else he was having some sort of dream. He still couldn't move his arms and legs, but he felt as if he were drifting through the air or was being carried — he couldn't tell which. From afar someone was calling his name, and he tried to answer, but no sound came from his mouth. *It must be a dream,* he decided, *but I must wake up.* He had to force his eyes open. There was something he had to do. It was something urgent, but he couldn't remember, for the life of him, what it was. Then someone was shaking him. And his ribs were being constricted so he couldn't draw a deep breath. Then he was drifting again painlessly.

Suddenly his eyes flew open. He blinked several times and then focused on a fly-specked ceiling, illuminated by the wavering light of a coal-oil lamp. For a few moments he couldn't remember what had happened. Then he vaguely recalled being struck. He had no headache. He put his hand to his forehead. There was no bump or soreness. But his senses seemed fuzzy, heavy, as he pushed himself to a sitting position on the floor.

His senses came alert immediately. Sitting calmly on the opposite side of the small room, with legs crossed and watching him, was Ho Ming. Flanking him were two hard-looking Chinese that McGraw took to be *boo how doy.* As his glance rested on them, he thought they could have been two of the same men who had captured him and Casey in Ho Ming's office that awful night. With a sinking feeling in the pit of his stomach, he pushed himself heavily to his feet.

"Well, we meet once again, Mister McGraw," Ho Ming said with no trace of a smile. "You and your friend, Mister Casey, are causing more and more trouble."

With a chill, McGraw swung his head around to be sure Casey had not also been captured, but Casey was nowhere to be seen. He barely listened to what Ho Ming was saying as the realization struck him that this was the man Casey had trusted as an informant for many weeks. No wonder they had been picking up only a little opium here and there. It had all been just a diversionary tactic to keep the law busy so the main shipments could be smuggled in unmolested.

All this passed through his mind in a flash, yet he tried to keep his face impassive. Why hadn't he borrowed Dr. Watson's revolver? At least he could have put up a fight. But then he remembered he had been armed with his Colt Lightning and still had been surprised and taken prisoner the last time he had run afoul of these hatchet men. Ho Ming was eyeing him critically, as if trying to decide what to say or do next. The hard planes of Ho Ming's face, the heavy brows, the shiny black hair pulled straight back into a queue behind, the western-style black suit he wore — all brought back thrills of fear in McGraw's stomach as he vividly remembered the night he and Casey had been dropped into the rock cave to drown. With an effort he thrust these thoughts from his mind and forced himself to concentrate on this man before him.

"Your escape," Ho Ming was saying, "was very good. Very lucky, maybe." His mouth was a grim line. "You know you must die to warn off the others. Your men are frightening away our supplier. You must die with much pain, so your body will be found. Then the police will not try to stop the opium. You understand?" The hooded, slanted eyes peered at him as if trying to make a dull-witted child understand why he must stay after school.

"Is that why you killed Kevin O'Toole and chopped off his head?" he almost shouted, his own voice sounding strange in his ears.

There was no flicker of recognition in the impassive face of Ho Ming. Finally he shook his head and shrugged. "I do not know this . . . O'Toole?"

"Like hell," McGraw muttered.

"Never mind this talk. It is time. I have a plan for you. This time you will not escape. Business, you understand."

A chill went up McGraw's back. This man would as soon kill, even torture, as he would step on a cockroach if it got in his path — thoughtlessly, dispassionately. No one could appeal for mercy to such a man.

At a nod from Ho Ming the two tong enforcers grabbed McGraw from either side. They did not search him. Apparently that had been done while he was unconscious. They gripped him like two giant vises. Solid muscles underlay the quilted padding they wore.

McGraw didn't know what was coming or where he was being taken, but he suddenly decided he wasn't going quietly. As they reached the door, he leaped up, slamming both feet against the door frame and did a back flip, breaking loose from his surprised captors. But, quick as two jungle cats, they pounced on him, and the three hit the floor. McGraw yelled with all the power of his lungs until one of the hatchet men slapped a callused hand over his mouth. McGraw bit down and had the satisfaction of feeling gristle and bone grind under his teeth until the warm, salty taste of blood was in his mouth. The Chinaman bellowed and swung a free fist at his head. It caught him a glancing blow as they struggled, but the force stunned him. He stopped yelling, and the two *boo how doy* chattered back and forth at each other in sing-song Chinese, gesturing.

They yanked their dazed captive to his feet and dragged him

roughly through the door. One man grabbed McGraw by the back of his collar and twisted his left arm up behind his back in a hammer lock that nearly wrenched his shoulder out of place. He gasped involuntarily as the pain cleared his head. He went the way he was being shoved, now unable to shout with the fist twisting his shirt collar tightly around his neck. Through a mist of pain, McGraw heard Ho Ming's voice behind them, saying something in Chinese.

They forced him, stumbling, down a long flight of stairs into a large room. They stopped at the bottom, and, while the two burly guards held McGraw, Ho Ming said something more to them in Chinese. An overhead coal-oil lamp was casting a dim light, allowing McGraw to see that they were in some sort of subterranean kitchen, perhaps below a restaurant. Two wrought-iron cookstoves lined each of two side walls, with black stove pipes leading up and out through the walls near the ceiling. Three small windows were on each side of the room at the ceiling, presumably at ground level to admit some light and air during the day. The air was heavy with a melange of lingering cooking odors, stale grease, and rotting garbage. The floor was of flat flagstones, while the walls and the foundation of the building were of mortared rock up to a height of some six or seven feet, then brick the rest of the way up. The ceiling consisted of wooden beams and the planked floor above.

McGraw took all this in at a glance. The room was unusually warm, probably from the stoves, still holding the heat from the day's cooking. His attention was drawn to one thing that dominated the center of the room. Sunken into the floor was a rectangular cooking pit, covered with an iron grill. Above it, about the height of a man's head, was a metal venting hood with a pipe leading through the ceiling.

It was toward this pit that his captors thrust him, and his stomach revolted when he saw what they were about to do.

They pulled his coat off, dragged him forward, and threw him down on his back on the greasy grill, stretching his arms and legs out, fastening them to the four corners with several turns of soft wire. The grill was still warm, and he could feel it through his shirt and trousers. Ho Ming came forward and turned a crank at one end of the grill, lowering it a few inches. Then he stepped on a bellows and pumped it several times, blowing up a cloud of fine ash from the coals. McGraw felt the heat intensify immediately. Ho Ming said something to the hatchet men, then walked around the grill, inspecting the soft wire fastenings himself. McGraw could feel the wire cutting off his circulation already as Ho Ming took a couple of extra turns on the wire.

Ho Ming stopped and looked down at McGraw. "Nothing personal, you understand, but we must show those who would stop us that we will not be stopped."

"You're going to cook me alive?"

"As I said, your death must be an example to the others."

"My torture and death will not scare off the police. It will have just the opposite effect. They will be outraged. The police will tear Chinatown apart. They'll wreck every damned opium den and gambling house. Even if they don't get you, there will be nothing left of your business. They will stop the flow of the drug to the city. Think, man! Think what will happen if you kill a white man in Chinatown. My death will *not* help you."

McGraw twisted his head to look at Ho Ming. The hooded eyes gave no indication he had even heard. Instead, all he said was: "Screaming will not help you. There is no one to hear." He said something in his native tongue, and the hatchet man who had wrapped a rag around his bleeding hand grinned slightly as he cranked up the grill about a foot. The other man took two coal scuttles full of charcoal and scattered them under the gridiron. The injured one then began pumping the foot bellows. As he did so, he watched McGraw's face who remained impassive, although the backs of his legs and his back were getting uncomfortably warm. He could feel the beads of perspiration beginning to form on his forehead. At first he gritted his teeth, but then he thought this was no time for false pride. If he screamed before the grid got really hot, he might fool this grinning assassin into abandoning his pumping of the bellows. No sooner thought, than done. McGraw's screams rent the air and echoed off the rock and brick walls and floor. Yet he felt that most of the sound was going up the hooded vent above him. He threw back his head and screamed with all his strength and volume. Through squinted eyes he saw the Chinaman at his feet give a few more pumps on the bellows, then back away.

Ho Ming said something from behind him, and the three of them started back up the wooden stairs toward the upper floor. McGraw continued to yelp as the trio disappeared, slamming the door behind them.

The heat began gradually to increase as the new charcoal caught fire. He might as well save his voice, he reflected ruefully, because it would only be a short time before the pain of the fire would wrench involuntary screams from his throat anyway. He worked his wrists and ankles to see if he could find any slack in the wire fastenings. There was none. What would happen? His clothing would catch fire. He would feel and smell his flesh scorching, and his hair would probably be set ablaze. But would the excruciating pain cause him to pass out before that? He hoped so. He had heard that very hot flash flame could sear the nerve endings and be virtually painless. But this fire was not that hot and not that quick. It would only gradually get hotter and hotter, grilling him like a stuffed pig. That's what this pit was designed for — slow cooking.

Fear and the increasing heat were causing sweat to stream from every pore. Apparently it wasn't necessary to keep pumping the bellows to bring this fire to its cooking strength. He glanced at the windows high along each wall. It was still dark outside. He had no idea where he was in relation to the opium den where Sherlock Holmes presumably lay in a stupor, but where were Dr. Watson and Casey? Had this Captain Moreland shot Watson as he ran? McGraw remembered nothing after he had thrown himself into someone's legs and caused the first shot to be fired. After that he had been hit, presumably by Ho Ming, and knew nothing until he had awakened in this building.

He squirmed as he felt the glowing coals beginning to scorch his back and legs. He was stretched tight and could hardly twist part of his body at a time away from the inexorable flames. He could hear his own sweat sizzle as it dripped onto the glowing charcoal. He coughed as the poisonous fumes of the smoldering charcoal enveloped him. Maybe he would pass out from asphyxiation before he burned to death. That might be more merciful.

While he had a little time, he would use it in one last desperate effort. He opened his mouth and screamed and yelled in case someone might be within hearing distance. He whistled, he screamed, he shouted, he called out Casey's name and Dr. Watson's. He filled the room with noise of all kinds, hoping some of it was leaking out the small open windows at ground level near the ceiling. But finally the time came when the fumes robbed him of breath, and his throat grew so raw that he could hardly croak. He twisted and strained, but only succeeded in causing the wire to cut into his wrists. In addition to the charcoal fumes he could smell cotton scorching. He began to pray silently. It would not be long now. The pain was intense.

Suddenly he was aware of something scrabbling at one of the windows. He tried to yell, but only a cracked sound came from his throat. He twisted his head to see where the sound was coming from. Burning rivulets of salty sweat trickled into his eyes.

"Help!" The cry was barely above a whisper.

"McGraw!" A head was thrust through the glassless opening. It was Fred Casey.

"Here!"

The head disappeared to be replaced by a pair of long legs. Then the torso, and finally, Casey was hanging by his hands and dropping lightly to the floor. The nickel-plated Smith & Wesson appeared in his hand and swept the room in an arc to be sure there was no one in the dim corners. A wave of relief flooded over McGraw as his friend cat-footed to his side.

"You O K?"

"No," McGraw replied weakly. "Get me loose before they come back."

With one more look around Casey shoved the gun inside his belt and began untwisting the soft wire from McGraw's wrists. In a few seconds his arms were free. Casey grabbed him by the shirt front and yanked him to a sitting position so he could free his own ankles.

The sound of a bolt being slid back sounded from the door at the head of the stairs. McGraw fumbled frantically with the wires on his ankles as the door swung open, and one of the burly *boo how doy* started downs the stairs. He caught sight of Casey and jumped back with a startled yell, reaching under his jumper for a weapon. Casey's gun sent off with an ear-shattering roar in the confined space, and splinters flew from the top step. The hatchet man stumbled backward and flung the door shut as Casey fired again.

McGraw rolled off the gridiron and, ignoring his aching, burned body, staggered to his feet.

"Is there another way out?" Casey demanded.

"Only that door and the windows."

"Damn! We'll have to shoot our way out."

"Let's try the windows."

"Too high. Nothing to stand on."

The door was flung open again, and a tongue of yellow flame leaped from the barrel of a revolver. The wild shot ricocheted off the stone floor and clanged against one of the iron stoves. Casey snapped off a shot, and there was a yell of pain as the figure disappeared from the doorway again.

"Cover me," McGraw shouted as he threw himself against one of the stoves and gave it a hard shove. The stovepipe was wrenched loose and came clattering down in a shower of black soot. The adrenaline was flowing, and another hard shove brought the stove under the window where Casey had entered. "Now! Let's go!" McGraw leapt to the top of the stove. He could just reach the window sill.

Still watching the door at the top of the stairs, Casey backed to the stove and leaped up beside McGraw. He dropped to a crouch. "Stand on my shoulders."

McGraw did as he was told and was able to get his elbows through the window and muscle and scrabble his way until the upper half of his body was outside. He wriggled all the way out just as he heard another shot from below, then an answering blast from Casey's revolver. McGraw lay flat and reached back and down inside. "Give me your hands!"

McGraw saw the two hatchet men now creeping down the stairs, and Casey fired again. This time the one in front grabbed his leg and collapsed into the man behind him. The room was full of acrid powder smoke. Casey quickly turned, and McGraw gripped both his arms. It was only a matter of seconds before Casey scrambled up, with McGraw pulling on him. A shotgun roared inside the room, and the wooden window frame shattered.

"Ahhggh!" Casey rolled away from the opening, grabbing the backs of his legs.

"You're hit!"

Casey rolled to one side, his hand coming away bloody. "Only a few pellets. I can run. Let's go!"

The two were on their feet and flying down the alleyway. The fog was as thick as ever, and the night as black. No lights were showing in the alley, and no street lamps.

They ran to the end of the block, turned, and sprinted up the center of the deserted street. McGraw was thankful for the cover of darkness and fog. It had to be late. No pedestrians were anywhere about.

Only after they had run, flat out, for three blocks, some of it uphill, did they finally stagger to a stop, gasping, knees like rubber. McGraw's breath was rasping in his throat, and his heart was pounding. They continued walking with wobbly steps. Both were so breathless, they couldn't speak.

"Are . . . your . . . legs . . . hit bad?" McGraw finally managed to gasp.

"I don't think so . . . have to check 'em when we . . . get somewhere in the light."

McGraw looked back. There was no sign or sound of pursuit, as they walked one more block in silence, recovering their wind. The adrenaline was ebbing, and McGraw could feel his back and legs stiffening badly. The raw, burned spots were stinging with sweat. He was covered with black soot from the stove pipe and from smoke. His clothes were full of charred holes. He guessed Casey must be hurting as badly or worse. His friend still wore the coat he had gotten from the tramp. His hat was gone, and his face still grimed with dirt, but his major problem at the moment was the blood soaking through the backs of his pants legs where some of the pellets had sprayed him.

McGraw didn't know where they were, but they had apparently run out of Chinatown. At the next corner he peered at the street sign in the fog, dimly illuminated by a nearby gas light. Sutter Street. He leaned wearily against a closed and shuttered store front. Casey sagged against the lamp post, breathing deeply. "By God, I don't think I can take many more of these."

"I know what you mean," McGraw panted. "We need to get our wounds treated."

"Give me a minute," Casey said, his breathing still labored. "Station house is only . . . a few blocks away. We'll have somebody there go for the doctor."

In the silence that followed, McGraw became aware of the clacking of the cable running in its slot under the vacant street, and from somewhere in the mist-shrouded distance came the clang of hand-struck fog bells — bells that guided the ferries to their slips in the harbor. The familiar, quiet sounds of the night were a reassuring comfort. In spite of the danger and fear and the injuries inflicted on them by murderous men, the normal world was coming back into focus.

Chapter Twelve

"I guess Holmes and Watson got away to Los Angeles," Jay McGraw said as he and Fred Casey walked into a tiny seafood restaurant and saloon in the Mission District about thirty-six hours later.

"Sure did. They took the cars down the coast at nine this morning."

"I'm sure that was a night they won't forget," McGraw said, leaning on the end of the bar.

"You're right. Wish I could've gotten to know Holmes better. He's an odd duck. Maybe all geniuses are. I was brought up in a family with southern Ireland roots, so I never had much respect for the British in general, but Holmes must be one helluva detective. Wish I could've gotten him involved in this opium smuggling business, to see how he would have approached it. Up to now this whole case has been a rather messy, hit or miss operation to me."

"Hit or miss it may be," McGraw nodded, signaling for a waiter, "but the other night was definitely a hit. I just wish you could have been there to hear that conversation. I feel sure it was legitimate. They weren't aware there was anyone else around."

"Did you write down everything you could remember, word for word, like I asked you?" Casey inquired.

"Sure did, as soon as I got to my room. Fell asleep in the middle of it, but finished as soon as I woke up. Think I got nearly all of it."

The waiter approached, and they ordered grilled shark and

potatoes. There were several vacant tables in the place, but neither of them felt like sitting, as McGraw signaled the bartender for two steam beers.

"What would we do without Doctor Donnelly?" McGraw said, remembering the midnight messenger they had sent to roust out the police surgeon. He had shown up, puffy eyed, a half hour later to remove the lead pellets by lamplight in the back room of the California Street station house.

"Yeah, I can hardly sit down at all. There was more of that damn' buckshot in my backside and legs than I thought."

"The doc's experience with bullet and arrow wounds in the cavalry has sure given him a deft touch. I was watching him work."

"You're right about that. Except for a few of the deeper ones, I hardly felt him taking out most of that shot."

"Those two big slugs of whiskey he gave you probably helped deaden the pain some," McGraw suggested with a grin.

The waiter brought their food and set it on the bar.

"It's a damn' shame that Captain Moreland got away," McGraw remarked. "If we could have nailed him, that would have just about put a stop to this whole business. They talked like he was the major supplier. Most of the opium apparently wasn't coming in on cargo and passenger ships from the Orient, after all."

Casey nodded, spearing a bite with his fork. "But now at least we know who we're after. The boys won't be wasting a lot of man hours searching passengers and cargo. I would have been satisfied just to get my hands on Ho Ming."

"To hell with Ho Ming," McGraw replied, raising his beer glass. "Here's to you for saving my life. If you hadn't gotten there when you did, and taken one helluva chance, I would've been grilled crisper than this fish."

"We're about even then. You figured a way to get us out of

that cave. How are those burns, by the way?"

"Just a few patches of skin and some hair missing. The doc greased them up pretty good. It'll take a while for all these scabs to grow new skin under them. Just have to watch out for infection. Had to get rid of my shirt and pants, though. Burned full of holes. You should've seen the look on Missus O'Neal's face when I gave 'em to her to make rags out of. She didn't ask any questions, and I didn't volunteer any answers. I'm sure she's wondering what kind of a crazy man is interested in her daughter." He chuckled and took a long swallow of beer. "By the way, you haven't told me the details of how you found me the other night."

"Well, I heard the shot but didn't know where it had come from. As a policeman, I instinctively wanted to go investigate. But then I remembered where I was, and what I was doing. I figured it was some argument between tong members and decided to wait. I was just about to go inside and warn you to be on the alert, when Watson came running around the corner and told me what had happened. By the time we got back into the alley, we couldn't find anyone. Of course, the fog was so thick we couldn't see six feet, and there was no light anyway. We fumbled around in the alley, feeling our way around, but couldn't find a thing. And time was wasting. So I sent Watson for help. Told him how to get to the California Street station house. I knew with his bad leg, he'd have to find a hack, or it would take him a long time to get there. But we had to have help. While he was gone, I kept looking." He paused to chew a bite of bread. "I don't know how much time passed. It seemed like hours, but probably wasn't more than twenty or thirty minutes. I thought I heard my name. It's a good thing you kept on yelling because I was able to gradually home in on the sound. Turned out you were in the cellar of a big restaurant at the far end of the alley on the same street. I didn't figure you'd have had time to get very far, and, sure enough, there you were."

"I'm sure glad you kept looking."

"Watson finally got to the station house and brought back three men, but by the time he directed them to that opium den and they had searched the alley, we were long gone and, apparently, so were Ho Ming, the hatchet men, and Captain John Moreland. Watson stayed at the House of Celestial Delights when the three men on the Chinatown squad returned to the station house."

"And found Doctor Donnelly working on us there," McGraw finished.

"When they found out where you'd been, they went back and searched the place but, of course, found nothing except a little blood on the cellar stairs, a few bullet holes, and that stove you'd shoved over under the window."

"Who owns that restaurant?" McGraw wondered aloud.

"Probably owned by some tong member. Ho Ming may even have a financial interest in it. At least he had access to it after it was closed for the night. No doors or locks were broken."

McGraw shifted his stance and put a foot up on the brass rail to ease one of his sore legs. "What did the chief say when you gave him the news?"

Casey took another bite of potatoes and didn't reply immediately.

McGraw looked up. "You did tell him, didn't you?"

"Not yet," Casey said, chewing thoughtfully.

"Why? The quicker the squad gets the information, the quicker they can put pressure on in the right place."

"Not really sure. Just a feeling. I'll tell the men, of course. But as far as reporting this through channels . . . because of our injuries and the fact that you and I were temporarily off duty when that incident happened . . . I'm not technically required to give a report of what happened. I've just hinted that it was a private thing . . . never gave any indication that it had anything to do with this department's campaign against the opium traffic. I might have to wind up paying Doctor Donnelly out of my own pocket."

"What's the next move?"

"I'm giving it some thought. Meanwhile, we have time. I probably won't have to be back on duty for a few days, and you won't, either."

"And I won't be able to play baseball," McGraw added regretfully.

Casey looked up with a slight smile. "Spend a little of your time getting sympathy from that pretty O'Neal girl at your boarding house."

"Huh! Afraid she's not susceptible to this sort of thing."

"Too bad. She must be a hard one."

"Not really. She's just had to perform a lot of drudgery all her life. She's not impressed by my injuries. Thinks I ought to have my head examined for what I'm doing . . . although I do think she's secretly envious of all the mystery and excitement my jobs have brought with them."

They ate for a few minutes in silence, as the small eating place grew crowded with the lunch time rush. Men elbowed up to the bar as the tables filled, so McGraw and Casey talked only of trivial matters until they had finished, paid their bill, and retired to the sunshine outside.

"Let's walk down toward the waterfront," Casey suggested. "I need to keep moving to prevent stiffening up."

"Aren't we a couple of sad-looking cases!" McGraw laughed. "Both moving like we're octogenarians."

"We're damn' lucky to be moving at all," Casey snorted.

McGraw stretched his stride slightly, aware of the greased, gauze bandages wound about both thighs and one ankle.

"What did Ho Ming say to you before he put you on that grill?"

"Not much . . . other than you and I were becoming a real nuisance, and that he was going to kill me in such a way as to make an example of what would happen. Indicated he wanted to scare off the rest of the special squad and the police from interfering in the opium trade in Chinatown. Basically the same thing you and I figured out when they tried to kill us the last time. These people remind me of Apaches. They like to torture their victims, to strike terror in the hearts of any other enemies."

"Hmmm . . . he didn't say anything else? Anything that might give us more information about their operation?"

"Can't recall anything of importance. When I realized he really meant to kill me, I blew up and accused him of beheading O'Toole to make an example of him, too."

"Oh?" Casey glanced over sharply. "What did he say?"

"As I remember, he just looked blank and acted as if he had never heard of O'Toole and didn't know what I was talking about."

They walked on a few steps without speaking, while Casey absorbed this, gnawing thoughtfully at the corner of his black mustache. "Have you got the paper you wrote down their conversation on?"

"Sure. Right here." McGraw pulled a folded sheet of paper from his shirt pocket and handed it over.

Casey stopped and sidled out of the way of the other pedestrians as he unfolded and read the dialogue. "At least our squad's nightly patrols on the Bay seem to be doing some good," he remarked. "That's where I've had the men concentrate since we stopped getting those false leads from our so-called informant, Ho Ming. Moreland mentions here that he's afraid to come into the Bay. If it was being brought into the Bay, I wonder where they were bringing it ashore? It's a cinch that ghost schooner never docked at the wharves down here, or it would have been spotted. Of course, there are many miles of shoreline in the Bay, and they could've landed it almost anywhere. Alcatraz is out of the question since it's occupied by the Army. Besides, trying to row or sail across to the city from there in small boats in the dark would be very difficult, especially while trying to avoid being seen. And my men have questioned fishermen, yachtsmen, harbor pilots, ferry crewmen . . . many of the people who would have occasion to be on the Bay at any and all hours of the day and night. And nobody admits to seeing anything that might be suspicious . . . especially any Chinese in small boats. A few of them did mention seeing that unlighted and unmarked schooner."

"What about Angel Island?"

Casey shook his head. "There's an Army post there, too. Moreland would never risk transfer at Angel Island. And many miles of the shoreline of the Bay are shallow oyster beds and mud flats at low tide, so you couldn't run a ship of any size in close. Of course, there's Sausalito and quite a few other places where the water is deep enough, but they wouldn't want to unload across the water from the city, or they'd have a long way to haul it by small boat, or would have to transport it by wagon or horseback a hundred miles or more all the way around to get back to San Francisco. No, I believe the drops are being made right in the Bay, probably less than a half mile off the city. I believe the transfers are being made to small boats while the ship is hove to, or drifting, or anchored short, probably on moonless nights or in the fog, and then brought into some private dock or boathouse. It had to be arranged and carefully co-ordinated. I may be wrong, but I think that's the way it's done."

"Why not just seal off the Golden Gate to see if you can snag that schooner coming in?"

"Plugging the neck of the bottle sounds easy enough, but the strong currents, the fog, and the darkness make it almost impossible. The Bay has a big area, but it's relatively shallow. Every time the tide changes, a lot of its water sucks in and out through that opening, so you can imagine how strong the current is. You've got hundreds of ships and boats of all sizes, coming in and out through there. A police steam launch, if we had one, cruising back and forth right in that area could probably hold its position in the current. But it would take a big chance on collisions, and still it might miss the ghost ship. If we could somehow put two or three or more boats there, it would just increase the congestion and the danger." He shook his head. "I'm just glad to know the stuff is aboard one ship we can focus on. There are hundreds of small, ingenious hiding places the opium could be smuggled in by individuals or stashed in freight or baggage. But now I think the amount coming in that way is negligible . . . you know, people bringing in a little for their own use, like that hollow trade dollar we found."

"So what have we got so far?" McGraw asked.

Casey resumed a slow walk. "All right, here's the way I see it . . . the facts are these. The board of supervisors appoints a committee to study and report on conditions in Chinatown. This report causes a big uproar in the newspapers and from the public. I recruit a squad of men from those who patrolled in Chinatown . . . trustworthy men, as near as I can judge. Kevin O'Toole is one of them, and a baseball teammate of yours as well. O'Toole is seen talking to Blind Boss Buckley, for what purpose we don't know. Buckley later denies knowing or meeting him. O'Toole is found dead and mutilated a day later in Chinatown. If there is any connection to the opium smuggling, we don't know it at this time. While this was going on, the men on our special squad made a few arrests and seized a few small amounts of opium from Chinamen at various locations in and

153

outside the Bay. These arrests were due to the tips that came from Ho Ming. Then I am lured to one of Ho Ming's whorehouses in Chinatown, allegedly for a meeting. You accompany me, and we're both captured, thrown into a cave, and almost killed. And it is made to look as if Ho Ming is a victim as well, even though he isn't thrown into the cave with us. Then Ho Ming disappears, and we begin to presume he's dead. To make up for the small successes we are no longer getting from tips, I order stepped-up boat patrols every night in the Bay. Apparently they're partially successful because you accidentally overhear that Moreland is now afraid to bring his ship into the Bay. This confirms rumors you heard earlier of a ghost ship. At the same time you find out Ho Ming is still alive and one of the ring leaders in the opium smuggling. You overhear Moreland mention a boss he wants to deal with, presumably somebody above Ho Ming, but we don't know who that is. Ho Ming tries to kill you again. Basically, those are the known facts. From there, it starts to get a little murky."

Casey paused as they approached a warehouse near the waterfront. He half leaned, half sat against a hogshead near the wall of a building and seemed to be observing the horse-drawn drays, moving slowly away from a steamer being unloaded at a long wharf, but apparently his eyes were looking inward. "Just about everything else is supposition, hunches, suspicions, odd coincidences, and just plain guesswork. For example, what do we know about O'Toole's death? Nothing other than he was beheaded with a medieval European axe and then his body dumped in an alley in Chinatown. We don't know why or by whom, or whether his death has anything at all to do with his work on the police opium smuggling squad. We also don't know what business he could have had with Blind Boss Buckley. For that matter, was Buckley involved in the murder, or is he involved in the opium trade himself? Probably, but that is pure speculation, based on what I know of some of his other shady activities."

"Did you dig up anything on O'Toole's private life?"

"Well, we located an old address for his mother in his personnel file and sent her a telegraph message. If she got it, she hasn't replied. We found a casual girl friend . . . a Tessie Waters. Neither she nor any of his other acquaintances that we've identified ever saw him again after that ball game. He just seems to have vanished until he turned up dead the next day. Never returned to his boarding house that night."

McGraw absorbed this information.

"There's another thing I found strange."

"What's that?"

"This Tessie Waters told me he spent a lot of time hanging around Buckley's Saloon. That seems odd to me. O'Toole was big and blunt-talking, more prone to action than talk. There was nothing devious about him. As far as I know, he had no interest in politics. Why would he hang around with all these would-be politicians, lying bribe-takers, and favor-seekers? The people at Buckley's were not his type at all. There are plenty of saloons in this town, most of them catering to one type of clientele or another . . . sailors, factory workers, businessmen, bankers, sportsmen. He would've had no trouble finding a saloon that was more in tune with his character and personality."

McGraw shook his head. "I don't know. Maybe we didn't know the real Kevin O'Toole as well as we thought we did."

"Either that, or he had a particular reason for spending time in the Star of the West."

"And what reason would that be?"

"Could be he was working with or for Blind Boss Buckley. Whether it had anything to do with opium, I don't know, but I'd bet my reputation it was something illegal. And I'd also bet that, whatever it was, led directly to his murder."

"Where do we go from here? Concentrate on nailing that Captain Moreland and his schooner?" McGraw asked.

Casey shook his head. "The conversation you overheard indicated that Moreland had a large shipment he's received some payment for already but was hedging about delivering on schedule. He even threatened to take it north to Victoria, British Columbia. By the way, I've sent a telegram to the constable there to be on the lookout for this schooner with no markings and this Captain Moreland. Trouble is, I couldn't describe him or his ship, since we haven't seen either of them. For all we know, he puts a name to his ship, has forged papers, and goes by some other name when he lands there. Anybody who's had experience as a blockade runner during the War between the States, and has probably been into some sort of illegal activity . . . be it smuggling or piracy . . . ever since, is certain to have thought out and planned for just about any contingency."

"That's true," McGraw agreed, drawing in a deep lungful of the fresh sea breeze. "Maybe we can hope for a falling-out between thieves. The way they were arguing, maybe they'll do each other in."

"Don't count on it. Even if one of them got so provoked as to kill the other, someone else would just step up to take his place. Nobody's indispensable. It's nice to hope that these criminals and Chinese hatchet men and highbinders would cancel each other out, but I'm afraid it's up to us if anything really effective is to be done." He folded his arms across his chest and stared out across the waterfront where some gray and white seagulls were wheeling and crying and diving for scraps of fish. "Right now I'm keeping the men on their usual nightly patrols on the Bay, even though I've canceled searching the ships and cargoes down here." He gestured with his head toward the docks. "We don't know what deadline for delivery they were discussing, and without finding Ho Ming we won't know. From the heated conversation they were having, I'd have to surmise that the deadline is soon . . . within a few days. You said he did mention something about a week. If Moreland does decide to make his delivery as scheduled, maybe my men will be lucky enough to intercept his ship. If not . . . ?" He shrugged. "Then we've let another load slip by us. One thing I do want you to do, though, is keep your appointment with that Chinese prostitute next week down at Salinas. You never know, that might lead to something."

McGraw was surprised, but said nothing. When they had discussed this before, Casey had been pessimistic about it. Maybe the chance break of finding out about Moreland and Ho Ming had changed his mind. Now any chance meeting might have promise.

"Here's a hundred dollars in greenbacks," Casey continued, taking out his leather billfold and counting out some tens and twenties, and glancing about to be sure no one was close by. "It was all I could scare up. Make it last, and make it count."

"This girl looked to be fairly high class, more so than your average sing-song girl. I don't know what kind of money she was thinking of. We didn't get around to discussing specifics."

"She couldn't be too high class, or she wouldn't be working in Salinas," Casey retorted.

"You've got a point there," McGraw admitted. "But apparently she's somebody's favorite . . . somebody she claims is in the know."

"We'll see. Just be very careful."

"You don't think I'm going to get careless after these last two experiences, do you?"

"That restaurant where you were almost grilled is under the watchful eyes of our Chinatown squad," Casey advised. "If

157

there was anything going on there, besides serving customers food, we'll know about it."

"Unless they move their meetings or operations somewhere else."

Casey nodded. "Getting hold of anything in Chinatown is like trying to pick up a blob of mercury off a laboratory table . . . it just slips and slides and sometimes breaks into a lot of little pieces you can't get any kind of grip on."

"Let's walk down to Italy Harbor," McGraw suggested, changing the subject. "I promised Katie I'd pick up some fish for her mother to fix for supper."

Casey straightened up with an obvious twinge of pain, and set his legs in motion. "The Filbert Street wharf it is, then. The more I keep my blood flowing, the quicker I'll heal up."

Chapter Thirteen

"Ouch!"

"Be quiet, you big baby. I'm not hurting you!"

Katie O'Neal pushed McGraw face down onto the quilt and continued rubbing a salve onto the three or four small scabby areas on his back and shoulders. She worked her fingertips deftly, but gently, around the burned areas, oblivious to the stares of a few strollers passing nearby on the sunny grass of Golden Gate Park.

"These things are healing pretty quickly," she observed. "The scabs are beginning to flake off around the edges."

"*Ow!* Don't do that!" he howled good-naturedly as she flicked some dry scabs away with a fingernail.

"I'll bathe these spots in hydrogen peroxide as they heal, and that will keep them from scarring."

"Where'd you learn so much about nursing?" McGraw asked.

"Hard necessity. I had to help my mother doctor my niece and nephew when they were little and lived with us. Also my grandfather before he died. Things I just picked up here and there from older people and from books. We didn't usually have any money for doctors," she stated matter-of-factly. "Home remedies, mostly. Sometimes they worked, and sometimes they didn't. O K, now, I'll have a look at those spots on your legs."

"Oh, no, you won't. I'm not taking my pants off in front of you, especially here in public."

"Oh, for heaven's sake! All right, then, here's the salve. You can dose yourself later." She replaced the top of the small jar and set it aside, as McGraw rolled over and sat up, slipping his shirt back on gingerly.

She eyed him as he buttoned the white cotton shirt. "Did you say they actually tied you to a big grill and built a fire under you?" She wiped her hands on a handkerchief she had pulled from a pocket in her skirt. "You know there was nothing about it in the newspapers."

"We weren't on official police business," McGraw answered. "And Casey wanted to keep it quiet for now." He glanced at her suddenly serious demeanor. "By the way, I wouldn't recommend that restaurant. They burn their meat, and it's full of gristle." He grinned, but she didn't change expression.

"Do you realize you've almost been killed twice in the past few weeks?"

"Don't remind me."

"I read in the newspaper just this week that Police Chief Pat Crowley says San Francisco has double the murder rate of New York City, which is much larger. If I remember rightly, there is one murder for every eleven thousand people here. But just in Chinatown there is something like one murder for every twenty-two hundred people. What do you think of that?"

"I think I'd better be more careful . . . especially in Chinatown."

She shook her head. "You're hopeless."

"Most of those murders are just the tongs' hatchet men killing off one another, fighting to control the vice."

"And you put yourself right in the middle of it. When are you going back to your job with Wells Fargo?" She avoided his eyes as she plucked absently at a sprig of grass.

"Depends on when this opium smuggling is brought under control."

"What if it's not?"

"Then maybe toward the end of the year. I'm only hired by

the police department on a temporary basis. I've worked as a temporary before, about three years ago during that big robbery at the U. S. Mint."

"I remember," she nodded. "I didn't know you then, but I read all about it."

"As a result of that, I got my job as an express car messenger for Wells Fargo. Since then, I've seen about all I care to of the route between here and Chicago."

"You've led a rather adventurous life for someone who's still in his twenties."

"Better than being bored to death. I've recently seen what boredom can lead to."

"Oh?"

"That English visitor . . . the detective, Sherlock Holmes, I told you about."

"Oh, yes. But one of these days you may not survive one of these so-called *adventures* of yours. Do you ever think about that?"

"I've probably had more injuries playing sports than I've ever had working or running up against criminals."

"You *know* it's not the same. Your sporting opponents aren't out to kill you."

"Sometimes I'm not so sure about that," he laughed.

"Well, I can see you're not going to take this seriously," she said, slightly irritated. "Of course, you can do whatever you want to. All I'm trying to say is that I would be very grieved if something happened to you."

He looked quickly at her downcast eyes and that lovely face, framed by the dark hair. She actually cared for him. He couldn't believe his luck. He silently reached over and took her hand.

After a few moments they rose, and McGraw folded up the quilt they had been sitting on as Katie brushed off her long skirt. He put the quilt and the jar of salve in the rented buggy a few yards away. The horse stood, hipshot, stretching his tether to munch on the leaves of a nearby bush. McGraw was glad it was mid-week, because there were relatively few people in Golden Gate Park. On Saturdays the park was crowded with fashionable people, driving rigs from the livery of J. Tompkinson.

The couple walked slowly away from the rig, hand in hand, in the brilliant sunshine, wandering in the general direction of the Francis Scott Key Memorial, whose white marble shape loomed in the distance. It was five days after McGraw's brush with death in the depths of Chinatown, and, though the memory was still vivid, the entire experience had begun to take on an unreal quality as the days passed, as if it were some horror story he had read. At least, he wasn't having any nightmares about it. But the healing burns on his back and legs were a constant reminder that it had been real enough. This girl beside him was real as well. He ruefully reflected that he had told Casey she was unmoved by his injuries. She had proven to be just the opposite. Her compassion was something that affected him deeply, although he hoped her feelings for him were prompted by something other than pity. He knew she had been seeing a well-to-do man named Harvey Sullivan, the son of an Oakland banker. McGraw had seen him two or three times when Sullivan had come to pick her up at the boarding house. McGraw remembered how excited she had been the first time Sullivan had arrived. She had nervously checked her hair in the vestibule mirror in the front hall before opening the door for him. McGraw had tried not to eavesdrop from the top of the stairs that evening as Mrs. O'Neal greeted the visitor. But the tone of the mother's voice indicated an almost fawning attitude toward this wealthy young man who had come to escort her daughter to dinner and the theater. McGraw knew this was the type of suitor Mrs. O'Neal wanted to encourage.

McGraw had retired to his room and had glanced out the

front window at the light, spring carriage with the black leather seats and the varnished spokes, pulled by a pair of matched grays. That had been no rented rig. It had probably been built to order by the Pacific Carriage Works. He had experienced an involuntary twinge of jealousy as he had seen Harvey hand Katie up into the elegant buggy.

And now he experienced another slight twinge of unwelcome jealousy as he recalled that evening. But that was then, and this was now. He didn't care if she were still seeing Sullivan, and didn't want to know. He had never mentioned Harvey Sullivan to her, but he had not seen the banker's son at the boarding house in two or three weeks.

"Why so quiet?" she asked, startling him out of his reverie.

"Just enjoying the beautiful day . . . and the company," he said, smiling at her. He wasn't about to tell her what had been running through his mind. Some things were best left unsaid. "The Stormy Petrels have a game this afternoon," he remarked. "Would you like to go with me?"

"I wish I could, but mother's expecting me to help with the laundry. I had trouble just getting away for a couple of hours this morning."

"Probably because she knew you were going with me," McGraw observed dryly.

"My mother doesn't dislike you, you know."

"I'm just not her first choice," he grinned.

"Jay McGraw, I'll make my own choices, thank you," she said, her blue eyes snapping. She slipped her hand into his as they resumed their stroll. "How are the Stormy Petrels doing without you?"

"So far, I've missed only one game, not counting today's. They lost the last one, but not because I was missing from the lineup. Tub Moran put Jim Scala in my position, and he hit three-for-four and scored two runs. If he keeps that up, I may

163

be riding the bench when I get back."

"I doubt that. Moran would find a place for both of you."

"Tub may just keep me listed as disabled. When I talked to him the other day, he didn't seem too happy that I kept getting myself banged up. I almost had to miss a game earlier because of that cut on my arm."

"Speaking of getting yourself banged up, as you call it, what kind of dangerous situation are you getting into next?"

McGraw briefly considered confiding to her that he would be meeting with a Chinese prostitute the very next night in Salinas, but some quick instinct warned him against it. It was a confidential assignment, and she might inadvertently mention it to someone else. Better just to do his job and tell her about it later. And, he had to admit to himself, he would rather she didn't know he was meeting with a prostitute. "Just some routine questioning of some people who might be able to give us some leads," he replied with a vague wave of his hand.

"This opium and gambling and crime in Chinatown has really given our city a bad name, hasn't it? I've even seen articles about it in magazines like *Harper's Weekly*. Our reputation is spread all over the country. I have a girl friend, Marcella Stewart, who had a cousin come and visit her from Saint Louis. And guess what the first thing was that girl wanted to do when she got here? She wanted to go to Chinatown and smoke some opium. It was supposed to be so daring and wicked. She wanted to have something exciting to tell her friends back home. She said the first thing everyone wants to know about San Francisco is about Chinatown, the tong wars, the slave girls, and the opium dens. It's ridiculous, especially with all the interesting and beautiful things we have here."

"Well, I don't know of anything that's going to change that, human nature being what it is."

"I suppose not. I just wish all this campaign against opium smuggling was over. It's too dangerous. I won't rest easy until you're back on that train, working for Wells Fargo again."

"That messenger job isn't all that safe, either," McGraw said, referring to a wild shoot-out with robbers and a flight from his train in a gas balloon a year and a half before — a tale he had earlier related to her.

"Maybe not. But it's safer than this."

"Don't worry. I have no wish for a one-way trip to Cypress Lawn. I love my life too much. And I plan to get into something that's a little more boring . . . eventually."

He grinned as she gave him a disgusted look.

McGraw was beginning to doubt the sing-song girl would show up for their appointment. He slipped out his watch and checked the time — six thirty-five. He had been lounging near the bathhouse in Salinas for more than a half hour.

Three grimy, sweat-stained men McGraw took to be ranch hands came past him, talking and laughing, and entered the bathhouse. He waited another quarter hour. Finally he decided she was not coming. She had forgotten, she had lied, or she had been unable to obtain the information she had promised to get. Because of the scabs McGraw had not intended to soak in a hot tub of water tonight, but now he went inside, paid the old Chinaman, and decided, as long as he had come all this way, to have a relaxing bath before going to the hotel where he had spent the night the week before.

A female Chinese attendant escorted him to one of the partially partitioned wooden tubs where she poured in a bucket of steaming water. As he disrobed, she went for a bucket of tepid water. A few minutes later he slowly lowered himself into the tub.

Almost before he could relax, a small, silk-clad figure was

beside the tub. "Did you bring money?" the silvery voice asked quietly.

McGraw looked casually around. The attendant was gone, and the three cowhands were splashing and talking in three tubs on the opposite side of the room. He reached for his pants on the low stool beside the tub, slipped out his billfold, flipped it open, and held it low to the floor with one hand so only the girl could see the edges of several greenbacks, protruding from it.

"Tell me what you know," he said in a low voice.

"Fifty dollar first," she countered in a low, hard tone.

McGraw deftly edged a twenty-dollar note out and, dropping the billfold, crumpled the bill and held his fist out to her. "Twenty for now, until I know if your information is valuable," he said, a pleasant smile on his lips.

"Girls will bring opium tomorrow on the *Orient Moon* to San Francisco."

"How many girls and how is it hidden?"

"Six. Pads under dress. Here." She put a hand to her breasts.

McGraw smiled inwardly. "Anything else?"

"No."

He thought quickly. "I'll see you here again Monday night about this same time."

She shook her head slightly as he dropped the bill into her hand. "The man visit me Tuesday. I know more then."

"All right. Wednesday night, then." McGraw slid the billfold back into his pants pocket.

She made a barely perceptible bow and glided silently away.

Trying not to hurry, McGraw climbed out of the tub, patted himself dry with the rough towel, wincing at the sore spots. He slipped his clothes on over his still damp skin and went outside. The sun was down, but the sky was light in the long summer evening. The girl was nowhere to be seen. He stepped back inside.

"Where is that girl . . . the one in the green silk who was in here a few minutes ago?" he asked the old Oriental in charge of the bathhouse.

The old man looked at him with no expression. Finally he pointed. "Hotel."

"Does she work there? Does she live there? She's a prostitute. Does she have a master? Are there other girls?"

At this onslaught of questions the old man looked blankly at him again. This time he just shook his head, as if he didn't understand.

McGraw slipped his silver badge out of a leather pocket in his money belt and showed it to the old man. "I'm a policeman."

This statement and the sight of the badge elicited no more information. The old man said something in Chinese, and then a couple of halting words in English. "Girl." He pointed again. "Hotel."

McGraw gave up, replaced his badge, and started down the dusty street to the hotel where he had already checked in as soon as he had arrived. He had known the last train north for the day would already be gone before his meeting with the girl. He couldn't quite classify her with others of her race and profession. In the city nearly all of them were under bondage to a slave master who had them working out of houses. Maybe it was different here and in other remote parts of the state where Chinese slave girls had been dispersed. Maybe there wasn't as much business. Otherwise, why would this girl be soliciting business in a bathhouse and, at the same time, have some influential client who visited her once a week from San Francisco? Was she free-lancing, or was she bound to some master who directed her activities and took a generous share of her earnings? However she was operating, she must be doing it out of the only hotel in town. He had to find out where she was and what room she was in, even if it meant pretending to solicit her favors. Today was Thursday. In the morning he would catch the train back to the city, alert Casey, and try to intercept the six arriving slave girls to see if they, in fact, were smuggling opium. Whether or not the tip proved out, McGraw would be back here on Tuesday night to see if he could somehow discover who this prostitute's well-connected client was. He mentally kicked himself for again having forgotten to get the girl's name.

The first thing McGraw did when he reached his hotel was to inquire at the desk about the Chinese girl, describing her to the clerk as best he could.

"I'm sorry, sir. We have no Orientals at all registered at the hotel presently."

"Have there been any Chinese girls registered here within the past two weeks, even for as little as one night?"

"No, sir."

McGraw decided not to show his badge, hoping the man behind the desk would voluntarily tell him the truth. And he didn't want the fact that he was a detective generally known here, if he could help it. The girl probably suspected, but that couldn't be helped. Besides, a San Francisco detective had no jurisdiction in Salinas.

"Have you been the only one on duty here?"

"Yes."

"So you would have known had any Chinese girl checked in or out."

"Certainly. And the other clerk who comes on at midnight would have mentioned it, had he seen one."

"Why is that?"

"Because it's unusual for any Chinese to stay at this hotel. About the only Chinese we see around this town are the two families who run the laundry and the bathhouse. But they have their own houses. They don't stay here."

"You never have any passing through who want to put up here for the night?"

The clerk gave him an exasperated look. "Sir, I've told you all I know. Why all this interest in the Chinese?"

"Personal reasons," McGraw answered, moving away from the desk.

"I assure you, sir," the clerk called after him, "we run a clean, respectable hotel here. We don't allow just *anyone* to be a guest of this establishment."

McGraw continued on to the stairs and climbed to his room on the second floor.

The following morning, at sunup, McGraw had a quick cup of coffee in the hotel dining room, checked out, and walked to the nearby depot, just in time to board the northbound train for San Francisco. Upon reaching the city, he caught a horse-drawn trolley that took him to within a block of Casey's rooming house. Casey was at home and had just finished bathing in the tub down the hall from his room. His legs and lower back were healing rapidly from the peppering of shot he had caught, although he still had to treat a few of the tiny wounds, keeping them disinfected.

"Good thing that window frame stopped the biggest part of the load," he remarked, opening the door to his room. "Come in and sit down."

McGraw tossed his small traveling kit onto the bed and sat down in a cushioned armchair.

"What did you find out?" Casey asked, buttoning his shirt.

McGraw briefly related the information he had obtained. "Do you have any idea what time the *Orient Moon* is supposed to dock?" he asked.

"No, but we'll find out. Come on."

They walked two blocks and caught a cable car that took them to Marker Street where they hopped off and caught another one going toward the Ferry House at the foot of Market. From there they walked to the Pacific Coast Steamship Company which posted a list of all arriving and departing ships each day.

"There she is . . . the *Orient Moon*," Casey said, running his finger down the list. "Due in at three o'clock."

"How can they be sure of that?"

Casey shrugged. "It's always an estimate, but she's a steamship and more likely to keep a schedule than a sailing vessel. She's coming direct from Hong-Kong and will be docking at Pier Six." He slipped out his watch. "We've got plenty of time. Since we're not officially on duty, I'll alert the boys at the California Street station to meet the ship. As soon as I take care of that, we'll grab some lunch." He glanced at McGraw. "I can't wait to see what comes down that gangway."

At three thirty-six that afternoon a small steam tug nudged the high, iron-hulled steamship, *Orient Moon*, into her berth alongside Pier Six. Thick hawsers were hove from the main deck, caught, and looped over bitts ashore, securing her with crossing fore and aft spring lines. With a shrill blast of her steam whistle the tug backed away, swung about, and thrashed away in a welter of dirty foam. Deckhands were busy rigging the gangway while others set up booms for the aft cargo hold. Orders rang out in rapid-fire Chinese.

Debarking passengers were lining the rail. As soon as the gangway was in place and secured, the passengers began to stream off, carrying various bags and parcels. Jason Neal and Bernard Kohl, members of the special opium squad, were stationed at the foot of the gangway, out of uniform. Casey and McGraw were standing a few yards away, watching the passengers filing into the customs shed just behind them.

About fifteen people, including several Caucasians, passed them before six young Chinagirls, obviously traveling together, came down the gangway, ushered by a Chinaman, well dressed in western-style clothing. They were all accosted and asked to step aside as they came onto the pier.

McGraw was too far away to hear what was being said, but he saw the two officers show their badges and then guide the girls and their escort toward the customs shed. McGraw and Casey closed in behind the group, and McGraw could hear the girls talking to the officers in halting English, explaining that they were Californians who were returning from a visit to relatives in China. As proof, they named California Street and one of them said she had an uncle who lived on DuPont Street. Neal and Kohl were paying no attention.

"Hear that?" Casey asked quietly. "A well-rehearsed ploy to keep the authorities from thinking these are slave girls, headed for sale to masters like Ho Ming. They are coached in speaking English, memorizing street names, even to studying maps of the city in a clumsy attempt to make us think they've been here before and have a legitimate reason for being here now."

The girls and their male escort were taken into one of the small rooms under the customs shed, and the girls were ordered to disrobe. The girls looked at one another, and the man with them protested vigorously, but McGraw could see that his indignation was mostly bluster. The girls chattered excitedly among themselves in Chinese, but Jason Neal firmly repeated his order, and finally they saw they had no choice and reluctantly complied. When they had finished, a half dozen buxom Chinagirls had been transformed into six rather flat-chested Chinese girls and several small cloth packs of opium were piled on the table. Their male escort, whose name was Mar Tan, tried at first to disclaim any knowledge of the hidden opium, but, when he saw no one was listening to him, he lapsed into a sullen silence.

All seven of them were arrested, and McGraw and Casey helped the two officers escort the prisoners to the substation and holding jail on California Street. They walked the entire distance, since there were no paddy wagons available. Chief Crowley's plea for a system of police wagons had been turned down by the board of supervisors for economic reasons. Consequently arresting officers usually got plenty of exercise. The three paddy wagons the department owned were usually confined to use in dangerous situations and violent crimes, and seemed to be constantly in use.

At the station the seven Orientals were fingerprinted for possible future reference, the black smudges being added to a growing file on the city's arrested criminals. They were then charged with opium smuggling and jailed, pending a hearing.

"Now, *that* makes me feel good," Casey remarked with a smile of satisfaction as he and McGraw left the station house.

"Well worth the twenty dollars I paid for the tip," McGraw added. "But I'm afraid it's going to cost more the next time. If I can somehow get the identity of her informant, maybe we can track him to the source."

Casey looked thoughtful. "This was almost too easy. I don't want to look a gift horse in the mouth, but I'm always a little suspicious of anything that comes that easy." He turned to McGraw. "By the way, let me ask you something. Did you see this girl solicit any other customers in the bathhouse the night you first met her?"

"There were no other customers there at the time."

"What about last night?"

"There were three other men who came in together, but she never approached them. Of course, she was looking for me, since we had arranged to meet. . . ."

"But she didn't solicit them on the way out?"

"She never approached them while I was there."

"Doesn't that strike you as odd?"

"What are you getting at? Maybe she had a customer waiting somewhere."

"I think maybe you are being set up as a target. This girl appears out of nowhere and offers to sell herself. When you tell her to leave, she offers to sell you information about opium smuggling. Supposedly she's a prostitute, but she doesn't solicit any of the other men in the bathhouse. Why not? Then the bathhouse owner tells you she's at the hotel, but the hotel clerk denies any knowledge of her. Maybe I'm seeing ghosts where there are none, but we've had two very close passes with the hereafter, thanks to the *boo how doy,* and I don't want another one."

"Listen, Casey, I don't think I'm being set up."

"How do you know that?"

"I can't explain how I know. Just a feeling. You weren't there. First of all, how did this girl know I would even be there the first night? I didn't know myself until about thirty minutes before. I decided at the last minute to spend the night after the ball game because the train was three hours late. The second reason is, I just made some frustrated, off-hand remark that I didn't want anything she had to offer, unless she could tell me who was smuggling opium into San Francisco. She heard the remark, and it was only then that she offered to sell me information. It was totally unplanned. Besides, why would they want to set me up? Any hatchet man could kill either one of us on the street in Chinatown any day and probably escape into the crowd. Both times they tried to murder us, they tried to make a horrible example of our deaths. If they wanted to do it cleanly, they would have no trouble. No, I don't believe this girl poses any threat to me."

173

"I'm going with you Tuesday night. Both of us may be able to intercept this man, whoever he is."

"I'm not sure that's a good idea. First, I have to locate the girl. If she happens to see me, she won't think anything of it because she doesn't know what my business is in Salinas. But if there's someone with me . . . I don't know . . . she might suspect something."

"I'll stay out of sight. I think I need to be there."

McGraw grinned. "All right. If you think you'll be healed well enough by Tuesday."

"I'll be as healed as you are."

Chapter Fourteen

By Tuesday, McGraw and Casey were, in fact, well on their way to recovery. As they sat down to an early supper in the small hotel dining room in Salinas at four forty-five P.M., McGraw was feeling very good. By some judicious questioning and the payment of twenty dollars, along with some bluffing with his badge, he had just loosened the tongue and the memory of the formerly reticent hotel clerk, Oliver Bledsoe. Bledsoe had come forth with the information that a Chinese prostitute by the name of Kem Ying was, indeed, working at the hotel. There were two of them. She and one other girl, Toy Gum, came and went with their gentlemen friends to a room on the first floor of the hotel. They never registered but shared enough of their earnings with the management to more than pay for the use of the hotel. The hotel, the Tremont by name, was a small one of only sixteen rooms, eight on each of two floors. For the application of another precious ten dollars, the clerk disclosed that these girls had regular, moneyed customers, some of them solid citizens of Salinas and a few from surrounding communities. But when the girls weren't entertaining these well-to-do gentlemen, they were not above picking up a few more dollars by soliciting whoever happened to be bathing at the Chinese bathhouse. Bledsoe swore he did not know of any regular customers Kem Ying had from San Francisco.

"The local folks pretty much know what's going on here, but as long as it's kept quiet, everyone has a kind of common agreement to say nothing about it. Sometimes a few of the womenfolk raise Cain with the sheriff and, to placate 'em, he'll come over here and ask us to put the girls out for a time. But, before long, everything's back to business as usual," Bledsoe had ended with a smirk.

"Who do these girls answer to?" McGraw had asked.

"We don't know, and we don't care," the clerk had replied with some self-importance. "For all we know, the girls may be working on their own. But, as long as they pay as well as they do, and nobody complains too much, we're not asking any questions." He had added: "These are two high-class girls."

McGraw had pumped the suddenly informative clerk for all the information he could get for his twenty dollar bribe, and, as he and Casey sat down to eat, he was satisfied that he had learned all he could from Oliver Bledsoe.

"So far it all fits," McGraw said, buttering a piece of bread. "The high-class clientele, the soliciting in their spare time in the bathhouse. If they're free-lancing, they're out to get as much money as they can, and selling information would be an easy way to add to their income."

"A dangerous way, too, if her well-connected city client finds out," Casey mused.

"When was a prostitute's life ever designed for safety?"

They ate in silence for a few moments.

"How do you want to handle this?" Casey asked. "You were able to get the room number, but we don't know how many clients they have per night, or for sure which girl is yours, so we're still somewhat in the dark."

"Let's do it this way . . . there's an evening train down from San Francisco on Tuesdays, Thursdays, and Saturdays. Let's assume this man isn't already here so we'll keep out of sight and watch who gets off the train. Shouldn't be many passengers debarking here. In any case, we'll just keep an eye on any men who head for the hotel."

Casey nodded. "What kind of gun did you get yourself?"

McGraw patted the holster he wore in plain sight on his right hip. "I went back to the old reliable . . . a Forty-Five Colt single-action. Lunenberg had a good used one."

The southbound train was due in at seven forty-five, and the hotel was located just across the dirt street and down about a block from the depot. In fact, the Tremont depended for much of its business on rail travelers.

After supper, still having time to kill, McGraw and Casey strolled down the hallway and found room **Six**. Oliver Bledsoe told them neither of the girls was in at the moment as far as he knew.

"Haven't seen 'em around all day," he told them. "But they don't register, so we don't keep the key behind the desk for them. They have their own. You might say the room is rented to them on a semi-permanent basis." He glanced at the two serious faces before him. "Oh, my, I hope there's not going to be any trouble here that will reflect badly on the hotel," he fretted, wringing his hands.

"Not if we can help it," Casey replied. "You say you haven't seen either girl today?"

"No. But I'm due to go off duty in just a few minutes, at six o'clock. It's not unusual that I haven't seen them. They work nights, after all." He smiled. "They could be sleeping. As a matter of fact, it's just as well for our business that they're discreet. Can't have them traipsing around here in broad daylight, soliciting gentlemen."

McGraw and Casey meandered through the hotel but saw only three other guests — three men they didn't recognize — eating in the small dining room. So the two detectives went down the street to the bathhouse, which had only two other patrons. They both decided a good hot soak would be in order for themselves.

They emerged from their indulgence, refreshed and relaxed,

about seven and sauntered to the depot. A man, his wife, and two children were in the waiting room with their baggage. From snatches of their conversation McGraw learned that the children — a boy of about eleven and his sister, about nine — were going to southern California to visit relatives.

The long summer twilight gradually began to fade, and the stationmaster came out of his cage to light the Rochester lamp, hanging from the ceiling of the waiting room. McGraw was bored and kept glancing at the big wall clock. There were few people coming or going in this small depot. Only one man in a baggage handler's dark blue jacket and stiff-brim cap was trundling a cart down the platform. The iron-wheeled cart was piled with boxes and mail sacks. He stopped the cart and then disappeared around the side of the station. McGraw's thoughts were drifting toward Katie O'Neal.

A half hour later they finally heard the approach of the southbound train. It came puffing in at seven forty-three, right on time. The American Standard locomotive chugged past the platform and ground to a halt about thirty yards down the track in a cloud of steam.

McGraw and Casey, by pre-arrangement, drifted apart, lounging toward opposite sides of the room to watch the debarking passengers. Casey edged out onto the platform, leaned against the wall, his hat pulled low over his eyes.

A portly man in a bowler hat and a sample case stepped down from a coach and went into the depot. Two matronly ladies were handed down by the conductor, being careful not to step on their long dresses as they managed their handbags. From one of the other day coaches came a middle-aged man in a black suit, carrying a small leather grip. McGraw's attention perked up. Who was this? The face wasn't familiar. But he was just the type of well-dressed man he imagined he might be looking for. He scanned the three coaches anxiously, but no one else was getting off here. The side door of the baggage car was slid open, and the messenger was looking out, but no one was there to load the mail and baggage, so he jumped down and went over to the iron-wheeled luggage cart to start loading it himself, glancing around, as if looking for help.

But McGraw's attention was focused on the well-dressed gentleman who had gone over to talk to the stationmaster. McGraw nodded surreptitiously at Casey and then looked toward the frock-coated man with the leather grip. He walked over next to the man and pretended to study the schedule, chalked onto a blackboard on the wall by the stationmaster's window.

". . . at five fifteen," the stationmaster was saying. "Change in Oakland for Portland. One way, or round trip?"

"One way. I may have to spend some time there," the tall passenger replied, reaching inside his coat pocket and extracting an expensive sealskin billfold to pay for his ticket.

As this exchange was going on, McGraw sauntered over and dropped down onto the bench next to Casey a few yards away. He looked out the windows at the messenger, sliding boxes into the open door of the baggage car. Without looking at Casey, he said quietly: "I don't think this is our man. He's buying a ticket to Portland."

"That doesn't mean anything. All we know is that the girl said he was from San Francisco. He may do a lot of traveling. We don't know anything about him."

"Do you recognize him?" McGraw asked under his breath, leaning forward, elbows on knees and staring at the oil-soaked wooden floor.

Casey scrutinized the black-suited man again. "Nobody I ever saw," he replied quietly. "But he may be some big businessman who's involved in the drug trade and just comes down here to indulge himself with his favorite Chinese girl."

The stationmaster stamped the ticket, tore it off, and the man paid with greenbacks. He tucked the ticket into the billfold, replaced the billfold inside his coat, and picked up his bag.

"Let's go," McGraw said.

"Wait until he gets outside. We can't be too obvious. There's no crowd to blend into."

McGraw glanced at the wall clock. It was eight fifteen. With a blast on the steam whistle, the train lurched into motion. McGraw watched the lighted windows of the coaches slide away into the gathering dusk.

When they emerged onto the street, the black-suited man was about fifty yards away, walking briskly toward the hotel.

"We'll make sure this is the man, and then find out if he registers to spend the night. We'll get whatever name he uses, and then see if the desk clerk knows who he is."

But when they opened the door to the hotel lobby, McGraw knew something was wrong. Here were at least a dozen people, milling around the desk, many of them hotel employees. The cook had come out of the kitchen and joined the waitress. Two women McGraw took to be maids by their clothing were talking excitedly. And the whole crowd was looking down the hallway.

Casey and McGraw elbowed their way through the cluster of people to the desk. But the clerk was not there. The man they had been following stood at the edge of the group, looking bewildered.

"What's going on? Where's the clerk?" McGraw asked of nobody in particular. "What happened?" he demanded a little louder when he got no answer.

"Someone's been killed!" a wide-eyed maid at his elbow replied.

"Who?"

"One of those Chinese whores."

"And good riddance it is, I say," the other maid put in.

"Now maybe they'll go some place else to take care of their business!" She sniffed.

McGraw felt a twinge in the pit of his stomach as he lunged after Casey who was already three paces ahead and going down the hallway toward room **Six**.

Just then the door opened, and a man with a sheriff's badge on his vest came out, escorting an ashen-faced Oliver Bledsoe by the arm.

"I don't want anything disturbed in there until I can get the doc down here," the sheriff was saying.

Bledsoe nodded dumbly.

"You understand?"

"Yes."

"Who the hell are you?" the sheriff asked as Casey drew him up short.

Casey's badge appeared in his hand. "Detective Fred Casey of the San Francisco police. This is Jay McGraw, my partner."

The sheriff nodded, looking perplexed. "Sheriff Joe Cutliffe."

Casey drew him aside, and he and McGraw briefly explained why they were here. He asked: "What happened?"

"Somebody just murdered one of these Chinese prostitutes, Kem Ying. Stabbed her."

"The killer got away?"

"Apparently out the window."

"How long ago?"

"Less than thirty minutes. I've got my deputy outside, trying to pick up his trail. I've got to go help him. You can come with me, if you like."

"Rather take a look inside the room."

"Go ahead, but don't disturb anything."

"Right."

The sheriff proceeded up the hallway, pushing back the

curious onlookers. "Go on back to your business. We'll take care of this."

Bledsoe, looking shaken, went back toward the lobby.

Casey nodded toward the door, and he and McGraw went in, closing the door behind them. The room was small, but an open door connected it to an adjoining, almost identical, room. Apparently the two sing-song girls shared these adjoining rooms. McGraw's attention was immediately drawn to a red smear on the white sheets that were partially dragged to the floor. Casey took the low-burning lamp from the table and turned up the wick, then brought it over for a closer look at the form on the floor. "Kem Ying" the sheriff had said. McGraw grimaced at the sight the lamplight revealed. Lying face up, between the bed and the wall, was the girl McGraw remembered. But now the beautiful, almond-shaped eyes were half closed and fixed in death. She was naked to the waist, and the perfect skin made her look like a wax figure. A ghastly, jagged gash just below the sternum still oozed blood to join the mass of gore that had coagulated farther down in a huge stain. Her life's blood.

McGraw felt a wave of revulsion wash over him at the sight of this brutal, senseless act.

"Is that the girl?" Casey asked.

McGraw nodded.

"Well, whoever did this has shut her mouth for good." Casey moved the lamp, looking carefully about the body. The light gleamed off a huge, blood-stained knife, lying partially under the bed. He set the lamp on the floor and crouched, taking a handkerchief from his pocket and gingerly lifting the knife. "Left his calling card. Look at the size of this thing!"

It was not a knife at all, but a double-edged sword, about two feet long with a straight cross guard. From the look of the blood on it, the weapon had apparently been driven completely

182

through the girl, withdrawn, and dropped where it lay. Casey handed it to McGraw who lifted it carefully with his handkerchief, holding only the edges of the blade near the cross guard.

"Another antique?" Casey asked.

"No. This looks new. In fact, there's a name stamped up near the hilt. Looks like Colby and Sons."

"That's the name of a firm that makes a lot of stage props," Casey said. "Killed by a sword of medieval design made for a stage play."

McGraw replaced the sword where Casey had found it. Casey turned the lamp down and set it back on the table.

"Shall we go see if we can help pick up his trail?" McGraw suggested.

Casey shook his head. "A man who has just committed murder and is running scared can go a long way in a half hour. We're not familiar with this area. It's just gotten completely dark outside, and most important of all. . . ." He paused and regarded McGraw. "This murder may have nothing at all to do with the man we are looking for. That man in the black suit out in the lobby who just got off the train could very likely be the man we're looking for. Possibly he just got here too late. The customer just ahead of him killed Kem Ying. Either that, or she got on the bad side of one of the tongs, and they had her assassinated by one of their hatchet men, judging from the way this was done. It's very possible that Ho Ming, or someone like him, found out she was passing secrets about opium smuggling to you, and eliminated her."

McGraw's mind was in a whirl. He felt like walking away from all this and telling Casey he was going back to his job with Wells Fargo, but he quickly put the thought from his mind. He began to examine the room for anything the sheriff might have overlooked in his hasty inspection. Nothing else appeared to be out of place. The small rug was soaked with water since the porcelain pitcher and bowl had been broken in the struggle. There was nothing under the bed. He unlatched and swung open the girl's wardrobe in the corner. It was filled with various silk outfits — more than the ordinary sing-song girl would have. This girl, indeed, had some wealthy clients. He was getting ready to swing the door shut when something incongruous caught his eye. Something black was crumpled on the shoes in the bottom. "What's this?" He pulled it out. "A man's jacket. Looks like some kind of uniform."

Casey was on his knees, searching the bottom of the wardrobe. "Look at this." He held up a stiff-brim porter's cap. "And this." He held up something that looked like a mouse. "A fake mustache." The wardrobe yielded nothing else.

"What do you make of that?" McGraw asked. The shield on the front of the pillbox cap was blank.

"Hmmm. . . ." Casey looked from the jacket to the cap to the mustache. "Throw that stuff back in there. We told the sheriff we wouldn't disturb anything."

They took another last look around and then let themselves out, pausing in the hallway just outside the door.

"Something that looks like a porter's uniform, with a metal shield on the cap that's blank, a fake mustache, and a stage sword. What does that suggest to you?" Casey asked.

"An actor."

"Right."

"Whoever killed her came in here in some sort of disguise and must have had that two-foot sword hidden under his jacket."

"But who, and why?"

"Obviously someone didn't want to be recognized and went to some pains to be sure he wasn't until he got inside her room."

"It had to be someone she was expecting, or she wouldn't

184

have let him in. Did you notice the peep hole in that door?"

"Yes. She probably recognized his voice, or was expecting him to be dressed like a porter and to be wearing a false mustache . . . somebody who came to her as a regular customer who didn't want to be seen by anyone else."

"Why a porter's outfit?" McGraw wondered.

"From the distance an audience would be from a stage, the fact that the metal shield on the cap was blank wouldn't be noticed. So this outfit could be used for a man to play the part of a porter, a Western Union messenger, a fireman, a cable car gripman, or any number of other occupations whose uniforms are similar."

"Another stage prop."

"Right. What I'm getting at is that it's a disguise that's so common, nobody would pay attention to it. We're only a block from the depot. If anybody saw this man, they probably just figured he was getting off work and had an appointment with Kem Ying. After all, these girls are in business here all the time."

"Did you notice any porters near the depot when we were there?" McGraw asked.

"Now that you mention it, I did, but I didn't pay any attention to him. He was just there . . . part of the background."

"I saw him, too," McGraw said. "Just a few minutes after we got there. He was pushing a baggage cart along the platform. But I don't remember seeing him after that when the train came in about forty-five minutes later. It stuck in my mind because I'm a Wells Fargo messenger, and I noticed the messenger in the express car looked pretty disgusted when he had to get out and load the mail and packages himself."

"What did he look like?"

"For the life of me I can't remember. Just proves what

Sherlock Holmes told us . . . constables and law officers need to be more observant."

"Well, we'll just turn this over to the sheriff and let him check it out. Whether or not the man who committed this murder is the one we're trying to find the identity of, we'll probably never know." Casey sighed. "We'll just get a good night's sleep and catch the train back in the morning. Too bad. This looked like it might have been a good source of information."

"Let's go see what Bledsoe has to say," McGraw suggested, noticing that the desk clerk had finished waiting on the two or three customers who had been at the desk.

"This is my night off. I should have been off duty over two hours ago," Bledsoe whined, glancing at the wall clock. "But Thompson left it all to me. I need a tall gin. My nerves are just shot since this horrid business happened." His pallid, clammy face attested to the truth of his words.

"Were you here when this happened?"

"No. There was nobody at the desk."

"A tall man in a black suit, carrying a leather grip, just got off the train and checked in here," McGraw said. "What name did he use?"

Bledsoe stopped fidgeting and gave him a surprised look. "What *name?* Why, his own name, of course." He shoved the registration book across the counter and put a finger on a signature. "Jeff Dunhill."

"You know him?"

"Of course. He's been coming here off and on for several years."

"Tell me about him. What does he do? Where is he from?"

Instead of replying, Bledsoe reached behind the counter into a key slot, pulled out a business card, and slid it across.

McGraw picked it up and read:

LOCKE & MONTAGUE
Importers of Stoves, Metals, and Tinware
Plumbers' and Trimmers' Stock, Tools, and Machines
English and French Hollow Ware,
House Furnishing, Hardware
Also sole importers of the Celebrated Diamond Rock and
Good Samaritan Cookstoves
100 and 102 Battery Street, San Francisco
Jeffrey Dunhill, West Coast Representative

"If you think he is somehow involved in this terrible murder, you are sadly mistaken," Bledsoe snapped.

"Why is that?"

"I've known this man for five years. Wouldn't harm a fly, no matter how provoked he got. Man of very meticulous habits. Never saw him associate with prostitutes."

"You never really know," Casey commented. "People very often have a dark side."

Bledsoe shrugged impatiently. "I'm just telling you what I observed. Besides, she was apparently killed before the train even arrived."

"Did you notice anyone in a uniform come through here just before the murder?" McGraw asked.

"Uniform?"

"Like a railroad porter or conductor."

"Why, yes, now that you mention it, I did."

"Did you happen to recognize him?" McGraw asked, trying to keep the excitement out of his voice.

Bledsoe frowned, shaking his head. "No, I didn't. He just walked through the lobby and down the hall. I was busy with some paperwork and just glanced up. I believe he had a mustache, though. Why? Was he involved in this?"

"Apparently."

"God! I let a murderer walk right past me."

"No way you could know," Casey said. "Was the man Chinese?"

"No. He was white. I do remember that much. About average height, I think."

"Did you hear any screams or sounds of a struggle?"

"No. I had gone back to the kitchen to get a sandwich since Thompson hadn't shown up to relieve me. I believe one of the maids heard some noise, though. The sheriff is questioning her. Here he comes now. Why don't you ask him yourselves."

The sheriff came up to them. He was tall and lean, and the thinning hair, drooping mustache, and bags under his eyes gave him the look of a Basset hound.

"Did the maid get a look at the man, Sheriff?" McGraw asked.

"No. She was passing the door and heard some noise . . . two voices, some banging around, and glass breaking. Then a short scream that was suddenly cut off. She rapped at the door and asked if Kem Ying was all right. No answer, and the door was locked. By the time she found Bledsoe and he got a master key to open the door, the killer was gone. The window was open, and the room was just as you saw it." He sighed and turned to lean his back and elbows on the high counter top. "No sign of him outside, either. Must've had his horse close by. My deputy is scouring the area where he might've gone on foot, but I'm afraid he's given us the slip for now. Maybe we can pick up his trail in the morning."

Casey briefly filled him in on the uniform and false mustache they had found in the wardrobe, and Bledsoe confirmed he had seen the man earlier.

Sheriff Cutliffe perked up. "As soon as the coroner gets here, I'll get in there and give that room a thorough going over." He shook his head. "None of this makes any sense. What motive could there be? Robbery? I'll have to find out if she was working for someone who took most of her money, or if maybe she had it stashed in that room, or even had an account in some bank. I'm afraid this is going to be a long, drawn-out investigation. Not only that, but I'm sure I'll be hearing from all the proper wives in this county, demanding that I run that other Chinese whore out of town."

He paused, and the ticking of the wall clock behind the desk was loud in the silence. It was eight fifty-three.

"Funny thing," Sheriff Cutliffe continued, "the maid mentioned after the noise stopped, she heard a man's voice, like he was still talking to someone. She could hear it plain through those thin walls and door. . . ."

"What'd she hear?"

The sheriff wore a puzzled expression as if he were trying to get his memory of the words just right, or was trying to make sense of what he was about to say. "She said she heard him say something about a short candle. . . ."

"A short candle?"

"No, that wasn't exactly it. She said . . . she said it sounded like a quote from some old poem. Oh, well, it was probably nothing."

"Think hard," Casey urged. "If it was that unusual, it may give us some clue."

Sheriff Cutliffe frowned in an effort to recall the words. "I'll call the maid. She can probably tell you exactly." Then he snapped his fingers. "It wasn't a short candle. It was a *brief* candle. That was it. Something about putting out a brief candle."

189

"It wasn't . . . 'Out, out brief candle . . .' was it?" McGraw asked.

"That's it! And there was more," the sheriff said.

" 'Life's but a walking shadow. A poor player who . . . ,' " McGraw prompted.

"You've got it. That's the quote." Cutliffe nodded vigorously. "Now, I ask you, are we dealing with a crazy man or not?"

McGraw felt a strange, sinking sensation in the pit of his stomach. He and Casey looked at each other.

"Shakespeare," McGraw said.

"Macbeth," Casey replied. "Who does that sound like?"

"Let's go."

"There's a livery down the street. I'll rent two horses."

"Hey! Where're you two going?" Sheriff Cutliffe yelled after them as McGraw dashed for the stairs to their room, and Casey ran for the front door. "Do you know who this killer is?"

"We'll let you know if we find out anything!" Casey yelled back over his shoulder as the door banged shut behind him.

Chapter Fifteen

"There's one thing we need to do before we take off, hell-bent, for San Francisco," Casey said, riding up and handing McGraw the reins to the other rented horse.

"What's that?" McGraw asked, swinging into the saddle.

"The depot."

McGraw followed as Casey spurred his horse down the block between the hotel and the train station. They jumped down, and Casey threw a quick loop over the hitching rail before bounding inside, McGraw close on his heels.

The stationmaster was still in his office, wearing a green eye shade and bending over a sheaf of papers under the soft light of a coal-oil lamp. He looked up quickly at the sound of pounding feet, echoing through the deserted depot.

"Has there been a train through here since the southbound at seven forty-five?" Casey asked.

"No. Next passenger train is at seven o'clock tomorrow morning."

"No trains since seven forty-five?"

"Just a local freight about a half hour ago."

"Going north or south?"

"North."

"Did it stop?"

"Long enough to take on water."

"How long has it been gone?"

The stationmaster consulted a silver pocket watch. "Hmmm . . . thirty-seven minutes."

"You said it's a local with several stops?"

"Yes," he nodded. "It'll reach San Francisco about seven in the morning."

"One other thing . . . is there a porter working here?"

"Yeah. A local fella name of Lopez. Older man. Just works part time when we need him."

"Does he have a mustache?"

"Why, yes, he does."

"Was he here tonight when the seven forty-five came in?"

The stationmaster thought a moment. "Yes. I remember seeing him. No, wait. He wasn't here when the train arrived. Don't know what happened to him."

"Thanks." Casey turned to McGraw. "Let's go."

They left the mystified stationmaster rubbing his forehead as they headed for their horses.

"How do you know he'll head back for San Francisco?" McGraw shouted as they thundered, side by side, down the dirt street out of town.

"He thinks nobody knows about him, so there's no need to run," Casey yelled back, the wind whipping his words away.

They galloped the horses for nearly a mile before easing back to a canter and then to a walk.

"Better go a little slower or they'll never last," McGraw said as their mounts blew and snorted.

"You're right. There's probably no chance we'll catch him unless he stops somewhere along the way."

"You think he's mounted, or did he hop that northbound freight?"

Casey shook his head. "I don't know. I'm just guessing he was in a hurry to get out of town. But once he's safely away, he thinks nobody suspects him, so he'll go back to his job as if nothing was amiss."

"Then we don't need to hurry."

"On the contrary. If we could catch him on the way back

to the city, whether on horseback or in a freight car, we'd have a little more proof that he was in Salinas tonight."

"What do you plan to do?" McGraw asked, thinking ahead. "Just confront him? We have no real proof that Captain Kingsley was in that room tonight or that he killed Kem Ying."

"I don't know yet. We have all night to think about it, unless we catch up with him. Can't reach the city until sometime well after daylight."

As it turned out, his estimate was several hours off. They had turned their mounts off the road to follow the railroad tracks in a vain hope of overtaking the freight, but by an hour after midnight they were forced to stop and dismount, unsaddle the horses, and hobble them near a stream under a wooden trestle. And it wasn't just the animals that were tired and thirsty. For Casey and McGraw the four hard hours in the saddle had rubbed their barely healed wounds on legs and buttocks raw and bleeding. They eased themselves down in the sparse grass to try to rest.

"Captain Kingsley isn't one of my favorite people, but I can't believe he's a killer," McGraw said, trying to reconcile the circumstantial evidence they had gathered.

"I've seen some unlikely criminals in my time as a policeman," Casey replied. "With criminals at his level, it's usually a step-by-step process. They work up to it. One thing leads to another, and they have to resort to more desperate and violent acts to cover their activities. Kingsley's a frustrated actor. I don't know much about his background, except that he appeared in some plays in the East and South. He drifted out West with a traveling troupe of actors and later got into politics."

"A natural progression," McGraw observed.

"With his flair for the dramatic, making political speeches was easy for him. He didn't come up through the ranks of the police department. He was hired as a captain after serving a term on the board of supervisors and making friends with a lot of influential people in the city. I don't think Chief Crowley was happy about it, but there was nothing he could do. Rumor has it that the chief put Kingsley in charge of this special project to quell the opium trade, knowing that when his effort failed . . . as it very likely would . . . he'd have somebody to blame and then could get rid of him. Looks like Kingsley was making friends with the enemy, so he'd have something to fall back on when he got the axe from the chief. He must have found out Kem Ying was tipping you about the opium shipments and had to get rid of her."

"I wonder if Kingsley knows I was the one who was getting the information?" McGraw asked. "I never gave her my name."

"Don't know. He may have forced your description out of her. Kingsley knows we were at the pier to nab those six slave girls loaded with the stuff. And we're officially off duty, recuperating, so there's really no reason we should have been there."

"One thing that still puzzles me is this porter uniform thing. Why the elaborate disguise? If Kingsley was visiting this girl every week and didn't want to be seen and recognized, why not just show up in a false wig and side whiskers, or something? It would have been fairly simple to come up with an effective disguise each week. Even if he knew he was coming to kill her tonight, why show up at the depot in a uniform where more people could see him? People who were expecting the regular porter?"

"I don't know. Some actors have great self importance. Maybe he wanted to make the whole thing more dramatic and complicated than it had to be. After all, 'the play's the thing' . . . to quote his favorite playwright." He shrugged. "Then again, we're not even sure the porter we got a glimpse of *was* Kingsley. It could have been this Lopez fella."

McGraw lay back on the grass and closed his eyes. He was

very tired, but the sting of his legs and backside prevented him from falling asleep. Yet, in spite of everything, he dozed. When he roused himself and struck a match to check his watch, it was a few minutes past two. The sky was completely dark due to a heavy overcast.

"We'd better get moving," he said, rousing Casey.

They resaddled and mounted up, splashing across the small steam and up the embankment to continue following the tracks. There was no chance of catching up with the freight now.

"What about Kem Ying's friend, Toy Gum? Has anybody questioned her?" McGraw wondered.

"I imagine the sheriff will be able to find her."

They lapsed into silence, each man with his own thoughts. The rest of that long night was a blur in McGraw's mind. It wasn't until a slight gray began to lighten the eastern sky that they forded another small stream and dismounted for a short rest and to let the animals drink. Then they started again, walking stiffly, and leading the tired horses to help dispel the fatigue of both man and beast.

The sun broke the horizon to their right, and its low rays assaulted their gritty eyes before the clouds blocked its piercing light a few minutes later. They trudged onward, heads down, minds numb. Many hours and miles behind them lay their first flash of enthusiasm and excitement. Now they just doggedly plodded ahead, their only immediate thought to reach San Francisco.

And finally they did. Their rented animals were staggering with fatigue when they turned them into the first livery stable they saw, with instructions to give them the best of grain and a rubdown. They caught a horsecar a half mile farther on, that had paused at its turnaround on the end of a run near the edge of the city, and sank gratefully into their seats.

They rode as close to the California Street station as they

could, and then walked the last three blocks. It was just after one in the afternoon when they arrived. They asked the desk sergeant on duty if Captain Kingsley was in and were told he had not been there that day. This was not unusual, since he often spent time in the field, city hall, at one of the other stations, or at court. He followed no fixed schedule and didn't even have to account for his whereabouts, as long as he made his reports to the chief and was responsible for what his men were doing.

How were they to find out if Captain Kingsley had been out of town? How to find out if he had been south to Salinas? Neither of them had officially returned to duty as yet, so McGraw suggested they go to Kingsley's house to see if he was home. Casey was dubious about this move but finally agreed. They first checked city hall, but no one Casey knew there had seen the captain recently.

"You know, now that I think about it, I don't know much about the man's habits. I usually just try to avoid him," Casey commented as they came out into a light drizzle that had begun to fall from the dark, low clouds. He paused on the steps of city hall. "I'm not about to go in and ask Chief Crowley where he is. I'd have to give some reason as to why I wanted to know, and I can't arouse his suspicions until we're sure about Kingsley."

"Maybe you could do it casually," McGraw said.

"I don't get into casual conversations with the chief," Casey returned. "I seldom have any occasion to talk to him at all. And I never see him in a social setting."

"Let's try Kingsley's house, then."

Kingsley lived alone in a well-built wooden house in the Western Addition section of the city. The house was located on one of the several planked streets that still remained in San Francisco. The planked streets, held together by thirty penny spikes, resisted the iron shoes of the heavy dray horses. Houses, sidewalks, and streets were all of the best wood.

"Does he own a horse?" McGraw asked, eyeing the front of the house with its curtained bay windows.

"Yes. Let's take a look around back to see if he keeps it stabled here or at some livery."

They paused to allow a bakery wagon to pass and then crossed the street and went between the houses. A small carriage building was just visible in the rear. No one was in sight on the street in mid-afternoon. All the houses appeared deserted. The windows in the back of Kingsley's house were shuttered.

Casey carefully lifted the latch on the double doors of the carriage house and eased them open. After a quick look around they slipped inside. A small black buggy with the top folded down took up most of the room. In the back was a stall occupied by a beautiful Morgan, but the horse was standing, head down, with its flanks flecked with dried foam. McGraw reached over the wooden barricade and put his hand on the animal's neck. The horse raised his head and snorted, but didn't move away.

"Look at his back," Casey said. "He's had a saddle galling recently."

A red plaid saddle blanket draped over the stall wall was still damp.

"No doubt he's been run hard. Helluva way to treat a horse. Looks like he was turned in here without even being cooled or wiped down."

"At least he's got food and water," Casey said, indicating a bucket of water in the corner and the grain in a wooden trough fastened to the wall.

"Let's try the house."

"Doesn't look like anyone's home," McGraw said as they went out and eased the doors closed. They went around to the front and up onto the small porch. Casey rapped the brass knocker and waited. Silence. He rapped again, louder and longer.

McGraw held his breath. He strained to hear any sounds of movement in the depths of the house. A horsecar clattered down the street behind them.

"There's nobody home," McGraw said, peering into the darkened interior through the large oval glass in the door.

Casey again rapped the brass knocker loud and long.

Silence.

"Let's go. He's not here," McGraw said, turning away. "We're wasting our time."

Just then he heard someone fumbling with the key in the lock, and the door was jerked open.

"Yeah? What is it?" Captain Thomas Kingsley stood there, holding onto the door casing, eyes puffy, collarless white shirt rumpled, as if he had just been awakened.

McGraw glanced at Casey who covered his surprise quickly. "Captain Kingsley, we're both recovered enough to work, and we're reporting back for duty."

Kingsley focused on them with difficulty. "What's that to me?" he demanded irritably. "Get a clearance from Doctor Donnelly and forward it through channels."

McGraw caught a whiff of whiskey. The man was in his cups, and it was only mid-afternoon. They had apparently awakened him from a drunken sleep.

"I understand I was to report to you, personally, sir," Casey continued smoothly.

"Mister, you don't come to my home when I'm off duty," Kingsley said, slightly slurring his words. He made a half-hearted attempt to stuff in his shirttail.

"We would have reported to you yesterday afternoon, but you were in Salinas, and. . . ."

The older man's face went deathly pale, and he staggered

back as if struck. "Where did you hear that?"

"Common knowledge," Casey said, pressing the attack. "You go down there every week to visit your favorite Chinese whore."

"How dare you! What's your name?"

"Lieutenant Fred Casey, sir."

"By God, Casey, I'll have your badge for insubordination!" Kingsley sputtered. But his words lacked conviction. He sounded more defensive than outraged. His pale face was suddenly beading with perspiration, and his rumpled shirt was beginning to cling to him. He was breathing heavily.

The fat was in the fire now. McGraw wondered how far Casey would press this. If they were wrong, Casey had probably gotten them both fired. If they were right . . . well, he braced himself for some violent reaction.

"Actually, Captain, my real reason for coming here was to warn you that the sheriff in Salinas is on his way here with a posse to arrest you for murder."

McGraw cringed inwardly.

Kingsley grew even paler and backed up another step, swinging the door wider. "What kind of crazy talk is this? You're out of your mind. Not only will I get you fired, I'll have you in court for defaming my character." He held onto the door for support, his knuckles growing white with the strain.

"You killed a Chinese prostitute named Kem Ying. Ran her through with a short sword. But I don't need to describe the details. You know all about that, don't you? The law is hot on your trail, Kingsley. I'd arrest you myself, but the crime was committed out of my jurisdiction, as you know. Besides" — and here he hesitated for what McGraw perceived as a fine dramatic effect — "you've been square with me a time or two, so now I'm giving you this tip that they're on to you. If I were you, I'd make the most of it."

Kingsley's eyes bugged, and a look of pure hate leapt from them. He apparently was sobering up quickly. He started to speak, spluttered, stopped, then started again. "Get out!" he managed to choke. His face had gone from clammy pale to beet-red. "Get out of my house! I'll make you pay for this before the day is out. Accuse me with your damned lies, will you?"

"You almost killed your horse getting back here from Salinas," Casey went on coldly. "I'm sure Sheriff Cutliffe will be interested in seeing him when he gets here. But then, he probably won't need to, since he has a witness to the murder." He started to turn away. "By the way, I don't think I would be standing there with my mouth open if I were you."

Kingsley slammed the door with such force that McGraw jumped back, expecting to see the beveled glass shatter. "Damn!" he breathed, glancing at his companion. Casey's eyes were snapping and his unshaven cheeks were flushed.

They went down the steps to the street and quickly walked away from the house, neither of them speaking. McGraw glanced back, but the house looked as deserted as it had before they knocked.

A horsecar approached, heading toward Market Street. They stepped out onto the planked street and boarded it.

"That was one helluva chance you just took," McGraw finally said. "I had my hand on my gun the whole time."

"Did you see his reaction?" Casey countered, eyes still snapping with excitement. "Had to throw some coal-oil down the rat hole to make the rat come out."

"He came out, all right. I think your bluff has been called. And we don't have the cards to back it. Circumstantial evidence is all we have."

"If that maid can identify his voice as the one she heard through the door, we have something."

"Not enough to make a murder charge stick in court."

"That along with the condition of his horse, the fact that he was away from duty for the past two days, and even if we can't find an eyewitness who might have seen him in Salinas, we may be able to find out if he owned or had rented the clothes or sword we found in the room."

McGraw shook his head again. "Not enough. He can always say those things were stolen from him, if he did own them. Even if it can be proven that he was a patron of Kem Ying's, it will only be an embarrassment, not proof that he murdered her."

"Well, the truth is, I just couldn't resist throwing a bomb in there on him just now. It was instinctive . . . a spur-of-the-moment thing."

"You know Sheriff Cutliffe isn't after him. The sheriff doesn't even know he exists."

"I know. But Kingsley doesn't know that yet."

"Do you think he bought that tale about you coming to warn him? He knows you've never had much use for him."

"If he's guilty, he can't afford to ignore my warning. If he's innocent, I'm out of a job and will probably have to leave San Francisco to avoid reprisals." He looked over at McGraw and grinned. "But I'm betting everything he's guilty as sin. And if he's guilty, he'll run. And if he runs, we'll be waiting."

"Which means we have to watch his house every minute from now on to keep him from slipping away."

"Exactly."

McGraw got up, and Casey followed. They hopped off the slow-moving car and started walking the nearly two blocks back to Kingsley's house.

"Keeping watch on his place won't be easy," McGraw said. "We're both so exhausted from lack of sleep and food, I don't know how we'll stay awake if this lasts very long."

"We'll just have to be tough. We can't take time out for either one right now."

"This is close enough. He may be looking out a window. We made sure he saw us go. We don't want him to see us coming back."

At a motion from Casey they detoured off the street between two houses and cut through to the next block. A dog barked at them from behind a tall board fence. They came along the parallel street, making sure to keep buildings between themselves and any possible sightings from Kingsley's windows until they were just below his carriage house. Then they carefully maneuvered up behind the outbuilding and waited.

The chill drizzle had started again, slightly heavier, and they huddled close to the wall of the carriage house, partially protected by the overhanging eaves. They didn't have long to wait. About ten minutes after they had settled in, McGraw heard the door slam. They peered around the edge of the building and saw the figure of Thomas Kingsley, muffled in a top coat and hat, emerge from somewhere in front of his house and start walking up the street. Casey and McGraw followed at a discreet distance for about three blocks, the two detectives, trailing from the parallel street, catching glimpses of their quarry now and then between buildings and shrubbery.

Then suddenly the police captain was gone. He had disappeared behind a house but never emerged on the other side.

"Where'd he go?"

"There! He must have caught that cable car going down the hill."

"Run! We can keep it in sight. That cable runs at a constant speed of seven or eight miles an hour. And it'll be stopping now and then."

They started off at a fast jog, their shoes smacking steadily on the wet paving stones.

"Can you see him?" Casey panted.

"He's aboard. Only one passenger. I recognize the hat."

McGraw cut between two houses, leapt a flower bed, and ducked the wet leaves of a low-hanging tree limb. Staying well away from the street, they were able to get ahead of the cable car. They reached Market Street, out of breath, but in time to see the cable car roll onto its turntable about a block away.

The dark-coated figure got off, looked around, and started off at a brisk pace away from them toward the Bay. McGraw and Casey saw him looking around, presumably for a cable car going in his direction as he strode purposefully down Market. His walk showed no sign that he had probably been drunk only a short time before. He spotted a cable car and nimbly dodged a passing wagon to reach and board it.

"Come on. We can't lose him now."

There were no hacks handy.

"Can we run it down?" McGraw asked.

"Here comes another car. Let's grab it."

They had to run back to the last corner to get the next cable car, and by the time the gripman had them rolling again, Kingsley was more than two blocks ahead. They stood on the back platform and peered around the side of the car, frustrated at their slow pace.

"Don't worry," Casey said. "He can't go any faster than we can."

"But we're stopping more often."

Finally they saw Kingsley hop off his car at a corner and start up Kearney Street.

"He's headed for Chinatown," McGraw said.

"You know, it could be he's just going to work at the California Street station," Casey remarked dubiously.

"At this time of day? And half drunk? Not likely."

Casey nodded. "Maybe going into hiding with his cronies in Chinatown. We'd better hurry to keep him in sight."

They leapt off a half block before their car reached Kearney

Street and sprinted ahead, dodging bowler-hatted businessmen and a few shoppers. By the time they reached the corner, Kingsley was over a block away, walking quickly, hunched down in his coat collar against the rain. There were an adequate number of pedestrians for McGraw and Casey to blend in at a fast walk without being noticed.

Kingsley turned once and looked back. McGraw quickly ducked his head, fearing he had been seen, but apparently the fading afternoon light and the fact that Casey was walking behind him, prevented the captain from recognizing them.

When McGraw looked up again, Kingsley was gone. McGraw experienced a moment of sudden panic. He riveted his eyes on the spot where he had last seen the dark-coated figure.

"I saw where he ducked off the street," Casey said, as the two of them broke into a quick trot. McGraw kept a hand on the holster that was flapping at his hip.

"Here. Slow down," Casey said, holding up his hand. They cautiously approached a Chinese eating establishment and casually glanced in the cluttered windows.

"No sign of him," McGraw panted softly.

"Let's go in."

They sidled in, hats pulled low and dripping with rain. The restaurant had only two patrons at this early supper hour. Kingsley was not there.

"You sure he came in here?" McGraw asked under his breath.

Casey nodded. "Check the kitchen."

An Oriental waiter watched stoically as they pushed past him and through the swinging doors. Odors of frying meat and spices assaulted their noses as two white-aproned Chinese cooks looked up.

"Out the back."

Casey signaled for caution as he eased open the door to the alleyway. Kingsley was disappearing at a fast walk around the corner at the end of the block. They slipped into the alley, filled with vendors' stands, small shops, and overhanging balconies. By the time they reached and turned the corner, Kingsley was turning into another eating house.

When they got closer, a chill went up McGraw's back under his damp coat, and he put a hand on Casey's arm. "This is the place where I was grilled in the basement," he said, eyeing the side entrance to the alley. Something that felt like a giant, unseen hand was holding him back from approaching the building. He fought down the feeling, put his hand on the butt of his Colt, and walked up to the front door. Two Chinamen came out the door, and McGraw caught a glimpse of Kingsley, hat and coat removed, sitting at a table, talking to a waiter.

"Doesn't look like he's running scared," McGraw said, stepping back around the corner into the alley.

"He took a few precautionary detours to hide his trail," Casey said. "But I don't think he knows we're here. He's just settled in to eat supper."

"I could eat a horse myself," McGraw groaned.

"I'll keep an eye on Kingsley," Casey said. "Here're two dollars. Run down there and get us a couple of whatever that vendor's cooking."

McGraw grimaced.

"I know. But I'm hungry enough to eat almost anything."

"Anything is what we'll get. Probably grilled rat."

"I don't *want* to know what it is. Just get something to fill my stomach."

McGraw walked back down the alley to a street vendor, pointed at what was being grilled over the smoking brazier, and held up two fingers. The food was some sort of meat rolled and cooked in dough. The chunky Oriental wrapped the two bullet-shaped objects in some old newspaper and took McGraw's two greenbacks without offering any change. He smiled and nodded, pretending not to speak English. McGraw didn't care. He took one of the greasy objects to Casey, and the two of them tore into the food like starving wolves.

When they finished, Casey crossed the street to take up an unobtrusive post, while McGraw stayed in the alley at the side of the restaurant in case Kingsley exited from a side door. As McGraw squatted against a brick wall, his hat brim pulled down and dripping rain, his eyes strayed to the ground-level window through which he and Casey had escaped in a hail of lead. No one had repaired the splintered wooden sash, and shards of jagged glass still framed the opening where the pane had been. Any blood stains on the ground had apparently been washed away by the rain.

Forty minutes dragged by. McGraw stood up, stretched, and groaned. He was in need of a good night's sleep, but there would very likely be no sleep for either of them again tonight, depending on what their quarry did. Then Casey was coming toward him from across the street.

"He's finished eating and gone somewhere else inside the building," Casey said tersely.

"Shall we go in?"

"No. We can't take the chance of him seeing us."

"We don't dare lose him, either."

"Are there any other doors besides these on the alley?"

McGraw shook his head. "There may be doors into the adjacent brick building. I think it's a warehouse."

"These buildings aren't usually built with connecting doors."

"You forget we're in Chinatown. They do as they please here regardless of any fire codes or safety laws. If they want a door, they cut a door."

"I don't think so. I know he disappeared into the back part of the building. He may have gone down into the cellar. Take a look through that broken window."

"Glad they haven't fixed it," McGraw grunted, squatting near their former escape route, and cautiously peering in. He jerked his head away, flattening himself against the wall.

"He's in there, all right. Smoking a cigar and talking to our old friend, Ho Ming."

"Ah . . . well, we know now that, even if it turns out he's not a murderer, he's still up to his eyebrows in this opium-smuggling business," Casey said.

They settled in to wait, Casey retreating to watch the front of the restaurant as before. McGraw walked part way down the alley and pretended to examine some jade ornaments in a wooden stall with a striped canvas awning. No one came out the side door. The alley grew less crowded with pedestrians as the supper hour wore on.

McGraw, by this time lounging back against a wall, slipped his watch out of an inside pocket and glanced at it. Seven twenty-two. The low-hanging clouds had brought on an early dusk. With the vanishing light his fear of being seen and recognized began to fade, and he sauntered back toward the broken window at the base of the wall. As he grew near, his nose identified the faint odors of cooking food and cigar smoke emanating from the jagged hole.

About ten minutes later Casey came striding across the street. "Come on. The pair of them just came out the front of the warehouse next door. There's a carriage waiting."

They emerged onto the street in time to see the door of the enclosed carriage slam. The team stepped off as the driver snapped the reins.

"We've got to find a hack . . . quick!" Casey said.

Only there was none in sight. They watched helplessly as the carriage wheeled around a corner and started north down toward the waterfront.

"Here we go again," McGraw said as they sprinted through the alley in an attempt to head it off.

"Glad it's mostly downhill," Casey panted after they had covered a block and were cutting to their left in an attempt to keep the carriage in sight.

It was then they saw a hack, hailed it, and jumped in.

"Just keep that black carriage in sight, without getting too close," Casey instructed the driver.

The slouch-hatted man nodded and clucked to his horse.

Casey and McGraw sat, facing each other inside the coach, panting and dripping. Casey pulled out a handkerchief and wiped the rain and sweat from his face. "I thought I was in pretty good physical condition, but running up and down these hills has shown me I'm not," he puffed.

"You forget, you've been up most of the night, riding nearly a hundred miles, and have had very little food."

"So have you."

"Who said I wasn't just as tired as you are?"

Less than a quarter hour later their hack rolled to a stop. McGraw stuck his head out of the side window.

"The carriage has stopped a little way ahead, sir," the driver remarked. "Two men just got out. Now the carriage is moving on. Shall I follow?"

"No. This will do," McGraw said.

They got out. Casey handed the driver the fare who tucked the coins into a vest pocket under his slicker and pulled his horse's head around, talking softly to the animal. McGraw and Casey used the vehicle for a shield as they ducked between two buildings. It was nearly dark now. They were somewhere near the waterfront, and a stiff wind was blowing in from the Bay. It had stopped raining.

A few lights were scattered here and there, from office windows, and farther down along the piers some storm-proof lanterns defied the wind, while partially lighting the stringers and wharves that led out to the moored vessels. But mostly, the warehouses and the ships were only bulky blocks of blackness.

Wordlessly they walked quickly down the street after Ho Ming and Captain Kingsley who had just passed beneath one of the last gas street lights. McGraw's fatigue was diminishing now, and he was beginning to feel the excitement of the chase. It was the thrill of unknown dangers that he was responding to. If he were still working at his Wells Fargo railroad messenger job, he would either be eating supper in his locked car as it rocked along the rails, or he would be back in the boarding house, wondering how he was going to spend the rest of his evening. *Did Katie O'Neal think he was still in Salinas on business?*

"Not so fast. We don't want to overtake them," Casey's quiet voice interrupted his musing. "They're going out onto that pier."

Casey and McGraw went cautiously forward, watching intently as the two murky figures climbed over the rail of a boat and dropped down nearly out of sight.

"That looks like one of those Italian fishing luggers," McGraw said. "What are they doing?"

"Getting ready to cast off," Casey said, the breeze bringing them the sound of squeaking blocks as the lateen sail was being hoisted.

"Feel like going for a sail?" Casey asked.

"If we want to keep 'em in sight, I guess we'll have to. But where do we get a boat without stealing one?"

"My men are still doing night patrol down here. They usually go out between eight and nine. If we hurry, we can use their police boat."

Without fear of being heard or seen in the windy darkness, they sprinted away toward Pier Seven where Casey indicated the various police boats were kept docked. Bernard Kohl and Jeff Brady, dressed in their dark blue uniforms, were lounging on the edge of the pier, smoking, when Casey and McGraw dashed up. They jumped to attention, startled.

"Lieutenant Casey, what are you doing here?"

"We thought you were off on disability leave."

"I'm back. Is this boat ready to sail?"

"Sure. We were just about ready to take off."

"Are both of you armed?"

They nodded in unison, their unspoken curiosity showing.

"There's a fishing lugger coming out of Pier Six with two or more men aboard. We have to keep them in sight."

McGraw and Casey leapt into the boat, while Kohl cast off the stern line and jumped in after them. The rudder was already shipped, and with McGraw's help Brady got the halyards loose and began hauling up the mainsail. The onshore breeze caught the partially raised sail and swung the boat against the pier. With a few more strong pulls Brady had the peak of the sail at the top of the mast and, with a quick clove hitch on a cleat at the base of the mast, tied off the halyard. The boom swung low over their heads.

"All set?" Brady asked.

"Let 'er go," Casey directed.

Brady cast off the bow line, gave the boat a shove, and scrambled in as the bow swung clear of the pier and the mainsail filled on the port tack. McGraw could see that the pair had a well-rehearsed drill.

"Which way?" Kohl asked from the tiller as they slid quickly away from the pier, leaving the dim lantern light behind them.

"Get beyond the end of the pier, and see if you can pick up a lateen rig," Casey instructed. "Boat's painted green with white trim. Also has a white sail. We should be able to pick it up off to starboard about a quarter mile."

The special opium patrol had started the summer with three fourteen-foot rowboats. These were adequate for poking around the waterfront and the many moored ships, but it was quickly discovered that something more seaworthy would be needed if they were to venture out into the Bay. So, in addition to the longboat they had captured the night McGraw had been knifed in the arm, Casey had petitioned Chief Crowley for two more boats that could be rowed or sailed easily by two men but were beamy enough and had enough freeboard to safely take on the choppy waters of the windy Bay. Surprisingly the money for these was forthcoming, and they had been quickly purchased.

McGraw breathed a prayer of thanks that they were in one of these boats now, a nineteen-footer, with a partially covered foredeck to prevent taking on water in rough seas. He crouched down on a thwart on the windward side. Three ships were docked, bow to stern, blocking the wind, causing it to swirl. Their mainsail backed and filled, swinging the boom from side to side. Brady took advantage of the time to spring up onto the foredeck and attach the jib. In less than a minute it was hoisted.

"Damn! I hope they're not out of sight yet," Casey fidgeted as the boat slowed. Kohl was doing his best to capture the fluky wind.

"They may be having the same trouble," McGraw said, as Brady crawled back in the boat and began taking up slack on the jib sheet.

After what seemed like an eternity, they cleared the end of the long piers and caught the full force of the unobstructed sea breeze from the port side. The boom slammed over against its restraining tackle, and the boat leapt up and forward like a thing alive. They heeled sharply to starboard, and white water came foaming along the sides.

After about a minute Casey said: "There she is."

McGraw strained his eyes, following the pointing finger. He could dimly make out a triangle of white on the leeward side, several hundred yards off.

"Don't lose them, Kohl," Casey urged. "This may be the break we've been hoping for."

Chapter Sixteen

McGraw watched the distant sail for two or three minutes. It didn't seem to be changing size. Apparently the other boat was parallel with them.

"Just hold your present course, and keep her in sight," Casey instructed the helmsman. "Those fishing boats aren't built for speed."

They were taking the wind and waves abeam, and the boat rode with a surging, rolling motion. McGraw was subject to seasickness but had never felt queasy in a small boat where the motion was usually quicker and more abrupt — and there was plenty of fresh air. In fact, though he had spent most of his life in the interior part of the country, he had become an accomplished small-boat sailor since moving to the Bay area several years before. For some unexplained reason he loved the sea and spent much of his free time strolling the waterfront, looking at the tall, raking masts of the ships that filled this major seaport. He and Katie O'Neal had spent several afternoons and evenings strolling the outer shore, the wind raking through their hair, and the cold surf creaming around their bare feet and legs. *Where is Katie now?* he wondered, as a vision of her lovely face surged into his mind's eye. *What would she say if she were in the boat with them this minute?* He smiled at the thought. She would probably be giving him hell for risking his life out here at night, sailing without running lights, as police boats were allowed to do if they felt it necessary. She would definitely not feel the thrill of the chase, as McGraw did. Hers would be the instinct for survival and safety — an instinct, McGraw had to admit, that was much more attuned to common sense.

The boat dropped into a trough, the bow pounded into a wave, and a heavy spray of icy water exploded over the port side. The pleasant vision of Katie O'Neal vanished as McGraw gasped and gripped the gunwale.

"Nothing like a good dousing to keep a man alert on his night job," Brady yelled, laughing. He reached under the foredeck and pulled out something, handing it to McGraw. "Here's an extra slicker."

McGraw wrapped it around himself like a cape, buttoning it only at the throat. Brady offered another one to Casey who declined.

McGraw wiped the salty water from his face and looked out to leeward. The other sail was gone! He quickly scanned the darkness for some sign of the dim white triangle, but Casey's calm voice came from the other side of the boat. "She's over on the starboard tack and coming this way. She'll pass behind us. Just stay on your present course for now. Then we'll tack over and run parallel with her again," he said to Kohl.

"Looks like she's beating out toward the Golden Gate," Kohl said.

"At this point it's hard to tell," Casey replied. "Just don't let her get too far away. We may have to close in a hurry."

They sailed in silence on a broad reach for another fifteen or twenty minutes, as McGraw watched the lateen sail gradually come into better view as the other boat angled away to cross their stern more than a half mile away. Since they were running with no lights, Brady was half lying across the foredeck next to the base of the mast, keeping watch for any sight or sound of other boats or ships. The boat they were chasing was also sailing without visible lights.

"Ready about!" came Casey's quiet, but intense, voice.

"Ready about," repeated Kohl.

Brady slid back down into the boat. "Come about."

Kohl thrust the tiller away from him, and the bow swung immediately up into the wind, the boat slowing, and the sails flapping. They ducked as the wooden boom swung across the boat, and the big mainsail filled with a snap. All but Brady shifted to the upwind side of the boat for balance as they tore away on the starboard tack.

For the next hour the two boats matched tack for tack as they zigzagged toward the Golden Gate. Kohl spilled wind from his mainsail to slow the boat and allow the lugger slowly to come abreast and pass hundreds of yards distant. Kohl had to alter course twice as outward-bound steam tugs passed, towing square-riggers. They gave the big ships plenty of room as the running lights on the huge vessels passed them.

"Tide's setting toward the Gate," Kohl remarked, "but the wind's blowing in, kicking up a helluva chop."

His observation was unnecessary, as far as McGraw was concerned. He gripped the gunwale as the boat slammed up and down, punching its way through and over the waves. McGraw was almost glad he couldn't see the marching succession of whitecaps, rolling toward them. He could only dimly make out the feather-edged combers as they surged under the boat, lifting and dropping it. Now and then a harder gust of wind heeled the craft over, and Kohl automatically corrected for the sudden push. Kohl had been on harbor patrol for several weeks now, and seemed to have a natural feel for night sailing.

"Where do you think they're headed?" McGraw asked, watching the distant sail as it seemed stationary in relation to their own movement.

"Don't know," Casey replied. "Ho Ming may be taking Kingsley to some safe haven. I can't imagine that both of them are making a break for it. Ho Ming especially. He wouldn't give up his profitable kingdom in Chinatown. Even though he's wanted for attempted murder . . . ours . . . none of our Chinatown squad has been able to find him to arrest him."

Kohl and Brady, since Casey and McGraw had suddenly appeared on the dock, had asked no questions. They had only obeyed orders. Casey now took the opportunity to brief them on what had taken place, beginning with the murdered Chinese prostitute in Salinas.

"Kingsley! That's hard to believe," Brady said, when Casey had brought them up to date.

"We have no hard evidence, mind you," Casey said. "That's why I took a big chance at trying to bluff him. But it's beginning to look more and more like he's mixed up in all this."

"I'm going to have to tack to get past Alcatraz," Kohl said after a time. The lights on the island were looming up, dead ahead.

They came about onto the starboard tack and were heading toward the city at an oblique angle. At nearly the same time the sail ahead tacked, angling for the Golden Gate. Just then a sudden brightness caused McGraw to look up. The onshore wind was shredding the rain clouds, and a half moon popped out to shed its light on them. It was a wild scene that was revealed. The surface of the black water stood up in white ridges. The hump-backed hills were only dim black shapes as they curved in toward the mouth of the bay, with now and then a shore light, winking in the distance. Off their port side, lights of the city swept up in grandeur from the harbor like hundreds of sparkling diamonds on black velvet. Besides the boat they were pursuing, McGraw could make out the red and green running lights and the sails of a half dozen vessels in the middle and far distance. No more than three hundred yards off he saw the bulk of a ferry boat heading for them, the lighted windows clearly visible on the upper deck. They were in the lanes of one of the steam ferries, plying between Marin County and the city.

Kohl corrected his course to pass well clear of the ferry. The lateen sail of the lugger was much clearer now.

"If we can see them, surely they can see us," Brady said.

"Let's hope they're not looking to be pursued," Casey replied. "For all they know, we're just part of the normal boat traffic out here."

"She's going to have to tack again to get out to sea," McGraw said, noting that the lugger was holding a steady course that would take it past the opening of the Golden Gate.

"They may be relying on the current to carry them out," Kohl said. "It really sucks out through that hole at ebb tide."

The sea wind came whistling in, unimpeded, through the break in the hills that was the Golden Gate. It pressed the boat down to starboard, its sails as rigid as carved ivory. The sails turned wind force into forward motion, and the vessel leapt and plunged across the waves, drenching them with icy spray. Kohl eased the boat's motion somewhat by slacking the mainsheet.

"They're not going outside," McGraw said finally. Nobody replied as they all stared hard through the flying spray into the darkness ahead, trying to focus on the small blob that was the lugger's sail.

The ragged clouds again obscured the moon as they lost sight of the distant boat for several long minutes.

"Where'd they go?" Brady asked, bracing himself against the rolling and straining to see across the dark expanse of wild water.

"Port your helm! Hard to port!" Brady yelled over his shoulder.

Kohl shoved the tiller away, and the bow came up several degrees into the wind, the sudden thunder of the flapping sails drowning out all other sounds. Brady pointed at a huge, dim outline of a sidewheel steamer crossing their bow about fifty yards away.

"That was too close," Kohl yelled as he swung the boat back on course, and the sails filled with a snap.

"Keep a sharp lookout for other vessels," Casey ordered Brady. "We'll watch the lugger."

"She's running in toward Sausilito," McGraw said, picking up the dim triangle of sail once more.

The stiff wind finally swept the night sky clear of rain clouds, and the lugger seemed much closer in the moonlight.

"Do you have a pair of field glasses in here?" Casey asked.

Brady reached under a thwart, pulled out a leather case, and handed it over.

Casey slipped out the glasses, braced himself, and focused. After a few seconds he lowered them. "Can't get a bead on them. We're bouncing too much. Looks like she's coming up pretty close to the shoreline."

After several minutes it became obvious they were overtaking the lugger.

"Do you want to close with them, sir?" Kohl asked.

"No. Pinch up closer to the wind if you can. When we get above them, we can come downwind in a hurry if we have to."

"They're dropping the sail," McGraw said.

"Looks like they've come alongside a wharf or a larger vessel with no lights," Brady added, trying vainly to steady the field glasses Casey had handed back.

They bore up to windward and narrowed the gap with the lugger. They could now see the boat had come alongside an anchored schooner. As they came up under the lee of the land, the whitecaps disappeared, and the water smoothed out some, even though they were still sailing at a good clip. Nearing the shore they could see a few lighted gas lamps.

"There's the Sausilito waterfront," McGraw said. "That

two-story frame building you can make out there . . . that's the Arborvilla Restaurant on Water Street."

"Drop the sails," Casey said quietly as the wind became fluky, and they lost headway.

They furled the main around the unshipped boom and stored it. Then they broke out two sets of oars, fitted them to the oarlocks, and McGraw and Casey manned them as they pulled the boat down toward the schooner, some two hundred yards away.

"Wish the clouds were back over that moon," Casey muttered as they pulled carefully, trying to muffle the noise. "Any look-outs aboard?"

"Don't see anybody on deck," Brady replied, focusing the binoculars.

"Are we going aboard?" McGraw asked.

Casey rested on his oars but didn't reply immediately.

"That may be the black-hulled ghost schooner," McGraw added.

"Yeah. Very likely Captain Moreland's ship," Casey agreed. "We'll just stand off to leeward and watch for a time."

"How long?"

"Maybe the rest of the night. We might even go ashore over there and keep our vigil. I just don't want to do anything prematurely and take a chance on losing it all now. We still have no hard evidence against Kingsley. If we go aboard and arrest him, he could always swear he was acting undercover to gain the smugglers' confidence."

They gave several strong pulls in unison and then let the boat slide to within about thirty yards of the schooner's stern. They gradually drifted to a stop as the ebb tide began to pull on them. A stroke or two was sufficient to hold them in place.

"If somebody comes on deck, we're sitting ducks," McGraw said in an undertone. "Those gas lights ashore are throwing just enough light to make us show up easily."

"You're right. Let's bring 'er higher up under the port quarter, opposite where the lugger's tied alongside," Casey answered.

They maneuvered in quietly, shipping the oars and fending off with their hands to keep the boat from bumping the schooner's black hull.

After a few minutes of silence, broken only by the lapping of water against the hulls, McGraw leaned forward and whispered in Casey's ear, "I'm going aboard to see if I can find out anything."

Casey shook his head vigorously.

"We may not have to sit here all night if I can find out what's going on," McGraw whispered urgently. "I'll take responsibility. If you hear anything breaking loose, come running."

Before Casey could protest, McGraw was on his feet and gripping the rail that was about two feet over his head. His wet, flexible shoe soles made almost no sound as he braced his feet against the ship's side and walked himself up until he could get a leg over the rail. He rolled over the wooden bulwark and dropped silently to a crouch in the deep shadow. He paused, his heart pounding, and listened intently. He heard only the sounds of the sea breeze in the wire rigging of the two-master and a creaking somewhere as the hull flexed slightly with the motion of the sea. The unattended wheel rolled its spokes back and forth as the water worked against the rudder. A sliver of light shone from a hatch slide that had been left partially open for ventilation.

McGraw cat-footed forward and crouched at the hatchway near the break of the poop. Muffled voices came up through the crack from the after cabin. He slipped his Colt from its holster. The walnut grip was slick and cold with sea water. He wiped the gun under his arm — one of the few dry spots left on him. He inched closer to try to see or hear what was taking place below.

He caught a movement out of the corner of his eye and whirled to face the danger, a chill going up his spine. But it was only Casey. Relief flooded over McGraw as his heart began to slow from his sudden fright.

Together they carefully eased the hatch slide farther open. ". . . bloody well put us on the spot coming out here," a voice with a British accent was saying. Apparently Moreland. McGraw could not see him as he edged one eye around the small opening, but he could see Ho Ming, sitting at a table facing his direction, and the hatless, black-coated Captain Kingsley with his chair slid back slightly, a drink in his hand, his wet, thinning hair plastered down across his forehead and shining in the light of the overhead gimbaled lamp. McGraw caught a glimpse of a man's feet and legs as he paced back and forth in the tiny cabin.

"I'll be the judge of that," Kingsley shot back waspishly. "You forget, I'm giving the orders here."

There was a pause in the conversation, and McGraw pulled his eyes back from the opening.

"So you are, so you are," Moreland continued in a more conciliatory tone. "So, what are your plans? Am I to still make the drop as soon as we get a good fog in here? As you well know, it was set for tonight, but the weather did not co-operate. We have moonlight out there now so bright the harbor patrol could pick out a punt at ten leagues."

"We need this shipment, so make the drop as soon as you can."

"I'll alert my men to be ready the first foggy night," came Ho Ming's voice.

"What about my pay?" Moreland asked.

"You've got part of it in advance," Kingsley replied. "The

rest will be paid to you on delivery, as usual."

"I want the rest in gold, not greenbacks. Gold spends better in other ports. And this is my last trip here for a good while."

"Why? Something wrong with our arrangements or our money?" Kingsley asked, a note of irritation in his voice. He also sounded as if his teeth were chattering. McGraw put his eyes to the crack again and noted that the police captain's face was white and his lips were almost a bluish tint in the lamplight. The drenching he had received, crossing the Bay, his heavy drinking earlier in the day, and his nervous flight were all beginning to take their toll.

"Give me another rum toddy," Kingsley said. "Damn! Can't you stoke up that stove? It's freezing in here."

Moreland poured him another drink without comment. "As I said, this is my last drop for some time to come," the British captain continued. "Things are getting a wee bit too hot for comfort." He gave a short laugh. "I haven't lasted this long as a blockade runner and as a purveyor of fine, illegal goods by taking foolish risks."

McGraw pulled his face back from the crack as Moreland came to the table and set the refilled tin cup down in front of Kingsley.

"And your coming out here tonight is putting me and my men even more at risk."

"I had to get out of the city," Kingsley said. There was a pause. "Damn the luck!" he exploded. "I didn't think there was a chance in hell that I'd be connected with that whore's death. Now I either have to go to jail and stand trial, and hope they don't have enough proof, or I've got to go on the run and become a fugitive. Either way, I'm finished as a police captain in San Francisco."

"Sorry, old boy, but how does that concern me? I'll just deal with Ho Ming next time I visit your lovely city."

"I'm not going back," Kingsley said suddenly. "Take me wherever you're bound next . . . Victoria, the Sandwich Islands, South America . . . anywhere. I can't take a chance on going to prison, or being hanged."

Casey had one eye pressed to the crack now, watching the drama unfold below.

"I don't know much about your politics here, but I seriously doubt that a well-respected police captain will be convicted of killing a Chinese prostitute," Moreland said.

"Are you saying my people are not as good as white men?" Ho Ming's voice asked in a deadly monotone.

"Not in the least," Moreland returned lightly. "Just making an observation about the realities of what takes place here. As you know, the Chinese are not well loved by the authorities."

Ho Ming grunted but said nothing further.

"Well, gentlemen, if I'm not making the drop tonight, I've got to take my ship back outside before the tide turns. It wouldn't do to stay anchored here all day tomorrow, now, would it?"

McGraw felt, rather than heard, the footfall on the deck just before something struck him. It whistled past his ear and hit the top of the right shoulder, numbing his arm. His Colt clattered to the deck. At the same time someone slammed into Casey, and they went crashing through the thin wood of the hatch slide and fell in a tangle onto the companionway steps. There was the muffled explosion of a gunshot.

McGraw jumped to one side and aimed a kick at the figure of his attacker, feeling the sickening pain in his useless right shoulder and arm. His toe connected, and the man cursed as he leapt for McGraw, pinning his arms in a bear-like hug. McGraw staggered, and they both fell heavily. He was vaguely aware of shouts and feet pounding on the wooden deck.

"Art's been shot!" a voice yelled. "Kill the bloody bastards!"

"You'll kill nobody unless I give the order!" Moreland yelled. "Bring me a lantern!"

"We got 'em, Cap'n!"

The sailor, pinning McGraw to the deck, must have outweighed him by a good eighty pounds. McGraw felt as if a boulder had fallen on him. The pain in his right arm was agonizing, as if he had just tackled a ball carrier in a football match and injured a nerve. He was aware of the man's bad breath in his face, and then they were surrounded by several more men. He saw the flash of a storm lantern and was jerked roughly to his feet.

McGraw had a sinking feeling in the pit of his stomach. They should have known to check for a sailor on anchor watch, even though Brady had seen no one through the field glasses.

"Bring them below. The rest of you men check to see where their boat is. See if these are the only two."

The sailors, who had apparently been roused from the forecastle, ran for the rails, and McGraw expected to hear shots as Kohl and Brady were discovered. Lantern light flashed in his eyes, half blinding him as he was shoved toward the companionway that was still littered with splintered wood. Casey was already below, but the steps were splashed with bright red blood. McGraw's heart sank until he realized that the limp form being dragged back up on deck was the one bleeding.

"Take him forward and see what you can do for that wound," Moreland snapped.

"Ain't no use, Cap'n," a man said, pressing a hand to the wounded man's throat. "Art's done for. I say we shoot the bastards now!"

"Shut up and get forward!" Moreland ordered. "And take that body with you."

Then McGraw heard no more as he was pushed down the steps into the cabin. Ho Ming and Kingsley were on their feet, staring at them, Ho Ming inscrutable as usual, and Kingsley's face betraying his bewilderment.

McGraw and Casey were made to sit on the cabin floor, their backs to the after bulkhead. Casey's left eye was puffy and swollen and was rapidly darkening as the bruise swelled.

Captain Moreland came down the steps, holding McGraw's .45 with practiced ease. It was the first time McGraw had seen him clearly in the light. He was a shade over six feet tall with black hair and a raffish mustache, both slightly tinged with gray. He was a lean and handsome man, probably in his late forties, with hazel eyes and a authoritative demeanor.

They were trapped. From the look on Moreland's face it was not going to go well with them. Casey had just killed one of his men. Unless Kohl and Brady somehow came to the rescue, he and Casey had seen their last sunrise.

Chapter Seventeen

Before anyone could speak, a blond, red-faced sailor ducked halfway down the cabin steps. "No sign of an extra boat, sir."

"Well, they didn't swim out here, so someone's dropped them off and gone. But never mind that now. Pass the word to Mister Hanson that we're getting underway."

"Yes, sir."

"Well, jump to it, man! We have to be out to sea before the tide turns. We haven't much time."

The sailor disappeared, and the sound of his running footsteps receded.

McGraw felt nauseous. Kohl and Brady had deserted them. They were armed. Why didn't they come aboard and take the ship? But this was a smugglers' ship, not a commercial or Navy vessel. All the men aboard were probably armed as well. They couldn't afford not to be. McGraw had seen at least six men. There may have been more. Yet . . . ? He glanced over at Casey, who gave him a slight smile and winked with his good eye. McGraw couldn't imagine what there was to be cocky about. Maybe Casey had been hit too hard. They were in the hands of these killers again, and he had an instinctive feeling deep inside him that there would be no escaping this time.

"You two are like a pair of ticks," Ho Ming said in his slightly stilted accent. "We cannot kill you, and we cannot get rid of you."

"Are these the two men who warned you about the sheriff from Salinas?" Moreland asked the San Francisco police captain.

"Yes," Kingsley nodded, still staring numbly at them, as if he couldn't comprehend their presence here.

They were apparently in Moreland's cabin, but it was as sparse and devoid of decoration as the lean Englishman before them. With one exception. Affixed to the bulkhead over his hammock on one side of the room was a large display case with glass doors. Inside were samples of various edged weapons — daggers with jeweled hilts, a dirk, a cutlass, a horn-handled Bowie knife, a rapier, a short, double-edged thrusting sword, such as McGraw had seen drawings of Roman soldiers carrying during the time of Christ. There was even a cane sword of the type that had been fashionable at one time among gentlemen in England and the Old South before the war. There were cavalry sabers, a curved scimitar, and several more ancient pieces McGraw could not identify.

"Please, gentlemen, resume your seats," Moreland said, motioning to Ho Ming and Kingsley, who retrieved their overturned chairs and sat down, well back from the table and facing the two prisoners. Kingsley shakily poured himself another cup of rum before he sat down. Some of the color was beginning to return to his face.

"I see you've noticed my collection," Moreland said, still standing and holding the Colt with careless ease. "Quite admirable, is it not? I spent many years and many pounds, acquiring that collection. Of course, several pieces are what you might call spoils of war. There are some rather rare and valuable weapons in that display case."

McGraw took another look. The hasp had been broken that held the small padlock. Two small, empty hooks and the faint outline of a weapon showed that one of his pieces was missing. And with a sudden twinge of nausea McGraw realized which one it was. As depressed as he felt, he couldn't help what he said next to their handsome English captor. "I believe I know where your missing Danish war axe is."

Moreland's expression clouded, and his bronzed face suffused with anger. He bit off a retort and controlled himself with an obvious effort.

"It's at the station house, stained with the blood of a good friend," McGraw continued, deliberately baiting him, impulsively throwing all caution aside. He knew these men did not intend to let him or Casey leave here alive. "It's stained with the blood of Kevin O'Toole, just as your hands are stained with his blood." McGraw watched intently to see the reaction his words produced.

"I am not a murderer," Moreland said. "That axe was stolen from me. Not that your friend, O'Toole, didn't deserve to die. He was on the verge of wrecking our entire operation, so one of the soldiers of the tong took care of him. Unfortunately they used one of the most valuable weapons in my collection to do it."

"A piece that was stolen from the British Museum," McGraw said.

"You have a very impudent mouth," Moreland said, "and considerably more knowledge than it will be safe to leave you with. I can safely say that I have never been guilty of murdering a man in cold blood, as you Americans say. I have killed only in self-defense, or in time of war. But I wouldn't be at all surprised if your superior officer in the police department didn't arrange a potentially fatal accident for the both of you." He looked pointedly at Captain Kingsley. "I believe he's had more experience at that sort of thing. In fact, it might be the only way he could arrange for his safe passage out of this country."

Kingsley gulped a swallow of his rum and glared at them. Clearly he was no longer giving the orders.

McGraw glanced over at Casey. His eye was nearly swollen shut now, but he still looked confident.

228

"You killed one of my men tonight," Moreland said, walking over to Casey who was sitting on the floor and kicked him viciously in the ribs. Casey doubled over with a gasp. Moreland's face had twisted with sudden hate, but relaxed as quickly into its normal, calm expression. "Well, don't lose any sleep over it, Casey . . . is that your name? Casey? Yes. Anyway, Art wasn't worth the powder it took to blow him to hell. He'll be food for the sharks when we're outward bound. Besides, we have Captain Kingsley here to take his place for now, although I doubt he'll be much of a hand at going aloft." He laughed at his own joke as he glanced at the paunchy, middle-aged police captain.

Kingsley drained his cup and scowled, brushing the thinning hair back from his forehead.

McGraw and Casey were not tied, so McGraw, during his exchange with Moreland, had been unobtrusively moving and flexing his right arm. The feeling and strength had come back quickly, leaving only some soreness on the top of his shoulder.

Captain John Moreland glanced upward at the thumping of feet on the deck overhead. "We'll be underway shortly. Have you formed any plans for your friends, here?" he asked Kingsley.

Even though he was clearly no longer in charge, Kingsley stood up and set his empty cup on the table. He took a deep breath. The rum seemed to have warmed him. His color had returned, and his lips no longer had a bluish cast. "They will join your sailor as food for the sharks. But, since they seem to have an almost supernatural ability to survive, I will make sure they are quite dead before they go over the side."

"Very well, but do it on deck," Moreland said coldly. "I don't want any more blood to clean up down here. I'm going topside to check on things." He tucked McGraw's Colt into his belt. "Ho Ming, your boat is alongside any time you're ready to shove off. Watch for me tomorrow night if the fog is thick."

He quickly went up the companionway, stepping carefully around the splintered wood and the spots of blood.

When McGraw looked back, Kingsley was watching him with a gleam of anticipation in his eyes, as a small, nickel-plated revolver had appeared from under his coat.

"What? You're just going to shoot us with that thing?" McGraw taunted him. He glanced over at Casey, who had been strangely silent through all this. Casey had a hand on his side where he had been kicked in the ribs, but otherwise seemed to be alert. He and Casey were now on their feet.

"What happened to your flair for the dramatic?" McGraw continued. "Don't we at least deserve to be dispatched with something exotic like a Turkish scimitar? Or General Lee's saber? Or a dirk carried by Edwin Booth when he played Hamlet?"

This seemed to give Kingsley an idea, as the police captain's eyes strayed to the display case on the bulkhead. "You think I won't," he snarled. "Moreland doesn't know it, but *I* was the one who took care of O'Toole."

McGraw started, his eyes widening at this short, frustrated actor.

"Yes, *me*," he gloated. "O'Toole, the big, strong athlete. Whacked his head right off and made it look like a tong killing. It had to be done," he continued briskly. "He had found out about Ho Ming and Captain Moreland. But, luckily, he didn't know about me." He smiled. "He came to me directly instead of to his immediate superior, I believe, hoping to curry favor at a higher level. A stroke of luck for me. I assured him he had made the proper decision and pretended to take him to a secret meeting at a deserted warehouse to introduce him to an undercover agent." Kingsley's lips curled in a demonic smile. "And he was rewarded to the fullest. Oh, I know what you thought of me . . . ridiculing me behind my back as a pompous, posturing weakling of a political appointee. But my physical strength and my cunning won out, didn't they? And the head of that fool, O'Toole, is at the bottom of the Bay."

McGraw fought to control the red veil of rage that was falling across his sight.

Kingsley moved toward the case. "So, maybe I'll use a rapier on you. Punch you full of holes so there will be plenty of blood in the water for the sharks. Let's see now. . . ."

Just as he passed in front of Ho Ming, Kingsley took his eyes off McGraw and looked toward the glass door of the cabinet. At that instant Casey came out of his quiescence and sprang at Kingsley, gripping his gun hand and driving him backward into the Chinaman. In spite of his swollen eye and his injured ribs, Casey was more than a match for the out-of-condition Kingsley.

As soon as Kingsley slammed into Ho Ming, McGraw leapt over the falling bodies and landed partially on Ho Ming. The Chinaman's hand was already under his coat, reaching for a weapon when McGraw hit him. And before McGraw could get clear of Casey and the captain, Ho Ming had his gun out. McGraw had a hand on the gun arm, but the man was quick and powerful. He jerked free, falling backwards. McGraw scrambled toward him, trying to deflect the weapon. McGraw got both hands on the Chinaman's wrist, forcing his arm upward, and preventing him from cocking the single-action revolver. Ho Ming twisted out from under him and began clubbing McGraw on the back of the neck with his free arm. McGraw attempted to knee him in the groin, but missed. McGraw threw his legs around his muscular opponent and took him down in a scissors grip.

McGraw was dimly aware of another deadly struggle going on next to him, but had no chance to look. McGraw ducked his head against the blows, taking them on his back, rather than on his head and neck. At the same time he squeezed with all his strength as he had done many times during college wrestling matches a few years before. He heard Ho Ming grunt as the air was forced out of him. With one quick movement McGraw slammed Ho Ming's wrist back to the deck and then jerked it forward with both hands. The dislodged gun flew out of the Chinaman's hand over McGraw's head, and glass crashed as the front of the display case was smashed. The Chinaman reached around with his free hand and raked fingernails across McGraw's face. McGraw felt the stinging of the cuts as the nails just missed his eyes. He let go of Ho Ming's right wrist and swung a backhanded blow at the head. Ho Ming ducked, and McGraw felt teeth tearing into his biceps. McGraw jerked his arm free and shoved away from Ho Ming, springing to his feet.

"What the bloody hell is going on down there?" Moreland's voice came from above.

McGraw instinctively lunged toward the watertight door at the foot of the companionway stairs, flung it shut, and shot the bolt.

Casey and Kingsley were still trying to gain control of the revolver. McGraw underestimated the strength born of desperation, or else Casey was injured worse than either of them first realized. Casey had not yet managed to dislodge the small gun from Kingsley, and, just as the pair struggled for it, the weapon exploded with a roar, and the slug buried itself in the overhead. Locked together, neither able to gain an advantage, they kicked and rolled under the cabin table that was bolted to the deck.

McGraw dared not try to help, since Ho Ming was stalking him, moving in a half-crouch. His black eyes glittered in the lamplight. The slicked-down black hair and the hard, flat planes of his face reminded McGraw of a weaving cobra. He threw a quick look at the smashed case but didn't see the pistol that had been flung into it. McGraw maneuvered to stay between Ho Ming and the case, and to keep the table and the struggling bodies between them.

There was a heavy thumping at the cabin door. McGraw knew he would have to end this quickly before anyone burst in and changed the odds. He knew that Ho Ming was unusually strong and decided not to close with him again. Instead, McGraw rushed around the table and faked a dive for the Chinaman's legs. Ho Ming took the feint and leaned forward to counter the move. Instead, McGraw came up with a right uppercut that connected solidly with the mouth and nose. Ho Ming's head snapped back, and he staggered sideways, crashing into the wall. Before he could recover, McGraw followed up with a kick to the midsection, and Ho Ming crumpled to his knees, doubled over. McGraw moved in quickly for the finish, but the Chinaman wasn't through yet. He sprang up with a wild swing that caught McGraw in the stomach. The punch seemed to paralyze his breathing. He gasped and covered up, trying to stall and protect himself from the expected rain of blows. Through a mist of pain, everything appeared to slow down. He saw Ho Ming back off a step, rock on the balls of his feet, and aim a vicious kick at McGraw's head.

McGraw started to react but was too slow. The toe caught him, sending a stabbing pain through his left ear. He fell away, buying time, and saw Ho Ming scramble across the deck on his hands and knees, searching for his gun.

Staggering, gasping for breath and fighting the pain, McGraw dove toward the Chinaman and caught him by the braided queue. Ho Ming's head jerked backward, and he thudded onto his back. But McGraw had not recovered from the blow to the midsection or the kick to the side of the head. He couldn't follow up. Ho Ming jerked, and McGraw felt the oily pigtail slide out of his grasp. The Chinaman sprawled on the floor and grabbed the revolver. McGraw saw him spin around on his belly, cocking the weapon as he turned. McGraw caught a glimpse of the bloody nose and the hate in his eyes as Ho Ming sighted down the barrel. McGraw threw himself sideways as Ho Ming squeezed the trigger. The roar of gunfire deafened him. He felt a bullet burn past his left hand. Then he looked, and Ho Ming had rolled over on his back, clutching the top of his left shoulder. His revolver lay on the floor.

Casey crawled out from under the table, gripping Kingsley's still-smoking small pistol. The police captain was lying unconscious on his back.

McGraw got to his feet, his chest heaving, and picked up Ho Ming's gun. "Dead?"

"Kingsley?" Casey panted. "No. I got him . . . a good one . . . across the temple with his own gun. He'll be out for a bit."

McGraw bent over Ho Ming. He was conscious, but there was no fight left in the wounded man. Casey's bullet had gone into the top of his shoulder but had not exited. His normally impassive face was twisted in agony. Sweat was trickling down his face.

The thumping and banging on the cabin door had stopped. Instead, they heard running feet overhead, and voices yelling. The ship was moving, and the gimbaled lamp overhead was swaying.

McGraw motioned for Casey to stand clear of the door. He reached around, slid the bolt back, and flung the door open. The stairs were empty. There was a lot of commotion on deck.

"Put another man on that wheel!" they could hear Moreland's voice ordering.

"The wheel won't move, Cap'n!" another voice yelled.

McGraw and Casey crept up the steps in single file, guns ready.

"Jerk it back and forth. It's just fouled with kelp or driftwood."

"Sumpin's got 'er jammed tight, Cap'n. She won't move more'n a few inches."

"Sir, we're drifting down on the beach," came another voice.

"Damn it! Let go the anchor! Drop the jib and foresail!"

McGraw eased his head above the hatch. The rumble of anchor chain sounded from the foredeck. McGraw raised his head cautiously and looked around in the semi-darkness. He saw the outlines of two men, struggling at the wheel, silhouetted by the gas lights ashore that seemed much brighter.

Moreland's tall figure was near the starboard rail, but the captain didn't see McGraw. He was looking up at the sails and forward to see if the anchor was going to bite and hold. Blocks were squealing as the outer jib descended its stay. Just then Moreland looked down and spotted McGraw and Casey. He yelled something and pointed at them.

McGraw sprang out onto the deck, with Casey at his heels. They dashed for the rail, but the crew members were heading them off. McGraw snapped off a shot at the first figure. The man jumped back behind the mizzen mast, and a stab of flame answered as he fired back.

"Hang on! We're going aground!"

Before McGraw and Casey could take two more running steps toward the port rail, the schooner struck stern first, and they were thrown to the deck, rolling into the scuppers as the grounded vessel heeled.

As they struggled to untangle themselves, there was a spattering of gunfire only a few feet away, and McGraw saw Brady and Kohl, climbing over the port rail, spraying shots in every direction. Then the roar of gunfire stopped, and there was a sudden and profound silence for a few seconds.

"Everyone stop right where you are! Get your hands up!

You're under arrest. This is the San Francisco police!"

McGraw had never been so glad to see the blue uniforms of his fellow officers. Casey and Kohl went forward, and McGraw heard two more shots before the three crew members there gave up and were herded back to the fantail with the two men at the wheel. They were all searched, disarmed, and their arms tied through the spokes of the wheel.

"Kingsley and Ho Ming are in the cabin," Casey said. "The Chinaman's wounded, and the captain's just pretty beat up. I don't think there's much fight left in them, but be careful. McGraw, go ashore and see if you can get some of those men to come and help take these prisoners ashore."

For the first time, McGraw noticed about a dozen men who had gathered on the Sausilito beach, drawn by the noise and the sound of gunfire. He handed Casey his larger caliber .45 and leapt over the rail, gasping as he landed, chest-deep, in the cold water. He waded a few yards ashore. Just as he came up onto the rocky beach, he remembered Captain John Moreland.

He turned and yelled back at Casey, but his friend must have gone down into the cabin, out of earshot.

"Brady! Kohl! Where's Captain Moreland?"

Apparently they were busy with the prisoners and didn't hear or answer. He ran along the beach, his mind racing. *Was Moreland hiding aboard somewhere, ready to ambush Casey and the other two?*

Just as he came out from behind the stern of the grounded schooner, McGraw caught a glimpse of a sail, bearing away from the starboard side of the stranded ship. It was the lateen sail of the fishing lugger that had been tied alongside. Captain Moreland was at the helm. McGraw reached for his gun in his waistband. Then he realized he had handed it to Casey. He looked on helplessly as the sail filled, and the boat bore away. He would never catch him if he had to get to the police boat moored alongside the schooner with its sails down. The men, looking on from the edge of the road near the top of the beach, would be no help, even if one of them had a gun. By the time he could get a weapon and fire, Moreland would be out of range or covered by darkness.

He looked around, frustrated. The beach was more small rocks than sand. He scrambled around and quickly selected a heavy rock about the size of a baseball. The boat was receding rapidly, going almost directly away from him now. McGraw estimated the distance at about thirty to forty yards. He took a quick hop-step to gather momentum and brought his arm overhead, throwing as hard as he could. The follow-through almost threw him down on his face as the rock whistled toward its target. There was a dull *thunk* as the missile struck. The figure in the stern slumped forward, and the boat slewed up into the wind, its sail flapping uselessly. The boat began to drift backward toward the shore.

McGraw watched for a few seconds, then, shivering in the cold, started up the beach to the cluster of curious men to ask for help.

Chapter Eighteen

"The prosecution calls Mister P. J. Buckley to the stand."

McGraw and Casey exchanged startled glances.

"Buckley? A witness for the prosecution?" Casey asked.

"What's this all about?"

There was a rustle in the crowded courtroom as Blind Boss Buckley made his way to the witness box by himself with the aid of his white cane. He was nattily dressed as usual in a brown suit and vest, white shirt, high collar, and a yellow cravat fixed with a diamond stickpin. His graying brown hair was slicked down. As he took his seat and was duly sworn, his eyes were only black spots imbedded in the thick lenses of his spectacles.

The prosecutor paced back and forth, his hands clasped behind his back. He was a handsome young attorney out of the prosecutor's office who was on his way up and full of self-importance. This was the biggest case of his life.

"Mister Buckley, would you please tell the jury in your own words what your rôle in this whole affair has been."

Buckley rested both hands on the head of his cane and turned his head in the general direction of the jury box where twelve men watched him attentively. "Of course. Chief of Police Patrick Crowley came to me about three months ago, shortly after the publication of the special report on Chinatown. He told me an all-out effort was going to be made by his department to limit or stop the flow of opium into this city, particularly into the Chinese quarter." He paused.

"And why did the chief come to you, a private citizen?" the prosecutor queried.

"He asked for my help. He wanted me to function as an undercover agent to discover what I could about this opium smuggling."

There was an excited stir in the courtroom. McGraw shot a flabbergasted look at Casey whose mouth had dropped open. The judge rapped for silence.

"And you agreed?" the prosecutor asked.

"Yes. I have certain connections in this city, and he felt I could use these to advantage."

"And did anyone else know of this arrangement?"

"No. It was strictly in confidence. Chief Crowley and I have known each other for several years, and I might add he is the most honest, upright man you could ever find. The people of San Francisco are fortunate to have him as their chief of. . . ."

"Yes, yes, go on," the prosecutor interrupted.

"In any case, I was to report directly to him and *no one* besides the two of us was to know of this arrangement."

"No wonder the word came down to leave him alone," Casey whispered to McGraw.

"He sure played dumb and lied to us when we talked to him," McGraw answered.

"A real *blatherskite*. Never knew an Irishman who couldn't lie like a professional when he had to."

". . . find out in your rôle as an undercover agent?" the prosecutor was asking. Even though the attorney had asked the witness to relate the story in his own words, he never missed an opportunity to interject comments or questions of his own, with an eye to the newspaper reporters in the courtroom who were busily scribbling on their note pads.

"Without revealing all my confidential sources as a saloonkeeper, I was able to discover that Ho Ming, the notorious highbinder, was the man in charge of the acquisition and distribution of the opium in Chinatown. He was the one who arranged the details of the contacts, the payments, the logistics of the operation. In other words, he was the foreman of the opium trade. Members of other tongs were not happy with this, but I am told by my Chinese sources that they would go along until this current investigation died down." He smiled a thin smile. "Our Chinese inhabitants are nothing, if not patient."

"What else did you discover?" the prosecutor persisted.

"To keep the police busy, Ho Ming arranged to feed them just enough information about the smuggling of a little of the drug here and there. But the greatest amount of opium was coming in regular shipments on the schooner of the English sea captain, John Moreland. In between these shipments, a smaller, but steady, flow was brought in from the Orient on the persons of imported slave girls."

McGraw noted Casey's face, flushing slightly with embarrassment at the mention of this deception.

"Can you tell us what you know about the murder of the policeman, Kevin O'Toole?" the prosecutor asked.

Buckley hesitated, shifting in his chair, as if collecting his thoughts. "Kevin O'Toole was a brash young lad. But he was a lot smarter than many people gave him credit for. As you know, he was a member of this special opium squad. He spent a lot of time in my saloon, playing poker, joking with the girls, plying certain people with drinks, and listening, always listening. Under that bluff exterior was a very shrewd policeman. He would have made a capable politician." He shook his head. "What a shame that. . . ."

"Go on with your story, Mister Buckley," the prosecutor prompted.

Buckley took a deep breath and again focused on his narrative. "In an operation as widespread as this opium trade, many, many men have varying degrees of information. And where many people are involved as workers, sellers, buyers, addicts, it is impossible to keep secrets. There are always leaks. At first I wasn't aware of what O'Toole was doing, but gradually I discovered he was using my saloon as sort of an unofficial headquarters to conduct an undercover investigation of his own. In his own very different way, he was doing the same thing I had been asked by Chief Crowley to do. But here is where I made a terrible mistake. . . ." He paused, and McGraw thought he could detect a moistening of the eyes behind the thick lenses.

This time the prosecutor waited without prompting. The packed courtroom was hushed. No one coughed; no one stirred. The pendulum of the wall clock swung back and forth, measuring the seconds in audible ticks.

Buckley composed himself. "I should have taken the lad into my confidence and shared information with him. But I didn't. I had given my word to the chief that our relationship would remain strictly confidential. I met O'Toole away from the saloon after a baseball game one day to see if I could feel him out, to see how much he knew about the smuggling operation. He told me nothing. I sensed that maybe he thought I was part of it. While I was trying to decide what to do, O'Toole apparently took it upon himself to go to Captain Kingsley with whatever information he had gathered. Neither he nor I, at that point, knew that Captain Kingsley was bossing this whole operation and taking a generous cut of the profits to insure that the opium smugglers were safe from police interference. When O'Toole told Kingsley what he knew, Kingsley murdered him."

"Objection!" the red-faced defense attorney roared, springing out of his chair. "Supposition on the part of the witness. It has not been proven that the defendant murdered anyone. That's why this trial is being held."

"Sustained," the judge ruled. "Mister Buckley, you will confine your remarks to those facts that you know first hand. The jury will disregard that last statement."

"That is all," the prosecutor said. "Your witness."

The defense attorney got heavily to his feet but spoke from behind the table. "What did you do with the information you had gathered about Ho Ming and O'Toole? Did you tell Chief Crowley?"

"Yes, I did. But O'Toole had already been found dead with all the marks of a tong killing."

"And, to your knowledge, did Chief Crowley do anything with your information?"

"I can't speak for the chief, but I heard Ho Ming was to be brought in for questioning. I don't know that he was. Ho Ming is a very hard man to locate sometimes."

"No further questions."

"You may step down," the judge directed. "Court will recess for lunch, and reconvene at one o'clock." He rapped his gavel and a buzz of conversation accompanied the crowd out the door.

"Makes you feel like a very small pawn on a very large chessboard, doesn't it?" McGraw remarked as they filed out into the sunlight.

Casey nodded. "Wish I had known about Buckley. It would have made things a lot easier."

"Well, not even Buckley or the chief suspected Kingsley until we got onto him and you bluffed him into making a break to escape."

"Yes. It's ironic that he's on trial for O'Toole's murder instead of Kem Ying's."

"Let's get a bite to eat. We're on the stand this afternoon."

Katie O'Neal was among the spectators in the pine-paneled courtroom when the trial reconvened after lunch. Fred Casey was called first and read a short report from the police laboratory positively matching the fingerprint on the Danish war axe to the right index finger of Thomas Kingsley. Then he gave a brief summary of his own rôle as the lieutenant in charge of the opium squad and their investigation, and how they had come to suspect Kingsley and the pursuit of him. Lastly he testified that Kingsley had bragged about killing O'Toole with the stolen antique weapon, just before he attempted to murder them aboard the schooner.

"Objection! Witness is implying that my client was involved in the murder of this Kem Ying girl."

"Overruled!" the judge said, indicating the jury was entitled to know what led to the chase that resulted in Kingsley's bragging of the O'Toole murder.

Then the defense attorney got his chance to cross-examine and tried to discredit Casey's story by depicting him as an irresponsible rebel who did not follow correct police procedure — accusing him of unprofessional conduct by leaning heavily on a personal friend who was not a permanent member of the police department. He accused Casey of making wild, unfounded accusations to Captain Kingsley's face and to the court concerning the Kem Ying murder. And, if Casey would do this, he couldn't be relied upon to tell the truth about the O'Toole murder, either. Casey was unshakable, calmly, but firmly, repeating his story.

When Casey finished his testimony and stepped down, McGraw could read nothing in the impassive faces of the jury. Then McGraw followed him to the stand, his heart pounding as it never had when facing real danger. He corroborated Casey's story, adding a few details of his own about the conversation he had overheard on the schooner before their capture. He carefully avoided any direct comments about Kem Ying.

Kingsley sat stonily through it all, staring at nothing.

The following day, the defense had their turn and, without

permitting Kingsley to testify, brought forth character witnesses from among the leading citizens of San Francisco who told, in glowing terms, about the generosity and public-spiritedness of the former actor. They testified that the defendant would have been incapable of such an act of cruelty.

In early afternoon the defense rested. Closing arguments followed. Then the judge charged the jury who subsequently retired for the evening to consider their verdict.

"I'm sure glad that's over!" McGraw remarked as he and Casey and Katie sat down to a special meal prepared by Mrs. Bridget O'Neal at her boarding house later that night. The other guests had been fed earlier so the family could eat undisturbed.

"It's not over yet," Casey said. "Juries are notoriously unpredictable. This is a murder case. They might decide our evidence wasn't strong enough."

"But what about that deposition Ho Ming submitted from his hospital bed, stating he was pressured into paying heavy bribes to Kingsley?" Katie asked. "Surely that will tilt the scales against him?"

"The fingerprint is the strongest evidence. But that science is so new, I wonder whether the jury will believe it."

"We'll see."

"All rise!"

The bailiff's booming voice cut through the hubbub of noise in the courtroom. The spectators rose as one, and stood silently as the twelve good men and true filed in through a rear door and took their places in the jury box.

"Be seated."

The crowd sat.

"Has the jury reached a verdict?"

"We have, your honor," the short, heavy-set foreman answered. He handed the bailiff a folded slip of paper who passed it to the judge.

The black-robed judge adjusted his gold-rimmed pince-nez on his nose and read silently.

"The defendant will please rise."

Kingsley stood.

The judge peered over his spectacles at him. "Thomas Kingsley, you have been found guilty of murder by a jury of your p. . . ."

The room erupted in bedlam.

"Order! Order!" The rapping of the gavel gradually quieted the tumult. The judge looked like a stern schoolmaster as he surveyed the crowd. When complete silence was restored, he continued. "It is the judgment of this court that you be hanged by the neck until you are dead, and that such sentence be carried out within thirty days of this date. And may God have mercy on your soul."

Another disturbance broke out as a woman on a back bench fainted, and the judge rapped the court into adjournment. Reporters rushed outside ahead of the crowd, some to file their stories, others to get interviews on the courthouse steps.

Katie threw her arms around McGraw and Casey on either side of her and gave them a convulsive hug.

"Justice is served," Casey said as the three of them made their way through the last stragglers to the door.

"What will happen to Ho Ming and Captain Moreland?" Katie asked.

"Ho Ming may recover from the bullet in his lung to stand trial," Casey replied. "If he does, it's my guess he'll be deported . . . save the state some money. As for Moreland, I don't know. He's not a citizen, either, and he's wanted for various crimes around the world. Since we caught him, he'll probably be tried here under United States law and get a substantial prison term."

"What about Kem Ying?" Katie asked. "Will that poor girl's murder go unresolved?"

"It won't go unpunished. Kingsley will pay with his life. And we're convinced he did it, from what we overheard him say, and the way he ran, even though he'll never be tried for it," McGraw said.

"Chief Crowley mentioned to me this morning that I have a pretty good chance at Kingsley's old job as captain," Casey said.

"That ought to change your mind about staying in police work."

"Well, maybe. I'll have to give it some thought. What about you? Are you going to finish out the season with the Petrels?"

"I don't know. Considering all that's happened, it's been a deadly season. I really need to get back to my job with Wells Fargo. It pays better."

"You have to see the team through to the end of the season," Casey countered. "After all, you're hitting more than three-fifty. They need you. Besides, who has a better throwing arm? You put Moreland out with that rock from at least a hundred feet away."

McGraw laughed. "It was a team effort. If Brady and Kohl hadn't jammed the schooner's rudder with that oar, we'd have been out to sea."

They paused on the steps, blinking in the mid-morning sunlight.

"So there's a good chance you'll be promoted," McGraw said. "Congratulations! A captain and not even thirty years old yet. There may be a major change coming in my life, too." He paused awkwardly as the two of them regarded him with curiosity. "I plan to ask Katie to be my wife."

She looked at him blankly. "You *plan* to?"

"I just did."

"That's the most off-handed proposal I've ever heard," she frowned.

McGraw's heart sank, and he could feel his cheeks burning.

"But I accept." She flashed one of her dazzling smiles, looked intently into his eyes, slipped her arms around his neck, and kissed him.

DARK EMBERS AT DAWN
STEPHEN OVERHOLSER

Like many a veteran of the Civil War, Cap McKenna went west to the Rockies to build a new life. But that new life changes forever the day he comes across an abandoned infant, whom he takes in and cares for until the baby's Cheyenne mother appears at his door. Alone and terrified, all the woman wants is to find the baby's father. Cap helps her locate him at the U.S. Cavalry encampment, but Colonel Tom Sully stands defiantly between the father and his family. When the desperate man deserts to be with his wife and child, Sully sends a detail after him and suddenly Cap finds himself caught in a deadly pursuit—ready to risk all for what he knows is right.

___4657-1 $4.50 US/$5.50 CAN

Dorchester Publishing Co., Inc.
P.O. Box 6640
Wayne, PA 19087-8640

Please add $1.75 for shipping and handling for the first book and $.50 for each book thereafter. NY, NYC, and PA residents, please add appropriate sales tax. No cash, stamps, or C.O.D.s. All orders shipped within 6 weeks via postal service book rate. Canadian orders require $2.00 extra postage and must be paid in U.S. dollars through a U.S. banking facility.

Name_____
Address_____
City_____State_____Zip_____
I have enclosed $_____ in payment for the checked book(s).
Payment <u>must</u> accompany all orders. ❏ Please send a free catalog.
    CHECK OUT OUR WEBSITE! www.dorchesterpub.com

SEARCH FOR THE FOX

Stephen Overholser

Benjamin Fox's father is legendary Confederate General John Fox, the Southern hero who, still in uniform in 1865, rode into Richmond and robbed the Atlanta Bank and Trust. Then "The Fox" fled Richmond, leaving his wife and infant son behind, and became one of the West's most notorious outlaws. In the summer of 1882, when young Benjamin sets out from Richmond to find his elusive heritage, he doesn't know what he will find. He can't know his search will lead him to a silver bonanza in Colorado, mule skinners and mountain men, road agents and merciless lawmen. Nothing has prepared him for the ways and wiles of ruthless bounty hunters. And he never thinks that one day his search will bring him face to face with the truth about the Fox . . . and himself.

___4745-4 $3.99 US/$4.99 CAN

Dorchester Publishing Co., Inc.
P.O. Box 6640
Wayne, PA 19087-8640

Please add $1.75 for shipping and handling for the first book and $.50 for each book thereafter. NY, NYC, and PA residents, please add appropriate sales tax. No cash, stamps, or C.O.D.s. All orders shipped within 6 weeks via postal service book rate. Canadian orders require $2.00 extra postage and must be paid in U.S. dollars through a U.S. banking facility.

Name_____
Address_____
City_____ State_____ Zip_____
I have enclosed $ _____ in payment for the checked book(s).
Payment <u>must</u> accompany all orders. ❑ Please send a free catalog.
        CHECK OUT OUR WEBSITE! www.dorchesterpub.com

SWIFT THUNDER
Tim Champlin

Lance Barlow is only nineteen when he starts riding with a Missouri militia group known as the Border Ruffians. He joins them seeking adventure, but their wanton destruction and murder of the Free-Staters is too much for him. Finally, after a brutal attack on a farm family, Lance can't take any more. He rebels and switches sides. He reunites with his best friend, a freed slave named Shadrack, and together the pair set off to ride with the newly organized Pony Express. But Lance gets more adventure than he bargained for when he is forced to rescue Shadrack from slavers. Still working for the Pony Express, the friends escape west to Utah, with the Missouri militia and a Marysville slaver on their trail. They have no idea that the real danger lies in front of them, waiting in the midst of Paiute country.

___4758-6 $4.50 US/$5.50 CAN

Dorchester Publishing Co., Inc.
P.O. Box 6640
Wayne, PA 19087-8640

Please add $1.75 for shipping and handling for the first book and $.50 for each book thereafter. NY, NYC, and PA residents, please add appropriate sales tax. No cash, stamps, or C.O.D.s. All orders shipped within 6 weeks via postal service book rate. Canadian orders require $2.00 extra postage and must be paid in U.S. dollars through a U.S. banking facility.

Name _____
Address _____
City _____ State _____ Zip _____
I have enclosed $ _____ in payment for the checked book(s).
Payment <u>must</u> accompany all orders. ❏ Please send a free catalog.
          CHECK OUT OUR WEBSITE! www.dorchesterpub.com

Behold a Red Horse

Cotton Smith

After the Civil War, Ethan Kerry carved out the Bar K cattle spread with little more than hard work and fierce courage—and the help of his younger, slow-witted brother, Luther. But now the Bar K is in serious trouble. Ethan's loan was called in and the only way he can save the spread is if he can drive a herd from central Texas to Kansas. Ethan will need more than Luther's help this time—because Ethan has been struck blind by a kick from an untamed horse. His one slim hope has come from a most unlikely source—another brother, long thought dead, who follows the outlaw trail. Only if all three brothers band together can they save the Bar K . . . if they don't kill each other first.

___4894-9 $4.99 US/$5.99 CAN

Dorchester Publishing Co., Inc.
P.O. Box 6640
Wayne, PA 19087-8640

Please add $2.50 for shipping and handling for the first book and $.75 for each book thereafter. NY and PA residents, please add appropriate sales tax. No cash, stamps, or C.O.D.s. All orders shipped within 6 weeks via postal service book rate. Canadian orders require $2.50 extra postage and must be paid in U.S. dollars through a U.S. banking facility.

Name_____
Address
City   State   Zip_____
I have enclosed $ in payment for the checked book(s).
Payment <u>must</u> accompany all orders. ❑ Please send a free catalog.
     CHECK OUT OUR WEBSITE! www.dorchesterpub.com

COTTON SMITH
DARK TRAIL TO DODGE

Tyrel Bannon knows more about a plow than longhorn cattle, but the green farm boy is determined to become a Triple C rider on the long, hard drive from Texas to Dodge, the "Queen City of the Cowtowns." But this is a trail that only the brave, smart and lucky can survive. Waiting ahead are Kiowa warriors, raging rivers, drought, storms . . . and vicious rustlers out to blacken the dust with Triple C blood.

___4510-9 $4.50 US/$5.50 CAN

Dorchester Publishing Co., Inc.
P.O. Box 6640
Wayne, PA 19087-8640

Please add $1.75 for shipping and handling for the first book and $.50 for each book thereafter. NY, NYC, and PA residents, please add appropriate sales tax. No cash, stamps, or C.O.D.s. All orders shipped within 6 weeks via postal service book rate. Canadian orders require $2.00 extra postage and must be paid in U.S. dollars through a U.S. banking facility.

Name_____
Address_____
City_____ State_____ Zip_____
I have enclosed $_____ in payment for the checked book(s).
Payment <u>must</u> accompany all orders. ❏ Please send a free catalog.
       CHECK OUT OUR WEBSITE! www.dorchesterpub.com

Genevieve of TOMBSTONE

John Duncklee

Tombstone in the 1880's is the toughest town in the West, and it takes a special kind of grit just to survive there. Ask the Earps or the Clantons. But among the gunslingers and lawmen, among the ranchers and rustlers, there is Genevieve, a woman with the spirit, toughness—and heart—the town demands. Whether she is working in a fancy house or running her own cattle ranch, Genevieve will not only survive, she will triumph. She is a woman who will never surrender, never give in—and one that no reader will ever forget.

___4628-8 $4.99 US/$5.99 CAN

Dorchester Publishing Co., Inc.
P.O. Box 6640
Wayne, PA 19087-8640

Please add $1.75 for shipping and handling for the first book and $.50 for each book thereafter. NY, NYC, and PA residents, please add appropriate sales tax. No cash, stamps, or C.O.D.s. All orders shipped within 6 weeks via postal service book rate. Canadian orders require $2.00 extra postage and must be paid in U.S. dollars through a U.S. banking facility.

Name_____
Address_____
City_____ State_____ Zip_____
I have enclosed $_____ in payment for the checked book(s).
Payment <u>must</u> accompany all orders. ❑ Please send a free catalog.
      CHECK OUT OUR WEBSITE! www.dorchesterpub.com

Graciela
of the
Border
John Duncklee

Jeff Collins knows horses. He works as a horse trainer on the Sierra Diablo ranch in Arizona, and he is mighty good at it. But he wants more. He's dreamed for years of having his own ranch. He sees his chance when he wins a blue roan in a high-stakes poker game. This isn't just any roan; it is carrying the foal of a great racehorse, and that foal is Jeff's ticket to his dreams. When that roan is stolen and herded along with other horses toward the Mexican border, Jeff knows where he has to go. But he doesn't know what will be waiting for him when he gets there. The border is a dangerous place, a harsh land filled with bandits and outlaws—and the woman who will change his life . . . Graciela of the border.

_4809-4 $4.99 US/$5.99 CAN

Dorchester Publishing Co., Inc.
P.O. Box 6640
Wayne, PA 19087-8640

Please add $2.50 for shipping and handling for the first book and $.75 for each book thereafter. NY, NYC, and PA residents, please add appropriate sales tax. No cash, stamps, or C.O.D.s. All orders shipped within 6 weeks via postal service book rate. Canadian orders require $2.00 extra postage and must be paid in U.S. dollars through a U.S. banking facility.

Name_____
Address_____
City_____ State_____ Zip_____
I have enclosed $_____ in payment for the checked book(s).
Payment <u>must</u> accompany all orders.☐Please send a free catalog.
    CHECK OUT OUR WEBSITE! www.dorchesterpub.com

Broken Ranks

Hiram King

The Civil War just ended. For one group of black men, hope for a new life comes in the form of a piece of paper, a government handbill urging volunteers to join the new Negro Cavalry, which will soon become the famous Tenth Cavalry Regiment. But trouble begins for the recruits long before they can even reach their training camp. First they have to get from St. Louis to Fort Leavenworth, Kansas, a hard journey through hostile, ex-Confederate territory, surrounded by vengeful white men who don't like the idea of these recruits having guns. The army hires Ples Butler, a grim, black gunfighter, to get the recruits to Fort Leavenworth safely, and he will do his job . . . even if it means riding through Hell.

___4872-8 $5.99 US/$6.99 CAN

Dorchester Publishing Co., Inc.
P.O. Box 6640
Wayne, PA 19087-8640

Please add $2.50 for shipping and handling for the first book and $.75 for each book thereafter. NY, NYC, and PA residents, please add appropriate sales tax. No cash, stamps, or C.O.D.s. All orders shipped within 6 weeks via postal service book rate. Canadian orders require $2.50 extra postage and must be paid in U.S. dollars through a U.S. banking facility.

Name_____

Address_____

City_____ State _____ Zip_____
I have enclosed $ _____ in payment for the checked book(s).
Payment <u>must</u> accompany all orders. ❑ Please send a free catalog.
      CHECK OUT OUR WEBSITE! www.dorchesterpub.com

ATTENTION BOOK LOVERS!

CAN'T GET ENOUGH
OF YOUR FAVORITE WESTERNS?

CALL 1-800-481-9191 TO:

- ORDER BOOKS,
- RECEIVE A **FREE** CATALOG,
- JOIN OUR BOOK CLUBS TO **SAVE 20%!**

OPEN MON.-FRI. 10 AM-9 PM EST

VISIT
WWW.DORCHESTERPUB.COM
FOR SPECIAL OFFERS AND INSIDE
INFORMATION ON THE AUTHORS
YOU LOVE.

 LEISURE BOOKS

We accept Visa, MasterCard or Discover®.